SAVE THE FATE

SAVE THE FATE

A WEDDING PLANNER MYSTERY

MARY KARNES

LEVEL
BEST BOOKS

To my husband of forty-plus years, Kenny. Thank you for being my friend, love, and rock all these years. I love you to distraction.

Chapter One

Saturday, June 21

Give your wedding planner a master list of all your vendors' duties. She will then be able to make sure all tasks are completed, even if they are not her own tasks.

T he night was winding to a close at our town's annual "Strawberry Moon" street fair. Why was the event called "Strawberry Moon"? According to Google, *The full moon names used by* The Old Farmer's Almanac *come from a number of places, including from Native Americans who lived in the northeastern United States. June's full Moon—typically the last full Moon of spring or the first of summer—has traditionally been called the **Strawberry Moon** to mark the ripening of "June-bearing" strawberries that are ready to be gathered.*

Brian, my old flame and new love, swung me around the makeshift dance floor. I was dizzy in a most delicious way. I looked up to smile at him, but he was looking past me. Whatever, or whomever, had captured his attention had also captured the entire party. Many of the dancers stopped swaying, others pointed. I even heard, "Oh my God, is that..." The entire crowd buzzed like a swarm of angry bees...now, I *had* to peek.

I looked over my shoulder. Oh...my...stars. It was Jack O'Malley in the flesh. Jen's Jack with a tiny blond on his arm. Jen, my best friend from forever; Jen, who was the owner of our town's coffee shop, 'The Perk.' And

Jack, well, he was the best athlete the entire of New England had ever put out. He was the hottest MLB player on the field these days, despite his rather advanced age for a ball player, and he had come home. I can't remember the last time I had seen him. I had heard that he came to see his family who still lived here, but he didn't catch up with anyone else, except maybe Brian. It was as if he was too good for the rest of us. I knew Brian had visited him through the years. They were about as good of friends as Jen and I were. But Brian and I had been so estranged for so long, I had a lot of catching up to do.

I frantically looked around for Jen. I finally found her, her mouth gaping open in surprise

just like everyone else, but only she was white as a ghost. Brian left me on the dance floor and

walked over to Jack. I would have appreciated an, 'I'll be right back, but whatever. I made my way to Jen. Some color had returned to her face, thank God. I looked around for Jen's husband, Jeff, but didn't see him anywhere. Had he come tonight? I tried to remember if I had seen him but couldn't. I did see Jen's two daughters; they didn't seem impressed by the adults' frenzy and were giggling with some friends over by 'The Fountain.' The fountain was more than a fountain in our little town. Every year, the high school students went to the fountain to have their Pre-Junior Prom photos taken, with their dates, with their friends. All the teens' families went too, it was another big street party. This tradition was repeated with the Senior Ball. Some of my brides were insistent that they have a few wedding photos taken at the fountain too.

"Hey, Jen," I smiled broadly after I made my way over to her. My smile was so wide my face hurt. We were being watched, and I didn't want to add more grist to the rumor mill. The town knew Jen and Jack's story, and I imagine most were interested in how this new development would play out. I wrapped my arm around her, still grinning like a loon.

"What's wrong with you, Katie," Jen finally shook herself and came out of her fugue

state. "You're grinning freakishly," and she laughed. Thank God.

"Everyone's looking," I tried to talk without moving my lips.

Jen shook me off. "Get a grip, Katie. No one cares anymore." I looked around me, yep.

They were all looking. They still cared.

Chapter Two

Sunday, June 22

Consult your wedding dress designer or salesperson to determine the best method for making your dress wrinkle-free and then plan to do this one to two days before the wedding.

T he next morning, I was in my office above Jen's coffee shop, seated behind my desk. My office was the first time I had space that was all my own since I was a teen and lived at home and reflected me and my sometimes-quirky personality…oh, and weddings, of course. I had a small reception area painted in grey-blue with two stormy sky-blue, (yes, think a hint of grey again), visitors' chairs, and a little table between them. I had a thing for fresh flowers, so this week's arrangement was a study in pinks. And it only cost me $5.99 plus tax from Whole Foods down the street. I had a little "kitchen area" cordoned off from the reception space with a burgundy screen. Behind said screen was a mini-fridge, a state-of-the-art espresso machine (I felt guilty for having an espresso machine when my office was above a premier coffee establishment, Jen's 'Perk, and my best friends to boot, but sometimes it was needed), and all the bells and whistles to have a proper coffee/tea-party. I loved my cups, saucers, and teapots. Did I have snacks? Well, a few, as I was always hungry, and my figure reflected this. I was still trying to lose those last five pounds of the fifteen I had gained while I was recovering from a bike accident in California. A door next to the visitors' chairs led into my office proper, and directly across from me was Jack O'Malley and to his right, his fiancée, Meghan. Turns out he was engaged to the perky little blond who had accompanied him to Strawberry Moon last night, and they'd come 'home' to get married. Guess who the lucky wedding planner was? And his fiancée? Well, she was a hometown girl too, although much younger than Jack and I, in fact, ten years younger.

Our engaged couple had met in LA when she was a vodka rep at clubs, and he, well, he played for the Dodgers, duh. Next, my eyes flew to Meghan's engagement ring. It was five carats if it was one. It looked to be a flawless, colorless emerald-cut diamond in platinum. Oh my!

"Katie!" Jack brought me back to earth with a smile. "Venue? We have to lock this down, as I mentioned we want to start a family soon, as in seven months." He grinned.

"Seven months?" I'm sure my confusion showed with my frown.

Meghan patted her rounded tummy. Ah…duh again. She was so skinny. A little extra roundness would be apparent, and this bump most definitely was. We were going to have to deal with dress issues, I was afraid. Meghan held up a long strip of, I could only assume, the baby's ultrasound.

"Here," she waved it to me. It seemed rude to not take it. So, I did, and looked at it briefly until Meghan snatched it up again, almost aggressively. It didn't matter to me. I could never make sense of those things!

"Well, congrats." I tried to keep the question mark out of my voice. "We will move things right along, then." I smiled awkwardly to hide my racing thoughts about how Meghan's pregnancy could impact our timeline of the wedding. I should have known better; I was in situations like this all the time. "If we're looking for a near wedding date, perhaps we should consider a weekday."

Meghan looked angrily at Jack, then her eyes welled up. Oh goodness, she was going to cry. Not another one, I mused with a jaded heart. I had a real sobber yesterday. *What was wrong with you?* I scolded myself. My job was to be sensitive and understanding. I blamed my attitude on my post-Covid crunch. So many weddings had been rescheduled. And it was taking years now to get caught back up. I'd been running around like a chicken with its head cut off.

My attention went back to Jack and Meghan. She looked a whole lot like her sister Marjorie: blond hair, well, I can't swear that blond is her natural color, brown eyes, cute little button nose, although I don't remember Marjorie being so well-endowed.

I'm pretty sure Marjorie had moved away my senior year, but I had heard she was back, just like me.

Jack cleared his throat. "Meg really has her heart set on a Saturday wedding date…this month. Can we make that work?" My head was spinning. This was June. June was once again the most desired month for weddings. Here in New England, the trend had been the fall, but we had come full circle, and June was back on top. It just wasn't feasible to make it all happen in a month. The first problem was the venue. Everything for a Friday, Saturday, or even a Sunday was booked out for the next eighteen months. Then there were tablescapes to plan, invitations to order, and a design team for decorations to be brought on board. Typically, it took twelve to eighteen months to plan a wedding for an "A" lister such as Jack. There was a media blurb to go out, security to obtain, as well as non-disclosures to be signed by all vendors.

I looked at them both, hard. They had to know I was serious. "I can make it work in a month's time, maybe less, but you have to realize some concessions will have to be made, like the day of the week you will be married." Meghan actually stuck out her bottom lip like a petulant toddler. Tears once again threatened. Her face was red and getting redder. Was she, was she going to…. Was she going to hold her breath? I looked at her in horror. My eyes drifted to the dark blue chaise lounge to my right. It was my pride and joy, and I was known to take a nap or two on it when brides got to me. I was wishing for such a nap right at this moment. The cashmere throw draped carefully on the chaise was particularly inviting. My little dachshund was parked on the chaise. I really shouldn't bring her to client meetings, but she was so darn cute, and as I was leaving this morning, I couldn't ignore the pleading look in her eyes.

"Jack," she whined. Thank God. She couldn't speak and hold her breath at the same time.

CHAPTER TWO

"No, Meghan," I said. " I'm afraid this is non-negotiable. Every venue within a four-hour drive is booked for a weekend date." If she was going to act like a child, I was going to treat her as one, but then I realized I was acting too coldly. I was being way too harsh. Hopefully, this was Meghan's one and only wedding, and it was my job to make it as perfect as possible. She sniffled pathetically.

"Meghan, I know this is disappointing. Have you considered getting married at the Hartford City Hall, it's gorgeous!" I tried to put enthusiasm in my voice.

The Hartford Municipal Building, also known as 'City Hall,' is a historic Beaux-Arts building. As it is only fifteen minutes from downtown Eastbury, it was a solid choice. In fact, many brides choose it for their photos before their wedding, or 'First Look.' A 'First Look' is when the bride and the groom see each other before the ceremony and take a series of photos. Doing so goes against tradition, but it has become quite a thing. And as a wedding planner, I sure do like the time 'The First Look' frees up time so the bride and groom don't have to endure a marathon photo session post-ceremony. But oh, you can't replace that 'AH' moment when the groom sees the bride coming down the aisle in her gown for the first time. There's nothing like it.

"Then we can plan a big Saturday celebration in a year, maybe on your anniversary, and show the town and all your friends and family how fabulous your new life is. The baby can be in your photos. You'll have your figure back." Now, I was appealing to her vanity. Meghan didn't react at first, then her face broke into a sunny smile, and I suddenly knew why Jack loved her. She had a beauty that came shining from the inside out.

"Yes," she whooped. "Yes!" She grabbed Jack's hand and squeezed. "Let's do it! Maybe we can have the wedding on our third month anniversary!" Good Lord. They had only been together two months? I glanced again at Meghan's bump. Did I have a bump like that when I was expecting Ellis at two months? Hard to say. I was not nearly as thin then as Meghan is. Well, Jack wasn't getting any younger. I guess he was ready to start a family. So, we would plan an elopement, not in the classical description, where the bride and groom run away and get married, just the two of them, but this

7

would be more of a micro-wedding.

Believe it or not, there is a lot to do for a 'micro-wedding,' or tiny wedding. This term came into being during the pandemic, and groups were limited to twenty to thirty people, including the bride, groom, and officiant. We had to get a florist, decide on florals, pick a photographer, make sure the bride and groom had their wedding attire, invite guests, and book City Hall. I'd make it beautiful for them. I loved a challenge.

I made a series of phone calls and texts as Jack and Meghan enjoyed a shot of espresso. I saw that my newly acquired luxury espresso machine housed in my tiny office kitchen area was needed.

I ended my final call. I still felt guilty serving coffee that wasn't Jen's. But I needed something to offer my clients, and it just wasn't feasible to run up and down the stairs from my office to her coffee shop to fetch it, I kept telling myself.

"Okay, team. We have an appointment at 9:00 AM tomorrow with Scott for florals, 10:30

AM is penciled in for Shay for wedding attire, then back here for a working lunch to tackle the guest list and how we're going to get the message out. We meet with Jeremy for photos at 1:30 PM, and Emilio from City Fish will be here at 3:00 to discuss the post-ceremony menu. City Hall in Hartford is booked for Saturday June 28th, we've got this!" I tried to put a positive vibe in my voice when the nerves began settling in. So much to do!

Chapter Three

Monday, June 23

Is your outdoor wedding being held in a season where the weather may be either hot or cold? If so, reserve both fans and heaters from your rental company.

I woke at 5:30 AM, so said my night table clock. Yikes, I wasn't ready to get up this early. I had laid awake long after my normal bedtime last night, going over every detail of Jack and Meghan's wedding.

I had to get it right. While it would be a tiny elopement, there would undoubtedly be a press-release photo, and, fingers crossed, I'd be mentioned as the official 'planner.' And there was the big shebang next year. No one said Jack and Meghan had to use me as their planner for that event, but boy, would it be great for business if they did. With the wedding just six days away, I'd have to beg my daughter Ellis to help me with a few details. Ellis had a summer job lined up at a local bed and breakfast, but other than that, she wanted to do nothing more than hang out with friends. Since we had moved here to Eastbury, CT, from California, Ellis had made good friends. I was thankful for that, as our reason for moving back home, well, to my home, was the break-up of my marriage.

A text came in from Jen:

Katie...Jack just texted me...yes this early.

I smiled. She knew I'd ask if he really had texted at this hour.

He wants to get the old group back together tonight at the Lucky Charm.

The town's dive bar.

I DON'T WANT TO GO.

Then don't go, I thought, then sighed. I needed my standby antidote whenever I got cranky. Coffee. But first, I needed to reply. I quickly thumbed back:

You don't have to go.

Yes, I do, she replied.

Yeah ya do, I responded.

She kinda did; the fall-out would be more miserable than just sucking it up and making an appearance. The town had an opinion, and they were often loud.

I lived with a sixteen-year-old. I didn't need any more drama, but it looked as if I'd be getting a front-row seat to some tonight.

* * *

I busied myself today first with the appointments for Jack and Meghan's wedding and then in the late afternoon with the mundane task of bridal paperwork. This was my least favorite activity in the wedding world. But timelines had to be printed and emailed to vendors, procession and recessions had to be organized. Some brides choose to organize their bridesmaids by height, others by how close their relationship is to her. What I love most about weddings today is that there is no right or wrong in how you organize your event. Just don't hurt others' feelings. Sometimes even that is hard, though. I had a bride recently whose parents were divorced—which, of course, is not uncommon. But what *was* uncommon was that they couldn't be in sight of each other. Not an easy task to orchestrate. And don't even get me started about the family photo session.

Somehow, after a too-short break for a salad, a couple of cookies, a cup of tea, and an orange, my day was gone, and it was time for Ellis to get home... then I'd have to get ready for the 'reunion' at 'The Lucky Charm.'

What to wear? I ultimately decided on a pair of comfy jeans and a long-sleeved button-down shirt. The shirt was grey-blue, my signature color, and had been washed so many times it was soft as silk. I threw on my favorite pair of Keds, and I was ready for whatever the night held.

If you had told me two days ago that I'd be sitting at Lucky's with the old gang, *including* Jack and Jen, I'd have given you a shocked stare. But yet, here we are. Lucky's was an Eastbury institution. It is where we would gather during a college break, where couples had broken up, and where a few had become engaged. I know, not the most romantic spot. Established in the 50s, I'd wager no updates had been made since. The tables and chairs were shiny, not so much from furniture polish, but constant rubbing of clothing of the patrons on the surfaces. The wooden floor was scarred, no effort had been made to smooth out the nicks and gouges on the surface. The bar, however, was a thing of beauty. The original owner, the great-grandfather of our current bartender, Rudy, was a master craftsman and had fashioned it over a period of a year with love and an artistry that was perhaps wasted on a bar owner. It was sleek and smooth and if rumor were to be believed, made entirely from a giant live oak from his property.

Eight of us round out our party. There was Brian and me, Jen and her husband, Jeff, whom Jen met in college, Will and Rose, and Jack and Meghan. Will and Jack have a delicate history. I'm actually surprised that Will and his wife, Rose, came tonight. In fact, I'm actually surprised that Will and Rose were even *invited*. Once upon a time, we all were friends, but an incident during our senior year of high school soured things between Will and Jack, and based on how quiet Will was tonight and how tightly he was wounded, I feared he might snap. Will's somber demeanor wasn't new. The few times I had been around him since I had been home wasn't unusual, but tonight, there was a brittleness to his quiet. I was honestly afraid of when, not if, he would snap. No one else seemed to notice the tension except Will's patient wife, Rose. Her face was a little pale, and she hadn't touched the beer in front of her. Rose frequently looked from Will to Jack, her face a study in worry. She must have felt my eyes on her as she looked over at me. I smiled, but she didn't. Will was getting more and more agitated. He was aggressively

11

peeling the label off his Budweiser, his movements quick and jerky.

I excused myself and headed to the ladies' room. I needed a break from the tension and drama. The restroom was cramped and barely clean. I splashed cold water on my face from the rusty faucet and patted my face dry with a brown paper towel. Luckily, I didn't wear a lot of makeup. My face would be a mess right now if I did. I looked in the mirror and shrugged. I'd do. I heard the toilet flush in the second stall, and a tall redhead walked out. She looked vaguely familiar, so I smiled, and so did she. I don't think either of us was up for 'don't I know you,' so we both let it go. She did have a beautiful, enameled metal St. Christopher hanging against her chest. I've always loved that bit of religious jewelry. I had a couple myself. Hers was a particularly luminous shade of green.

"Love your metal," I smiled my appreciation with my tissue-wrapped hand on the doorknob.

"Thanks," she said but with the enthusiasm of someone who had little to be happy about.

I knew I shouldn't engage, but I never could help myself. "All okay?"

She sighed. "Yeah, just a guy, ya know. He's married."

I had little sympathy. I was divorced because my husband had gotten involved with another woman who knew he was married, but she didn't care.

"I'm sorry," I said, and I was. But I wasn't talking about the redhead's situation.

* * *

Not much had improved in the open hostility between Will and Jack. I tried to diffuse the situation with what I thought were amusing stories of weddings gone sideways, from the bride who decided to leave her groom at the alter to the mother of the groom who wore white, but Will would not be drawn in. And it was only eight o'clock!

"Hey, Will," I raised my voice to be heard above the din of the bar. He reluctantly looked away from Jack and met my gaze. He was just too polite of a guy to ignore me. I felt Rose relax slightly beside me. But I couldn't hold Will's attention; he looked back to Jack as Jack seemed to say something rude to Jen.

Jen looked shocked. I don't know what was said, but it couldn't have been very nice. She looked crestfallen and then angry, balling her fists, but she kept them in her lap. And that was it. Nothing was said, but Will had his opening. He just reached over and punched Jack in the face. For those who knew Jack and Will, it wasn't out of the blue. It, in fact, was a very long time coming. Then all hell broke loose. Brian and Jeff grabbed Will, knocking over our high-top table in the process; Meghan screamed and threw her body onto a bleeding Jack.

"You monster," Meghan shouted, her face red with fury. Jack was bleeding through his nose and profusely. Meghan was trying to wipe his nose with a tiny little tissue, doing nothing more than smearing the blood around his face and onto his, I'm sure, uber-expensive shirt. He quickly shook her off and stood, choosing not to engage with Will.

"Come on, Will," Brian said. Brian had a now mostly docile Will by the collar of his shirt, Jeff had his arm around him. "Let's get you out of here." Poor Rose, she followed, weeping softly. I knew Brian would make this go away and that Jack wouldn't press charges. Surprisingly, the room quickly returned to the boisterous rumble.

I looked at Jen, and she rolled her eyes, dismissing the questioning look I had given her. What had Jack said to her? Jack was always the center of drama. Even though she had been a part of the origin of the fight, I know this time she was happy not to be cleaning up his mess. Meghan definitely wasn't as capable as Jen had always been. She was still hot, but was now attempting to put the ice pack Rudy had brought over onto Jack's face. She was none too gentle, and Jack jumped back with a yelp when she pressed a little too hard onto his nose.

I gathered Brian's and my things. "Let's go, Jen."

She didn't quite meet my eyes. "I'll wait for Jeff to come back in, but I want to talk. You okay with me coming over in a bit?"

While surprised, I, of course, agreed. Maybe she'd share what Jack had said to her.

"Sure," I raised an eyebrow at her in question. But she offered nothing more, just turned away, fiddling with her car keys. I guess I'd know soon enough what was on her mind when she stopped by.

Chapter Four

Will your outdoor wedding be held in warm weather months? If so, consider a program of the wedding details in the form of a fan.

I awoke cold and with a stiff neck on my "parlor" sofa at 5:07 AM (I know because I checked the clock on the sofa table). Why was I on the sofa, my pretty blue, but very uncomfortable sofa? Oh, yeah, Jen was supposed to stop by, and we were going to 'debrief.' I checked my phone. Nothing. I wasn't surprised that Jen didn't come by. It was odd that she even suggested it. But what *did* surprise me was that she didn't text to let me know she wasn't coming. That was *not* like Jen. I fired off a quick text to her.

Hey, what happened to you last night—you okay?

I saw the three little dots, reading or writing, I'm still not sure which. Then they went away. What the heck?

Then: **Sorry tired**

And me, **Okay, catch ya later**

And I would. Last night couldn't have been easy on her, and now she seemed 'off' – if one could ascertain when a friend was 'off' by a text. But having a teen in the house, I think I could. It was the little nuances one noticed, no immediate response, vagueness, etc. I'd go to the coffee shop after I got Ellis off to her summer job at the bed and breakfast. I went

15

upstairs to my bedroom, and grabbed my sweats from the slipper chair in the corner of my room and quickly put them on. I'd have to get properly dressed later, but this would do for now. As a business owner in town, I thought it was in my best interest to be professionally dressed *every time I went out*—exhausting!

I entered the kitchen to see the back of Ellis' head as she headed out the mudroom door. "Hey! Where are you off to? It's 5:30 in the morning, for goodness sake." I knew her shift at the local bed and breakfast didn't start until 9:00 AM.

Ellis turned and smiled, something I don't always see. She's a teenage girl, after all.

"Mom, it's not 5:30 in the morning. It's 8:30. The power went out last night." Her glossy chestnut ponytail swung back around.

Dang it all. The clock on the sofa table was plugged into the wall, I should have registered the blinking light on the digital time.; but why didn't I notice the correct time when I looked at my iPhone? I hated when the power went out, which it did frequently around here. Our electric wires were above ground in Eastbury. All the beautiful mature trees our little burg boasted were always being blown down by wind or falling down from a heavy snowfall. It got so bad last winter that I splurged on a generator.

"Well, have a great morning, Elle," I said grabbing a mug to brew a Keurig, not my famous percolator brew, but it would have to do.

"Thanks, Mom. I should be back around 1:00." And she was gone, the early summer morning blowing in with the hint of lavender from our bushes in the side yard as she shut the door. I put my coffee mug back into the cupboard and grabbed my favorite stainless steel travel mug. Chloe and I could do with a walk down by the river before I headed to Jen's coffee shop, The Perk. The gentle breeze that blew in as Ellis left had convinced me I wanted to be outside. I quickly brewed a Keurig in the travel mug. Coffee made, light sweatshirt zipped, Chloe on leash, I headed out. We weren't far from the Connecticut River. Far enough away that the bugs weren't complete pests, close enough to walk there. The morning was glorious. I smelled the damp/pungent scent of the rich Connecticut River Valley, and it smelled like...home.

Chloe and I started out on the trail behind our house; the cool morning air invigorated me. I shivered slightly. Chloe strutted along with her dachshund spunk. Should I have worn more layers? The mornings here were often cold, even in late June. I was almost to the town boathouse, and I saw lights, red and blue lights, flashing through the foliage. What the heck? As I got a little closer, I saw that a crowd had formed, held back by the ominous yellow crime scene tape. Oh God, what now? This took me back, not in a good way, to the murder I was accused of this past spring. I walked hesitantly to the crowd. I didn't see any friendly faces. As small of a town as Eastbury was, I didn't know *everyone*. I approached a group of women who looked about my age.

"What happened?" I inquired.

The apparent leader of the little mom's group looked me up and down. Apparently, I passed muster. "They found a body in the water."

"Oh, my stars!" I said, feeling horror at the thought. "Who is it?"

"No one's talking officially yet," said the leader, dressed from head to toe in lululemon yoga gear, "but my brother-in-law is with the Eastbury Fire Department, and he told my sister, who told me," (yes, that's usually how it worked), "that it's that famous baseball player who showed up at Strawberry Moon a couple nights ago."

The coffee I had been sipping on from my travel mug threatened to come back up. My stomach rolled. What the heck? Jack? I had just seen him last night. This could *not* be happening! I pushed around the gawking crowd of people, trying to get as close to the yellow crime scene tape as possible. I looked around wildly for Brian. Surly, he was on-scene. I finally saw him talking to a man whom I can only guess was the coroner based on the staff next to him with a gurney...and a body bag. He must have felt my eyes on him as he looked up. Our eyes met, and he very softly shook his head. "Go home," he mouthed. I did. And on the beautiful walk home along the grand Connecticut River, I felt tears fall. I hadn't seen Jack in years, but he had been a friend once upon a time, and there were people who had loved him.

I unlocked the mudroom door of my historic home. I loved my little abode.

I embraced all its idiosyncrasies, such as wavy windows, leaky roofs, I could go on and on. But sometimes, it did get tiresome. This morning, the door chose to stick, ugh. I finally wrenched it open just as my phone began to buzz its text notification. I entered, shut the door, and looked at my screen. It was Brian.

Does Jen know?

Oh my gosh! I hadn't even thought of Jen! I called her immediately, but it went straight to voicemail. I dialed right back. Maybe she didn't feel the phone's vibration; she always kept it on vibrate. Or maybe she had just heard about Jack from someone else and was too broken up to talk. Because even if she did act indifferently, I know how much Jack had meant to Jen at one time. Well, I'd just have to go over to The Perk.

"I needed a cup of joe anyway. My sweet little dachshund, Chloe, looked up at me with big chocolate eyes. 'More walk, please,' they seemed to beg. But she would slow me down as she sniffed every little leaf, a scrap of paper, or another dog she encountered.

"Later today, my love," I promised. And I meant it. I had to do my part.

It was only a three-block walk to the coffee establishment, The Perk Jen, owned, and where my own storefront was located above. Jen was so generous with me. She charged me next to nothing for rent. Good to have friends. I had great hopes that next year, my wedding planning business would be in the position to pay Jen the full market rate for my office rent.

The morning was still cool, not yet showing the heat of the day to come. The gentle breeze ruffled my hair. I was happy to be alive. Which brought me back to Jack. Grief hit me in a new wave. I entered 'The Perk.' Everyone loved this little shop. Yes, there were other coffee establishments in town, but the locals were loyal to Jen. And she made a mean cup of coffee. The cowbells on the door jingled merrily on the door as I opened it. I scanned the scarred old bar but didn't see Jen. Was she in the back kitchen area? I approached the side of the bar and leaned over to scan the back area. No, Jen.

"Is Jen here?" I asked Tally, Jen's right-hand barista, who worked most mornings.

"No," Tally shook her carrot top briskly while catching a double espresso shot in a glass shot glass. "She was supposed to open this morning, too, at 5:00. I slept through a text of hers asking me to open for her, so I didn't get here until about 7:00. Some of the regulars were waiting outside when I rolled in this morning. Not happy!" She made her eyes bug out comically.

"And Kate, I didn't want to mention this to anyone, but this isn't the first time she's unexpectedly asked me to open early for her—with no explanation. I'd quit if she weren't so darn good to me." She shook her head, whether at herself for being a pushover or at Jen's thoughtlessness, I'm not sure.

"And you haven't heard from her since?" I was worried now. To my knowledge, usually, nothing, and I mean *nothing*, kept Jen from opening her shop each morning. Even when she had an appendicitis, Jen went to work and waited until Tally arrived before driving herself to the hospital. Tally's admission was news to me.

"No," Tally was serious now, the worry apparent on her face. "And I heard about Jack. You don't think…"

What was Tally implying? I needed to tread lightly here. This scenario was just how rumors started. "I don't think anything, Tally, but that Jen probably had a situation where she neglected to communicate and ask you to come in and open. I'll get ahold of her, and I'm sure she'll reach out." I smiled but was afraid it looked a little forced. I turned to go.

"Wait, Katie," your coffee!" She filled a large paper cup with the roast of the day, slipped a sleeve onto the cup, snapped a lid on, and smiled. She was a doll. I had never paid for a cup of coffee at Jen's in my life. I dropped a five in the tip jar and skipped the condiment bar with all the creamers, sugars, and spice shakers. The fact that I didn't put any of the yummy half-and-half in my cup spoke volumes about my worry and urgency to get to Jen's house. I hustled out the door and made a sharp right down the street. Jen and her dentist husband lived at the beginning of the historic district of Main Street. I was about a five-minute walk away when my phone buzzed with a text. Thank God it was from Jen.

Sorry for not communicating – busy. Busy? That's all I got after being stood up last night, not to mention Jack and her 'no-show' status at The

Perk this morning. Not that Jen was answerable to me about anything, but I expected some sort of wild story. Anything but just a generic 'busy.'

Where are you? Important."

I heard about Jack if that's what's up. Sorry—unless it's an emergency—can't talk now

Then Brian:

Need to talk asap Where are you? On my way to your house now

Okay, I replied, and changed my destination to head back to my house.

I vacillated between worry and irritation, worry that something was really wrong with Jen and irritation that she was being a jerk. But I knew her. Something was off, very off.

It was apparent Jen didn't want to talk yet. I was just one house away from mine when I saw Brian's unmarked in my driveway. He was waiting on my coveted covered front porch. When I lived in California, I had always wanted a porch, but one, there wasn't room on the tiny lots in Orange County, and two, it just wasn't the California architectural vibe. Brian was pacing with agitated short steps. When he saw me walk up, he stopped, a frown on his handsome face.

"Where have you been?" His tone was harsher than I'd like or than was warranted. But he had just lost an old friend. I know he was stressed...and grieving.

"The Perk. Looking for Jen." Should I tell Brian I didn't find her? That something weird is going on with Jen? That she didn't show up at work this morning or here last night? No, not until I speak with her and find out what's going on. After all, Jen surely had a reason unrelated to what happened with Jack for acting oddly, and I didn't want her to face unnecessary police scrutiny.

"Let's get you a cup of coffee..." Do you have time?" When he nodded, I unlocked the mudroom door. I never used to lock my doors, but all that changed after a nasty incident this past spring.

He followed me in, leaving his work boots by the door. I didn't ask it of him but appreciated the gesture. I measured coffee and then water and added them both to the percolator, setting the gas flame on the stove just so. To enjoy my coffee, one had to wait. Instant gratification was not on a percolator's timeline. I gently reached for Brian's hand and guided him over to the loveseat positioned in front of my cold kitchen fireplace. It's June, but in New England, it can still be very chilly in the mornings. I sat next to him and opened my arms. He eased into them, putting his head in the crook of my neck and shoulder.

"Do they know anything?"

"No," came his muffled reply.

"How did he, was he…"

"No cause or manner of death yet. We'll have to wait for the medical examiner. I'm guessing drowning, though."

"How bizarre. Do you think it was…an accident?"

Brian disentangled himself and stood up. He rubbed the back of his neck in a distracted way. "I don't know Katie. Something's not right, though. We both know that. Jack drowning in the river? Come on. The state police will handle the case due to Jack's celebrity. Eastbury Police will be here to assist if needed. I'll probably be point on that end." I was surprised that Brian would be on the case due to his friendship with Jack. But our police force was small, and Brian and Jack weren't family.

"Their investigator arrived right before I came here. He can iron out this mess." He paced the small space of my kitchen seating area. "I'm actually here to ask a favor."

My curiosity was sparked. I stood, too. "Favor? Need help with the case?" I teased, even though it seemed a little inappropriate.

Apparently, Brian did, too, because he frowned, something he rarely did to me.

"Sorry, Bri," I said, chastened.

He sat back down again, his large legs spread wide. "Katie, will you go over and check on Meghan at the bed and breakfast? She obviously didn't take his death notification well when I made it. And not sure if it was the right time, but we did a preliminary interview right then and there. Was Jack was having problems with anyone, did they do anything after the bar, what time they got back from the B&B, etc." I embraced him. Brian never gave me details of the interviews. He must be more tormented than I thought. How awful for both Brian and Meghan to go through that. I know death notifications were the worst part of law enforcement. But wow, an interview about Jack's death right then and there. But then maybe she knew something important, and it needed to be addressed right away. "Her mom and sister left last night for a spa weekend in New York, before….before Jack." Brian's voice broke.

My heart hurt for Brian, and wow. I had not even thought about poor Meghan, who was pregnant, too. I took his hand and squeezed.

"Of course! I'll head over right now. Turn the percolator off in seven minutes, and give yourself a minute to rest with the coffee." My voice softened as I grabbed my keys. I'd drive to the B&B. It was right down the road, but I'd get there faster than walking.

"Room four," he said to my retreating back.

When I got to the B&B, I rushed in but didn't see Ellis. I quickly found room four and knocked softly on the door. Isabelle, the proprietress, and Ellis' boss this summer, smiled sadly at me when she passed by carrying a pile of towels. She'd obviously heard about Jack. I initially got no response to my knocking, but I tried again. "Meghan," I said softly. "It's Kate Ludlow. May I come in?" To ask her if she was 'okay' seemed like a ridiculous question.

I heard shuffling on the other side of the door. She seemed to be fumbling with the lock and doorknob, but the door finally creaked open. She only showed half of her tear-stained face.

"Kate," she said, but then broke into silent sobs. His whole body shook.

"Ah, Meghan." I eased the door further open, hugged her, and let her cry a little before guiding her to the loveseat set catty corner in front of the double windows.

"I, I can't believe it!" Meghan finally met my eyes, hers brown and filled with unshed tears. "It just doesn't seem real!"

"I know, I know Meg. It will take some time to sink in. How are you feeling?"

Her puzzled look surprised me. "Feeling? Destroyed, that's how." I saw a momentary flash of annoyance.

"Of course, but I meant with the pregnancy."

"Oh, fine, I guess." She stood and crossed the room to pick up her hairbrush and began brushing her long blond hair in slow, rhythmic strokes, her face becoming a blank canvas.

"Do you want to go to the doctor, just to check in, make sure all is okay, maybe they'll prescribe something." What I didn't know. What was safe for a pregnant woman to take? But she didn't seem normal, but then who would?

"No," she looked off out the window, not at me. I'm okay, and I'm sure the baby is too. My mom and sister will be here soon…"

"Yes, that's good." A soft knock interrupted her.

"Meghan," I heard Isabelle say through the door. "Your mom's on the house line. She says you're not answering your cell."

Meghan went to the door and opened it. She looked anything but grieved at the moment, more annoyed than anything. "I told her I was turning it off," she growled but stomped out into the hall, apparently going to answer her mother's summons. Isabelle gently closed the door as she left. Well, this was awkward. I peered around the luxurious room. I had always wanted to check these rooms out. Ellis is a 'Jill of all Trades' at the bed and breakfast. I had been sorely tempted to ask her for an unsanctioned tour. Now was my chance. I know it's rude. I know I'm crossing the line, but I went ahead and checked out Meghan's suite. Wow, it was swanky. I took a peek into the bathroom and almost swooned at the lovely antique claw foot tub. And were they…yes, yes, the bathroom floors were heated, I noted as I reached down to put my hand on the floor. I reentered the bedroom and admired the tasteful antique furnishings: Tiffany table lamps and a crystal candy dish with foil-wrapped chocolates from our own town's confectionery. I thought I should get back to the spot by the door I had been in when Meghan ran to the house phone when I noticed, mostly tucked under the crystal bowl, the ultrasound print-out Jack and Meghan had showed me when they were in my office. I looked at the door. No Meghan yet. I shouldn't…but I did. I picked up the printout and began analyzing it. But too soon, the doorknob rattled, and I quickly slid the photos back under the candy dish. I didn't have time to think, merely to compose myself before Meghan reentered. Not sure what, but something bothered me about that ultrasound.

I put my shaking hand rather awkwardly into my jean's pockets. Yep, still awkward. I don't think Meghan noticed, though.

She had come in a rush, her cheeks flushed as red as a Sea Breeze cranberry cocktail, which I bet she could use about now. Although being pregnant…Meghan flopped down onto the Victorian loveseat, definitely not a comfortable respite, from its scratchy heavy brocade fabric to its stiff contour.

"Meghan?" I queried.

"Uuugghh," she groaned rather dramatically, throwing her head against the loveseat's high back. "My mom and sister are stuck in the terrible Fairfield County traffic. She started to tear up. "I just want my mom." She sounded so young. "I knew something was wrong when he went out again last night after he dropped me off here when we got home. I was just so tired, though. I went right to sleep and didn't even realize he hadn't come home until this morning when I woke up. Then that terrible cop came and told me…" Meghan started to sob, and not in an attractive way. Poor thing. My heart broke for her. I sat next to her, gathered her bony little body next to me, and swayed with her.

"What time did Jack go out?" Was I rude to ask?

"What…" Even little Meghan seemed surprised at my rude, random question.

"Ah…" she continued, "about 9:00, I guess." I rocked her some more. 'My mom is staying here with us," she continued about her mother, "but she and Marjorie left really early to go the Elizabeth Arden in the city for the day. They invited me last night, but I was too tired."

"It's going to be okay," I mumbled. Was it, though?

Chapter Five

Will your outdoor wedding/reception be held in traditionally cooler weather? If so, perhaps a fun "favor" would be a small blanket for guests to keep cozy.

I awoke to a text from Brian: ***Have you heard from Jen? We stopped by her house and Jeff said she hadn't been home for a day. Looks bad for her, Katie.***

No, not since yesterday. My reply, but it didn't appear he was reading it—no bubbles.

When can you come to the station to make a statement? He responded.

Later today

I received a thumbs-up on my text.

The media had descended on little Eastbury like ants at a picnic. They were everywhere—Main Street, the Bed and Breakfast, the Fountain, I saw when I turned on the little TV this morning that Ellis and I kept on the kitchen counter. It was already set to a news station, and I did a quick flip to see if we were on every station. We were. Under an ordinary situation, it might be fun to see our local town square and shops on the news, but not under these circumstances. I imagine getting a cup of coffee today at The Perk would be a nightmare. And Jen had gone dark. I had heard nothing more from her. Even the one-line texts had stopped.

I smiled a good morning to Ellis who was loading her breakfast dishes in the dishwasher. Love that girl! I had turned the TV on at the right moment. There was a press conference being held. Brian introduced 'Scott Bennett' the state investigator on the case. I guess that's why I didn't get a text response from Brian.

"Thanks, Detective McAllister. Detective McAllister is our local liaison here in Eastbury. And before you start," Officer Bennett began, "I will be taking no questions today. The coroner has determined the manner of death to be homicide, and the cause of death is still pending more tests." There was an audible gasp from the crowd. I wish I wasn't surprised, but I wasn't. The reporters began yelling out questions, disregarding Officer Bennett's previous statement regarding questions. He held up a hand, and surprisingly, the crowd silenced. We are interviewing anyone who spent time with Mr. O'Malley in the last twenty-four hours leading up to his death and will update you when we have a person or persons of interest and then a suspect."

Ellis stopped loading her breakfast dishes to listen. "Oh my God, Mom, murder?" She looked stunned. I sat down heavily on a barstool. My first reaction was worry. If the police were interviewing all the people who had spent time with Jack the last twenty-four hours, my mind went immediately to Will and his little tussle with Jack. He was surely a good bet. And then my thoughts flew to Jen. What if she didn't turn up for a, sure to be requested interview? It would look awful for her. My mind was racing. I needed to do something to help Jen if she was incapable of helping herself or, for some reason, wouldn't. I might not know who killed Jack; it's just that Jen wouldn't have done it. But why had she gone dark right at this time? And what did Jack say to Jen that night to ruffle her feathers?

"Earth to Mom," Ellis said, waving a dish towel in my face.

"Sorry, Hon," I smiled weakly at her. "It's a lot to take in." I needed a cup of coffee. I stood up and reached for my stove-top percolator to begin the brewing process.

"Ah, yeah," Ellis agreed, "like a murder lurking around town." She was putting the last couple of lunch items in her cloth bag for work and then started in on putting away last night's dinner pots drying on the rack. Doing a little bit of everything from cooking to cleaning rooms at the Bed and Breakfast was good for her and for me.

"Elle…" I said in my most sincere voice. This whole murder thing looks bad for Jen as she's made herself scarce. It kind of makes her look guilty."

My mind was spinning, thinking of all the different scenarios, but I kept going back to that darn ultrasound. I'd have to go to my office to confirm something, but I really needed to see again the ultrasound photos I saw in Meghan's room at the Bed and Breakfast.

"Jen's missing?" The concern in her voice was apparent. Ellis loved Jen. Jen was not a new face to Elle when we moved here, and Jen's daughters had been so welcoming to Ellis.

"Well, she hasn't been at The Perk; Brian can't find her, and as of today, she isn't returning my texts. There's something wrong, I just know it, and I need to help her, Ellis."

Ellis stopped putting away the pots. "Of course, Mom. Can I do anything?"

"Funny you should ask, Ellis…" I shared my plan.

"Mom, no!" Ellis tossed a dish towel on the counter in a show of displeasure, "Despite what you might think, I actually like my job and don't want to get fired." She turned now to face me, her face stormy. I knew she looked like me when I was indignant. I wanted to laugh but knew it wouldn't be in my best interest.

Wow, this I didn't expect. I really thought Ellis would be down to do a little investigating, even if it was with dear old mom.

"Ellis," I whittled. "It would just be for a couple of minutes; no one would have to know. We could do it while Isabelle is cooking breakfast." I smiled my best smile. She didn't crack.

"I said 'no,' Mom. I'm surprised you don't see how wrong it would be to snoop in Meghan's room. She just lost her fiancé, and she's super nice." Ellis washed her hands at the sink, and I knew I didn't have much time left to convince her.

"That's exactly right, Elle, but this is to help Jen. How can you not want to help, 'cause I can assure you she's in trouble.

This stopped Ellis in her tracks. "Mom," she said with what appeared to cause her great patience. "How is snooping through Meghan's things and looking for an ultrasound photo helping Jen? And have you gone over to her house to see if she's there?"

Well, she had me there. "I don't have an answer to the first question, and to the second, I haven't been to her house, but I plan to right after the B&B. "But you know Jen. She'd never leave her girls, Jeff, and The Perk, especially now, if she weren't in some type of trouble. I have to start somewhere, Elle. I'm calling in a chip, Ellis." I stated dramatically, grabbing my light jacket on the back of one of the kitchen chairs. I was met with silence and an air of resignation. If one of us called in "a chip," there was not much to be done. And as we both knew, I had two chips to Ellis'…none. Ellis was still quiet. Hummm…

"Okay," I compromised, "I'll throw you one," meaning a chip. A chip was used for a favor, a grant of an unusual request, etc.

"Let's go, Mom. You kinda make sense. Jen's a super great mom. Can't see her leaving the girls." And the whirlwind that was my daughter grabbed my car keys. "I'll drive." Ellis and her learner's permit were going to be the death of me. I don't know if my parents lived through my practice driving. I'm not sure how I'd live through Ellis'.

* * *

As luck would have it, Meghan had gone out for a run. "Now is the time to clean her room," Isabelle had told Ellis. Could my timing be any better? I gloated as Elle snuck me in the side door and up the stairs to the second floor. But now that we were here, in Meghan's room, I felt bad. Maybe I shouldn't be here. I had no business snooping. But someone had been murdered, and my best friend was MIA.

Ellis was starting to look uncomfortable again. "Okay, Mom. You're here to do whatever hunting you're going to do. So…" she flitted her fingers in a dismissive gesture at me. "I'm going to go start on the bathroom."

Well, I was going to get started, too; I was wasting no time. I looked under the candy dish where I had originally seen the ultrasound photo. Not there, so I looked under the magazines, *inside* the magazines, under the table, on the nightstand...nothing.

"Did you ever think, Mom, that the ultrasound photo is precious to her and that Meghan has the ultrasound photo with her in her pocketbook?" Ellis asked when she reentered the bedroom and observed my obvious frustration at the missing ultrasound photos.

I looked around the room and noted the many designer bags Meghan had tossed around the room. Jeez! Did she need a different one for each outfit?

"How could you tell if one was missing?" That got a smile from Ellis. "And who takes her pocketbook on the run?" I cocked a brow at a disapproving Ellis.

I walked past Ellis, and I did a quick search of the ensuite bath, but again, there was nothing. I might as well make my exit. I walked to the room's door in defeat, but two steps away, I stepped on something. I looked down and picked up a screw. Huh. Then I looked up. There was a screw missing in a heater vent in the ceiling. And we know what that means; someone opened that vent, and I think I knew why. I dragged the desk chair over underneath the vent.

"Mom? What the heck are you doing? And quiet!" Ellis commanded at the screech the chair had made on the floor.

"Shush," I commanded. She watched in confusion as I dug through my cross-body bag slung around my side, withdrew my handy-dandy thirty-in-one knife, and opened the Phillips screwdriver attachment. I proceeded to unscrew the remaining screws of the vent and handed them and the vent cover to a hovering Ellis. I grimaced, put my hand in the opening...and withdrew the ultrasound picture. Now, why would it be *here*? I quickly reattached the vent cover with the screws, hopped off the chair, and grabbed the photo from Ellis. No time! I took a quick picture with my iPhone of the ultrasound picture and shoved it back into the vent via the slats.

"Put the chair back for me, will ya, Elle? I smacked a quick kiss on her cheek and skedaddled from the room, but not before checking the small hallway for guests or, even worse, Isabelle. I didn't know what it meant that

Meghan had hidden her precious ultrasound printout picture in the air duct, but it didn't bode well for 'nothing.' I need to talk to Jen; she was always my 'go-to' to hash things out with.

I successfully made my way out the front door of the bed and breakfast meeting, but no one I knew. I was glad, not so much for me, but I didn't want Elle to get in any trouble, sneaking her dear old mother in. However, a CNN van was parked across the street, and an NBC news van was parked behind it. There are no reporters to be seen, though. They were lurking somewhere, I was sure. As soon as I was clear of the Bed and Breakfast, I opened my photo app on my iPhone and looked at the ultrasound picture. I focused on the dates. They gave me pause. I'd have to go to my office and read my notes from my meeting with Jack and Meghan. But first, I was headed to Jen's house. When I got there, the house looked shuttered, and no one answered my repeated knocking. Well, it was a workday. I'm not sure where Jen's daughters were, their summer jobs were at The Perk and I'm assuming that Jeff, Jen's husband, was at his office. He was a much-loved dentist in town. I hated to, but it was time to check in with him.

I stopped my knocking and scrolled through my phone's contacts to Jeff's dental office. No use calling him directly. If he was in office, he probably couldn't answer anyway.

"Eastbury Family Dental," a melodious voice answered.

"Hi Carol, it's Kate McKenna. Is Jeff in today?"

"Hey, Kate. Crazy times here in town, right?" Those news people are everywhere!"

"Sure are! Is Jeff in?" Carol was sweet, but got off track easily.

"He's with a patient right now, Kate. Do you want to leave a message, or can I make an appointment for you?"

Oh, boy. "Ah…I'll just call him on his cell. Nothing important. Have a great day, Carol." And I clicked off. So, at least Jeff was accounted for. But what did he know?

* * *

Coffee time. I breezed through the front doors of The Perk, dismayed by the crowded tables and long line at the coffee bar. All these extra patrons had to be the media covering Jack's story, right? I didn't recognize three-fourths of the crowd. I guess I shouldn't be surprised; the media needed their coffee, too, and there were sure to be lookie-loos wanting to see the town where Jack o

O'Malley was killed. I searched out and met Tally's eyes. She shook her head slowly but held my coffee aloft. Thank you, Tally! I sure didn't want to wait in that crazy coffee line. I went up to the side of the bar and accepted it, thankfully. Tally smiled softly but didn't stay around to chat. Too busy. I didn't think Jen would be here, but I sure did hope so. I was ready to head back out when a customer by the window stood and, well, just exploded.

As he stood up, his chair toppled to the ground behind him, thankfully not hitting the woman seated at the next table.

"It infuriates me, that's all. I'm not trying to be difficult. But just when I think he's going to make things right, he goes off and gets himself killed!" The man's face was red, and I was worried for his health. He looked like he might have a heart attack at any moment.

"Calm *down,* Rodney," the blond seated at the table with him tried to grab his hand and pull him back down and into another chair at the table. The angry man righted his chair and grudgingly sat down. The blond looked around, as if hoping no one had noticed. Good luck with that. Everyone was looking, and waiting, it seemed, as one with bated breath to see what would happen next. I don't think 'Mr. Angry ' Man realized he was the center of attention. The blond, however, appeared mortified. Her face was cherry red, which sure did clash with her Kelly green polo dress, and she began gathering her things. Were they talking about Jack? The circumstances seemed to suggest that was the case.

My eyes met the blond's. Now my face was feeling very warm, and I worried about turning red. I always chattered when I was uncomfortable. I really shouldn't this time...but then...

"Do you, can I..." I stumbled over my words. Why did I do this? There was no reason for me to butt in. Somehow, I always seemed to think that

31

by speaking, I could somehow stem the awkwardness, but come on. It only made it worse.

The blond looked at me coolly and then adverted her eyes. "We're fine, thanks." And she began to gather their things.

'Rodney' put his hand over the blond's and stopped her progression. "Wait a minute, Lila; might as well ask some questions, see if anyone has some answers we don't." Was he referring to me? "Maybe she can shed some light on the situation."

They both looked at me, my mouth falling open. Why did I get myself in these fixes?

"Well?" Rodney sat back down and waved his hand toward me back and forth, as if to say, 'get on with it.'

"Uh," I said brilliantly. "Who are you talking about?" Dollars to donuts, it was Jack.

"Jack O'Malley, know him?" Rodney asked with a scowl, then a smirk.

I swayed a little. This day was all so bizarre. "Yeah, I knew him, but I don't know anything more than the police." The blond paled even more, and Rodney slapped the flat of his hand hard onto the table. Everyone really did look then, and the room got even more quiet.

"That son of a bitch. And he cheats me again. And you know I'm not just talking money, Lila." 'Rodney gave the blond a look. "If you knew him, do you have contact info on his next of kin?"

Can you say awkward? What to say and why was he asking *me*? "Um, if you want more information, the local police force may be able to help, or his fiancé is here in town." Yikes, was that a mistake to mention Meghan? Rodney was plenty angry.

"Meg? Meg's here?" His demeanor changed dramatically. He was no longer angry, but concern filled his face. I thought maybe this was the best time to make my getaway and did just that. I all but ran from 'The Perk.' I didn't find Jen, but I sure did find someone who seemed to hate Jack, and it appeared, with reason. What had he gotten himself into, and did it prove to be his undoing?

32

* * *

I watched from across the street as Rodney and the blond woman left rather abruptly. Were they going in search of Meghan? I wondered. I leaned against one of the ornamental streetlights that our lovely Main Street sported and sipped my coffee. I let my mind wander. I kept going back to the ultrasound. Okay, I thought to myself. Go up to your office and look at your notes from your meeting with Jack and Meghan.

I used the outside stairs to my office suite. I could either use those, or the inside access stairs. Handy if I need to get into my office and Jen's shop was closed. I entered my office and was not happy with the mustiness. I opened a window, and it groaned with the stress of it. The building was at least a hundred years old. I sat down at my desk and grabbed Jack and Meghan's file folder from the 'in basket' on my desk. I flipped through my interview notes. Ah ha! I knew there was something that didn't jibe. I wrote *Meghan due in seven months.* And when Meghan handed me the ultrasound, the due date indeed said January 11. I noticed it because that date was my grandparents' anniversary. I unlocked my phone and looked at the picture of the ultrasound. Oh, my stars! It was a completely different ultrasound. This one said the due date was November 11. No wonder Meghan had hidden this one. This brought up so many questions. Was the baby Jack's? If not, who was the father? How in the world did she get a fake ultrasound? Was this a motive for murder? Somehow, I didn't see Meghan as a murderess. She seemed to really love Jack. That had been apparent to me in the little time I had spent with the two of them Sunday morning. Who then? Well, that guy Rodney sure was mad. But there was another person who was mad too. Will. He and Jack had had that fight Monday night at Lucky's. I wondered if he had gone to the police station to give his statement yet. I made a snap decision. I was going to drop by Will and Rose's house. Rose was a hostess at a baby shower I helping out with—gratis. The sweet 'mother-to-be' had lost her husband last month in a car crash, so some ladies from our Parish wished to throw her a shower. I offered, as my contribution, to organize it all. Would it be a little awkward to just stop by Rose and Will's without notice? Yeah…but I'd make it work. I'd do it right after I made my statement at the police station.

* * *

I presented myself at our charming police station. It was a quintessential New England building with cedar wooden shakes on the outer walls. It really was too cute to be a municipal building. After the desk sergeant buzzed me in, I was taken to the interview room. Brian was there with the State Officer in Charge, Scott Bennett. I didn't have much to tell. But they seemed very interested in the fight that broke out between Will and Jack. Yes, Brian had been there too, but I offered a different perspective, or so it seemed to me.

I placed my hands on the cold metal of the interview table. I hadn't even been offered coffee. This did not make me happy. "Brian, you know as well as I do what that fight was about. It's been brewing for years. Everyone knows it."

Scott Bennett looked to Brian, as if to say, what the heck, Bro? But he kept his silence. Brian didn't answer me, just asked another question. "What did Jack say to Jen that got her so riled up at the bar?'

I hadn't expected that question, but I guess I should have, as I wondered too, and planned to ask her when she came over to my house that night. But she never showed.

"I really don't know," I said in all honesty. They dismissed me after that. I don't think they thought they'd gleam much more intel from me, except maybe what Jack said to Jen. On my way out of the interview room, I passed Will. Now really would be a good time to go see Rose for that 'drop-in.'

Could my timing be any more perfect? If I went to Will and Rose's house right now, I'd have Rose alone, easier to grill, I mean question her.

"Hey, Will," I offered.

"Hey, Katie," he replied, but he looked straight ahead and went into the station.

* * *

I was going to do it. I was going to go to Will and Rose's. Decision made, I got two texts at almost the same time, not unusual for me. One made me happy, the other distraught.

First: *Mom!* Ellis almost never used punctuation. The fact she did was significant. *Kevin wants to hang tonight at the concert on the green is that okay* (see no punctuation).

I smiled. Kevin was the middle son of my old high school friend, now library aid at the high school, Rainey. Kevin was a great kid, and *YES, Ellis*, I typed, *sure, home by curfew.* 'Concert on the Green' was a summer concert series every Wednesday in the Summer 'on The Green' smack dab in the middle of town. You could bring lawn chairs, or a blanket, and snacks if you wished. It was a gathering of all age groups and loved by many. I couldn't think of a more wholesome date.

The second text grabbed my heart with an icy hold. *Kate, Scott's* (the statie) *putting the pressure on to find Jen the fact that no one can put eyes on her doesn't look good. Thanks for coming in for your interview.*

So, the police couldn't find her either. Oh God. At least she had responded to me, even if it was a while ago.

My thumbs flew across my phone's keyboard.

Been looking for her too, so far, no Jen.

When was the last time you spoke to Jen?

She checked in the morning Jack's body was found.

I didn't have to look up Rose and Will's address, it was the home he grew up in. I had been there a few times in high school with Brian. When Will's parents moved to Florida, he and his wife, Rose, bought the home. That happened a lot here in Eastbury; homes change from parent to child. It's a win-win. The 'children' bought a home they knew the history of and were given a fair deal. The parents sold to someone they knew and trusted. There were no surprises, no bad deals. Or that's the way it usually worked, and I imagine this was no exception.

I hadn't called ahead to see if this would be a convenient time, which went against my personal sense of etiquette. But I didn't want to give Rose time to find an excuse to avoid me. She probably would sense I was nosing around in Jack's murder investigation. I wasn't sure of a warm welcome. I took a deep breath, fluffed the 'Whole Foods' flower bouquet I had brought, hey! Who doesn't like flowers? A sometimes-over-looked gem is the $5.99 flower bouquet from Whole Foods. Can you believe it? My heart was beating with anxiety. I never just showed up, anywhere, and never on someone's doorstep. I pressed the doorbell, but Rose probably saw me on her doorbell camera. Would she answer? I heard a dog bark; then his nails clicked on the floor, and finally, footsteps. Rose opened the door and smiled, if with a little bit of a question on her pretty face.

"Kate!" Rose was too gracious to say, 'What the heck are you doing here?' but I could see it on her face.

I awkwardly thrust the bouquet at her, not my best moment. But Rose took them gracefully.

"Why thank you, Kate," and this time, there was no masking the question in her eyes. "Please, come in. Will's at the police station being questioned. I already had my interview. Have you had yours?" She opened the door wider.

I walked into the house. "Yeah, just got back from mine. Thought maybe we could talk about the baby shower." Rose was too gracious to question my flimsy excuse for my impromptu visit. She pulled her beautiful golden retriever by the collar when she nuzzled me, probably smelling Chloe on me. "Presley, no! I'm sorry, Kate, but she's a people lover."

I rubbed Presley's head. "She's gorgeous." And she was.

"Come on in." Rose escorted me into the kitchen, and we perched on a pair of stools. "Coffee?" asked Rose as she simultaneously reached for a vase on top of her cupboards, filled it with water, and expertly arranged the bouquet. I imagine the top of her cupboards was a convenient place to store all the vases she had received with flowers over the years, but the varying sizes, shapes, and colors were a great vibe. I loved it. I was going to rethink how I stored my own vases at home. I liked seeing them all out.

"I'd love coffee," I answered honestly.

Rose made short work of my order, brewing a Keurig cup and offering cream and sugar. I declined both; my waistline would appreciate it.

Time to at least try to put this awkwardness aside and get right to the point.

"Rose, we know each other well enough, to be honest. I'm here about Will and Jack. I want to be totally candid here.

"Please do," she inserted, but didn't smile.

Yikes. Rose wasn't going to make this easy, not that I deserved it after this drop in visit.

I held up my hand as if to say, 'Cut me a little slack.' "Jen is MIA, and I'm trying to figure things out—to help her." Oh, there was history between Jack and Will…I thought.

"Maybe there's a reason for Jen being MIA." And she grabbed a tea towel and wiped at something invisible on the counter so as not to meet my eyes.

"Rose. You know Jen. She wouldn't hurt a fly…"

Now, she did meet my eyes, and she was angry. "And Will would? That's why you're here, isn't it, Kate? To snoop around and get some of the heat off Jen, but at whose expense? Will's, that's whose!" She met my gaze for gaze. Wow, I just realized I wouldn't want her for an enemy.

"Whoa, Rose. This is spinning in the wrong direction. I don't suspect Will." I did. "I'm just here, I'll admit, to try to figure out what's going on. To try to put some of the pieces together. If you really think I would suspect Will, then maybe others would, too, like the police. Maybe we can help each other." This last was brilliant, if I do say so myself.

The manic hand with the scrubbing tea towel stopped. I could almost see the wheels turning in her head, weighing the pros and cons of throwing in with me. She came around the island and sat down on one of the stools.

"Okay. What do you want to know?" She was watching me like a hawk, looking for tells or lying eyes, I'm sure.

"Well," I didn't want to offend this woman. But I'd probably have to, or this errand would be for nothing. "Was Will acting unusual lately, staying out late, unexpected absences…?" Will was the food and beverage manager at a swanky hotel in downtown Hartford. A big job with a lot of responsibility, but definitely not the career of his dreams. Jack had ruined those. I don't think I had succeeded in *not* offending Rose. By the look on her face, almost

37

outrage, but not quite.

"Wow, Kate. You go right for the heart, don't you?" Gone was the gracious smile I had been greeted with.

I wasn't going to sugar-coat anything. "Come on, Rose." You know as well as I do that the police are going to question everyone who was at The Lucky Charm the night Jack was killed. And everyone will share that Will and Jack had an altercation. But so did Jen and Jack. I'm trying to help Jen as she won't help herself. I just want some information. Let's help each other." Sometimes, I just wasn't a very nice person. I didn't want to help her, or help Will. I wanted to help Jen. And if I had to throw someone under the bus, I would. The question was, did she believe me? Would she trust me?

Rose looked down at her hands and absently picked at her raw cuticles. She raised her eyes to mine. "I'm just so worried, Kate. Will hasn't been himself, well, he's never been the old Will since he had the injury in high school, engineered no matter how 'accidentally' by Jack." Will had been every bit as good a baseball player as Jack and had a sweetheart of a full-ride scholarship to Boston College. During a practice, way back when, senior year of high school, the coach had divided the baseball team into two squads, and they were to scrimmage. As teen athletes tend to do, they got competitive, very competitive. The two squads were tied. Will, always the team's best batter, hit a honey of a ball and was rounding third, tying to score a run to win the scrimmage. Jack, the catcher for the opposing team, wasn't going to let that happen. When the centerfielder threw the ball in, Jack caught it and blocked home plate. Now, some say Will should have backed down, but it was a game of chicken. Jack should not have blocked the plate, and Will had to know the possible risk of injury to both. Will was the loser in the battle of the two. He tore his ACL and was never the same. He had to forfeit his athletic scholarship to Boston College. In fact, he didn't even go to any college, but stayed home and went into food service and eventually became the food and beverage manager at the same posh hotel in downtown Hartford he works at today. He married his high school sweetheart, Rose, and they quickly had three children in three years. To say that Will was bitter would be an understatement. Not only was Will's knee never the same, *Will* was never the same. He had become an angry man at the age of eighteen.

I leaned back. Rose's face was a mask of rage. Maybe I was looking at the wrong spouse. Could it, could it have been Rose? My gut said we were looking at a man. Was I being sexist? Maybe. I had to get Rose back on track.

"How has he been different lately, Rose? Has he been depressed, quiet?" Oh, boy, I sounded like I was an amateur psychologist.

I didn't think she was going to answer, but then she did, and she looked distraught. "He won't talk to me, Katie. I've tried and tried. I just found out about a rather ill-fated trip to spring training."

Wait, what? "A trip to spring training, like the Dodgers spring training in Camelback, Arizona? Like to see *Jack*?" This not only shocked me, but befuddled me. Why would Will go there? Seemed like the last place a guy with a broken dream of professional baseball would want to go. And how could that look good for him? "How did you find out?"

"Instagram. He told me he was taking a boys' trip to Atlantic City, who would want to go to that dump, I don't know. But he had been so off that I didn't complain. I thought maybe it would help, but it didn't."

"Instagram...did *he* post it? Did he go with anyone?"

"No, his buddy Rory. He's not quite that dumb." She smiled ruefully. "And he went with the same guys he said he was going to Atlantic City with."

"So why the lie? It seemed you were okay with him taking off with the guys..."

"I'm not sure, but probably because he knows I *hate* Jack. I probably wouldn't have agreed to him going to spring training, and he knew it." Why did either of them come to The Lucky Charm that night, then?

I was quiet, letting her talk. Her words gave me a creepy feeling again. She was so angry.

"Nothing good could come of going to Spring Training, and it doesn't appear that anything has."

"But why go?" I pressed. Rose just shrugged.

Oh. So much for hoping Rose would admit to having had an affair with Jack or something obscure like that.

She stood. "Now, Kate, I have to go get the kids, so…" Did she? Or was she just trying to get rid of me?

"Wait," I said. "Was there anyone else on that trip with him who might have wanted to go to see Jack? We know Will wouldn't have wanted to do it, but maybe someone else did." I didn't have any idea who this could be, but it could explain the trip.

"I can't think of anyone, Katie, but then I guess I don't know my husband very well." And neither could I.

"Thanks for the coffee, Rose." I paused here, then gently touched her arm. "It's going to be okay." How could I promise that? But it looked like she needed a little comfort, and I think I needed to give it. Maybe I was saying it for myself, too.

Chapter Six

Wednesday, June 25

Bug spray...If you're having an outdoor wedding, estimate how much you'll need for your guests and then double it. Make sure you have it all over the venue space: in the restrooms, on the bar, on bistro tables, everywhere.

I needed help. I didn't have Jen to talk to. Brian was all wrapped up with the staties. No. No, I thought, I won't call her. But I also knew I would. We had a business appointment anyway; it would be easy to ask for help...who was I kidding? It would be awful. But it was for Jen, I reminded myself.

I had just enough time before dinner to do my last work task for the day, and it was a doozie. This woman and I had history, old and new. Was it true that I had stolen Brian McAllister from her in high school? Well, kind of...Did she hate me, maybe a little...were we friends now? A little...

I pulled into a space in front of her real estate office, three doors down from The Perk. Well, if this meeting went south, I could at least drown my sorrows or quiet my rage, whichever applied at The Perk.

I hated to admit it, but Sarah's storefront was charming. It kept true to the historic lines, but the door was painted a delightful yellow, and the flowerboxes on either side of the door were always blooming and well-cared for. I gave a petal a little pinch on my way in. It would be just like her to have artificial flowers in those boxes. Alas, they were real. Who was her gardener? I was stalling. I pulled open the door and enjoyed the tinkling of the bells attached. It was my first time here, and I hated to admit it, but the office was warm and welcoming.

"May I help you?" Asked the serious receptionist. How did I not know her? But then, I don't know everyone in Eastbury.

I smiled at the receptionist with the perfect blond page-boy. "Hi, I'm Kate Ludlow, here to see Sarah."

She smiled then. "Katie Manet, wow, it's been a long time."

Well, this was awkward. Who was she?

Her smile grew. "Don't worry, Katie, no one remembers me from high school. I'm Elizabeth Kincade."

I wracked my brain...Elizabeth Kincade, Elizabeth Kincade....then, her image flashed into my mind's eye. Elizabeth Kincade was a very shy brunette who was frankly rather round. The woman before me was blond and all sharp angles.

"Elizabeth!" I stammered.

She giggled. "Don't worry about it. I've gone through a transformation and have a whole new career, thanks to Sarah. I had a rough patch," she added softly.

I'm not sure what surprised me more: Elizabeth's transformation from high school wallflower to stunner or Sarah's apparent bit of altruism.

"Well, you look awesome!" And she did, wowzah!

Sarah chose that moment to walk out of her office. She was dressed to kill in a black pencil skirt, cream silk blouse, and heels that would give me a nosebleed if I could, in fact, walk in them. Yep, still hated her.

"Hey, Kate, I see you've met Elizabeth." Sarah didn't smile at me, but she did at her receptionist. The warmth was returned.

"Yes, she had to remind me who she was, though." I sent a small smile Elizabeth's way.

To her credit, Sarah didn't take credit for Elizabeth's transformation or career move or even comment. "Coffee, Kate?"

"I'd love it," maybe Sarah wasn't so bad.

"Coming right up." Elizabeth popped up and quickly made her way to the rear of the common area where Sarah had organized a coffee bar. The equipment looked state-of-the-art. I'm guessing that Sarah's pop-ins to The Perk were for networking purposes, not coffee, not with this setup. Sarah led me back to one of the three offices in the suite, the other two being furnished but empty. Her personal office was a lovely space, filled with creams and yellows. Her desk was serviceable but not overly large, made of blond wood. Her desk chair looked like actual furniture, but I could see that it had all the components of an office chair. The two guest chairs were teal blue, but the color worked with the creams and yellows. I sat in one and was surprised at the comfort.

Elizabeth brought our beverages on a tray and deposited them on Sarah's desk without a word, but with a smile. I looked at mine and noticed it was my favorite 'fancy drink' I got at The Perk when I was feeling like I needed a treat, a non-fat cappuccino. I looked up at Sarah, surprised.

"What? It's my job to be observant." She smiled just a little. Sarah and I had had a moment last spring. We'd probably never be best buds, but I now respected her. Then again, never say never.

"So, what's up? How can I help you?" I asked Sarah.

"I'm throwing a baby shower for one of my clients and I want to have it in my home. It just seems too sterile to have it at the club." Interesting. As far as I knew, she had all her events at the Country Club, where she was a member. No usage fee, and easy clean up as well as adding a rarified vibe. But not another shower! Uuuggghh.

"Sure, Sarah, but why me?" Might as well get it right out there.

I hated Sarah Deloro in high school. The reason, well, Brian McAllister, of course. Because he was Sarah's before he was mine. Did I steal him? Well, kind of, but not really...After our 'moment' last spring, I wasn't sure where our relationship would go. I'm still not, but she was reaching out, and I would meet her at least halfway. All I'm sure, as far as Sarah Deloro is concerned, is that what you saw was what you got. If she was nasty, you knew where you stood. If kind, it was real. She was real, although I didn't always like her.

She put her own cappuccino cup down on the saucer before answering.

To buy herself time? "You know I hate to admit it, Kate. Are you going to make me?"

I was confused. Admit what? I gave her a quizzical look but didn't say anything.

Sarah smiled, then chuckled. "Okay! You're the best planner in Connecticut, maybe New England. And I'm not one to cut off my nose to spite my face. Never have been."

WOW. I couldn't believe it, and I'd hate to admit how much her statement meant to me.

I grinned back. "Well, okay then. Let's get started."

We finished the initial round of pre-event plans, and I closed my tablet. Now or never, I told myself.

"Sarah, Jen's missing." Not sure why, cause Jen was so close to me, but Sarah *loved* Jen.

"What do you mean, *missing*?" Sarah put down her cappuccino cup a little too hard onto the saucer.

"I mean, she's not home, and no one knows where she is. She's been in infrequent text communication with me since Jack was killed, but that's it." My leg started to bob up and down. I was nervous and worried.

"Stop fidgeting, Katie," Sarah scolded.

I stopped. But I wouldn't say I was sorry. I just glared at her.

"Have you poked around at all?" She knew me better than I thought. "Have you gotten any info from Brian?" I know it pained her to ask, but she did. I'll give her that.

"He's all tied up being the liaison to the state. But I did go see Rose, Will's wife today."

Sarah tapped a pen against her saucer and looked over my right shoulder, apparently deep in thought. "Good move. We all heard about his fight with Jack the night before he died." Her brown eyes bored into my blue ones with sudden intensity. "Did you get any good info?"

I lowered my voice. I'm not sure why. "Just that Will and a group went to spring training in April, *Dodger's* spring training..."

Sarah's mouth formed a perfect 'O.' "Are you messing with me?"

44

I shook my head. "Nope. Weird, huh?"

"Rose must be really worried about divulging that to you. Did she know about the trip? I can't imagine she did. She hates Jack." Sarah answered her own question.

Wow, it must be common knowledge that Rose didn't like Jack if even Sarah knew. What am I saying? Sarah knew everything about every*one*.

"How did she find out?" She continued.

"Instagram."

Sarah whipped out her iPhone and went to her Instagram, I can only assume. "Hooooo leeey Crap! There's Will in the flesh at spring training this past April. How did I not hear about this." Sarah handed the phone over to me. And sure enough, there was Will. Why in the world did Sarah Deloro think she should have known about this? Cause she knows everything, a little voice said. I started to hand the phone back to Sarah.

"Nuh-uh," Sarah held her hands back. "Look at the photo. What does it tell you? Look very closely."

I looked at the photo again, this time carefully. Yes, I saw a group of guys from high school whom I remember, but when I looked at all the characters in the photo, I noticed a woman with long red hair in the upper right of the pic. I hadn't noticed her before. "Who's she?" I asked both Sarah and myself.

"And that's what we need to figure out," Sarah said.

My eyes then shifted over to Elizabeth, and I lowered my voice. "Why do I think there's more to her story, Sarah?"

She shook her head ever so slightly. "I can't, Kate. She's had a real rough go, and I'm not going to pile on."

For someone who capitalized on gossip and used it as a form of currency, her prudent statement said a lot. I didn't see myself as a nosy person, but a lot was going on here in our tiny burg, and something told me Elizabeth just may be part of it, and maybe Sarah too.

Chapter Seven

Thursday, June 26

T he next morning, I fired off another text to Jen as I walked down the stairs. I know, not the safest thing I could do. I sprained my ankle last year when I tripped over my neighbor's garden hose because I was texting and not watching where I was going. It still gave me a little trouble.

Where are you Jen? Everyone's looking for you!

I saw the little bubbles appear, but then they disappeared, and...then nothing.

I grabbed a lukewarm cup of coffee from the percolator on the stovetop and flung myself down on the kitchen loveseat in front of my cold fireplace. I was impressed Ellis had made percolator coffee, but sad it was not hot. My own fault, I chastised myself. Get up earlier, Kate, I scolded. I'm going to have a fire tonight, I also promised myself. The weather was stubbornly holding on to late winter instead of spring.

I knew I should leave the sleuthing to the police, but I couldn't. Jack was my friend, and the state police investigator wasn't from here. I had read in the *Hartford Courant* the oldest consistently published newspaper in the country, that State Investigator, Scott Bennett was an early 'closer' and was hoping to make an arrest soon. This did not bode well for Jen. According to the same article, most interviewees' alibis had checked out, but with exception of one. Guess who? Of course, Jen. She wasn't coming forward. And not only that, locals may not talk to him—at least not frankly, which could hinder his ability to find the killer. I had to help.

KATE! DO WE HAVE A CALL NOW OR NOT? We all know that when a text comes through in all caps, the sender is yelling. Darn it all, I forgot my call with this season's bridezilla Janie. Janie, formally: Jane Covey Langford, was an attorney who had no time to plan a wedding but wanted to be involved in all aspects of it—the worst possible combination. This was all I needed.

My thumbs flew across my phone's keyboard. ***Sorry Janie—crazy times Can you still talk now?***

YES

She was still mad. I punched in the numbers. One ring and she answered. "Hi Janie, so sorry about the delay. Have you heard about Jack O'Malley? He was an old friend, and things are just crazy here." She wasn't a completely unfeeling person, was she?

"Oh Kate, I'm so sorry. Yes, I've heard all about that tragedy. I feel confident that his fiancée was taken care of in his trust." How could she be certain of that? Wait, was she their legal rep? I knew I couldn't ask, but food for thought.

"I know you were going to be their wedding planner, right?" Wow, it really was a small town.

"Yeah…"

I agreed that Jack would have provided for Meghan, especially with the baby on the way. But it all happened so fast. Did he speak to his attorney before he was killed, it kinda sounded like it from what Janie was saying? If so, it appeared that little Meghan might be a very wealthy young woman. Motive, after all?

But back to business. "Did you make a decision whether to have the strings play at the ceremony, or did you opt for the church organist?"

"Oh, the strings are locked down, I listened to some of their music on their website, and it's to die for." And we were off.

* * *

Next up was a venue site visit. I had a wedding next month at a beautiful old winery. Yes, we actually do have vineyards in New England! I was meeting the bride and the site coordinator. We were going to go over the venue's checklist, which included everything from guests' meal selections to linen colors to detail selection.

The main building of the vineyard was so quaint yet substantial. It was a two-story structure made entirely of river rock. I loved it. The building sported three fireplaces. I hoped on the evening of the wedding it would be warm enough in the day for a comfortable event, but cool enough to have the fires roaring cozily in the evening.

"Kate!" Sydney, the site coordinator for the vineyard, greeted me warmly. I was in the stone building's main room, looking out at the grape vines. It was so peaceful. "Did Hunter text you?"

"I don't think so," but grabbed my phone from my cross-body bag. "Oh, yes, she did."

Flat tire, so sorry will have to reschedule

"Oh, jeez, I just saw that text, Sydney. Sorry to break up your day, and come out for a no-show."

Sydney smiled. She had a very generous mouth and when she smiled you say every tooth she possessed, but it put a smile on my our own face.

"Come and have a cup of tea with me. I could use a break." That sounded good to me, although I'd prefer coffee, but I wouldn't be so rude as to suggest...

We were settled in her comfy office, thinking of English chintz and lots of flowers, and they were fresh, drinking hot Earl Grey tea.

Sydney had a good pulse on the community. I might as well pick her brain. She had lived here forever, and maybe she knew the redhead in Will's friend Rory's Instagram post from spring training.

"Hey, Syd, do you know the woman in this Insta post?" I asked as I pulled up Instagram and handed Sydney my phone."

Sydney took my phone and silently looked at the photo. "She does look familiar, but I can't say I know her, and Kate, it's not a very good photo." She grinned again, showing those lovely teeth.

"Yeah, I know," I responded.

"I'm guessing you don't know her either?" I nodded. "I'll keep thinking on it, and if it comes to me, I'll shoot you a text. So many people come into my world with all my events, sometimes I lose count."

"Don't I know it!" I agreed.

Chapter Eight

Friday, June 27

Every bride should have a wedding splurge. It is different for every wedding. Perhaps you will choose to go all out on the food, or music, or flowers or photography. This may mean you will have to cut back elsewhere, but you will be glad you did.

I had spent the morning refining the timeline for my next wedding. The average person doesn't think that being a few minutes late here and there makes a difference. Let me tell you, those minutes add up. As I often tell my brides, 'If you run late, you will still get married, you will still have your meal, but what will be lost will be the party time, as most entertainment (band or DJ) and venues have a hard stop. So, what you'll lose will be the fun time, the party time, at the end of the evening. And no one wants that. So, stay on the timeline! But then that timeline has to be very detailed yet realistic. Not easy, but I was pretty good at writing them.

Before I knew it, Ellis was done with her shift at the bed and breakfast and home, yelling for me.

"Hey, Mom, can Kevin come over and Netflix tonight?" Ellis looked hopeful. I don't know why she thought I'd say 'no.' I loved Kevin.

* * *

I was feeling domestic, so later that afternoon, I got out my Kitchen Aid mixer and assembled the ingredients to make my famous, in my own mind, lemon bars. I thought they'd be a nice treat for Ellis and her beau. Okay...I wanted them, too. I had been so good lately on my diet. My recovery from my nasty bike accident was long and ongoing. I'm proud to say I was still doing my PT exercises. My rather unsightly scar on my right leg hadn't improved all that much, and I was still hesitant to wear skirts. I wanted to hide it if possible. But let's face it, this was a stressful time, and I deserved a treat. Soon, the oh-so-sweet smells of the baking lemon bars were wafting through the house, and my thoughts turned toward dinner. Yuck, I hated to cook. It just seemed like a time suck to me.

"Elle!" I hollered to my couch-potato daughter. I guess she earned it. She rose early to work at the B&B and worked hard to boot. "How about pizza for dinner?"

"Frozen or delivered?"

"Frozen." I held my breath. I couldn't deal with a surly teen tonight.

"Fiiiinne." She drew out the word but was not going to raise a stink. Phew!

* * *

Gentleman that he was, Kevin arrived right at 7:00 PM, the agreed-upon time.

"Hi Ms. Ludlow, how are you tonight?" He entered our foyer and immediately took off his shoes, his socks were clean too. His mom, Rainey, my old high school friend, was raising her four boys well.

"I'm good, thanks Kevin, come on in." I ushered him into the room Ellis, and I used as a family/great room. There were actually two mirrored rooms that, a century ago, were former parlor and dining rooms, respectfully. I used the room across the foyer as a home office. I wouldn't be working there tonight. I would give the two fledgling lovebirds a little room to breathe. I'd hang out in the kitchen and curl up with a good book in front of my kitchen fireplace. I already had a fire roaring tonight. But not before I settled the two with my lemon bars and a beverage. I picked up my grandmother's

51

Desert Rose platter with my lemon bars artistically arranged. Ellis swooped in and grabbed it out of my hands.

"I'll take that, Mom," Ellis smiled and sauntered off. Okay, fine. I was hoping to chat a little with Ellis and her beau. I loved teenagers. They were just so...interesting. I stomped over to my wicker loveseat, which was placed just right in front of the fireplace, and picked up my Kindle and cashmere lap blanket. This throw was my own kind of security blanket. I loved its blue color and delicate softness, and I snuggled down. The next thing I knew, I heard Ellis yell for me. What the heck? I ran like a mad woman, and I entered the Great Room. Ellis burst out laughing, and Kevin tried not to. I smoothed down my ponytail when Ellis pointed at my hair, which I'm assuming was askew from my impromptu nap.

"All okay here?" I felt a little silly.

"Sorry, Mom." Ellis tried to look contrite for her screeching. "It's just this show." She looked back at the screen. They were streaming something on Netflix.

I curled up my leg and sat down on the armchair next to the sofa. "What about it?" My interest was piqued.

Kevin took over. Kevin was a good-looking kid, tall, sturdy, and blond. His grey eyes sparkled when he looked at Ellis. "Apparently, there is some sort of underground railroad type deal for abused women, and there's a big hub here in the Hartford area."

I raised an eyebrow at both of them. This was most definitely a good thing...but why did I get a screech from Ellis about his? "Cool," I said, confused. "This is great, but..."

"Mom!" Ellis interrupted me. "This new girl who works with me at the Bed and Breakfast shared something really personal with me. We were cooking breakfast one morning for the guests, and I don't know. I guess she needed someone to talk to and unburden herself. But anyway, she told me they ended up here because her stepdad had abused her mom, and they got help to move here through some network. Then she looked miserable for telling me. I promised not to tell, but well, here I am..."

I smiled gently at my tender-hearted daughter. "We won't say a word, will we, Kevin."

"Course not!" And he covered Ellis' hand with his own. She slid him a smile, but Kevin looked at me and quickly jerked his hand away. I smiled to myself. I better work on my persona. I wasn't an ogre. Oh my God! Was that how teens saw me? I felt my face blanch.

"Mom!" Ellis hissed. "Do you know what this means?"

Sorry, but I didn't. "What does it mean, Hon?"

I noticed that Elle had grabbed Kevin's hand back. Wait, was he blushing?

"I think maybe Jen has an alibi for the Jack thing, but she doesn't want to use it.

Wait, what? I felt my forehead crinkle in a frown. "What?" I brilliantly asked.

I actually saw this girl's mom talking to Jen after work one day. Well, I guess it was her mom. She looked like a mom, and she picked my friend up from the B&B." Now, her forehead crinkled in a thoughtful frown.

"Why was Jen at the B&B?" I queried, not on topic, but I was curious.

"She was delivering some baked goods. Focus, Mom!" Ellis was not the most patient.

Oh, my stars! Ellis could actually be onto something. "So, you're telling me that Jen was talking to this girl's mom and the mom had recently arrived via the domestic abuse 'under-ground railroad'?

Now Ellis looked a little uncertain. "I guess. I just thought it was a coincidence. Mom and I really wanna help Jen."

Me too, kid, I thought. But this just may be the reason Jen didn't want to provide an alibi. Because, without a doubt, Jen would never hurt a fly...would she? Oh, that woman and I were going to talk soon.

"Thanks, Elle!" I placed a kiss on top of her head. "And watch something a little more fun," I smiled at them over my shoulder as I went to find my cell phone so I could interrogate my best and oldest friend.

Jen, are you doing something with helping women in crisis? Is that why you won't come in? And by the way, what did Jack say to you that night at the Lucky Charm?

I saw the iPhone bubbles at work, but as usual lately, no response from

Jen.

Chapter Nine

Friday, June 27

I went back to the kitchen and snuggled back into my little cashmere cocoon. My thoughts went to Brian. I knew he was stressed. Jen was his friend, as was mine, and while she was hiding out, Brian couldn't get an alibi from her. He'd gotten them from 'everyone else'—I'd have to grill him on who's on that list when I see him—so it made Jen look bad.

I was furious with Jen. Of course, I was all about helping others, but how could Jen help those others if she was behind bars? Well, it was up to me now. I was going to be Brian's worst nightmare. I was going to get all up in the business of his investigation. Could our relationship survive this invasion of his work life a second time? Just this past April I had been involved in one of his murder investigations, only that time, *I* was the suspect. It all worked out, and we reconnected in the best possible way. Funny how we'd been quite the item in high school—he had been the love of my young life. If a grave misunderstanding hadn't gotten in the way, I think we might have ended up together. But then I wouldn't have my precious Ellis, and that's all I have to say about that! Now, we were quite the middle-aged item here in Eastbury. But as much as I cared for Brian, Jen had to come first this time. I knew the State Police and Brian were just hours away from making Jen the one and only suspect in Jack's death. Would I find love again if this relationship didn't turn out? At my age and in this small town, probably not. But I had to help Jen. I just hoped Brian understood enough to forgive me.

What's that old saying? 'Ask forgiveness, not permission.'

Thoughts of my relationship with Brian took me to thoughts of my ex, Grant. After he left me for the next-door neighbor in Orange County, CA a few years back, and I high tailed it back here. I thought the coast-to-coast buffer would work well. Now that I was finally back in a good headspace, happy, well-adjusted, in a healthy new/old relationship, who blows back into town (well, West Hartford), with a job promotion no less than Grant. And to make matters worse, he wanted to reconcile. Things hadn't worked out with the next-door neighbor, Heather, well, duh! And Grant can't handle being alone. What better way to 'get things back on track' than getting his family back. Thank God Ellis was as adamant as I that that wasn't going to happen. She loved her dad but had a good sense of her self-worth, and as she told him last year, "When you left Mom, you left me too, Dad. We'll never go back to how it was, but you'll always be my dad, and I will always love you. But it will never be the same, but different can be good too."

But let's just say Grant had always gotten what he wanted. Right now, he wanted me. Brian wasn't a fan. Speak of the devil, a text appeared on my phone screen.

Kate, how about you and Ellis join me for dinner tomorrow night at Max Burger? They have a great happy hour special going on

Ah, no. Before I could even respond, another text landed in my feed.

We need to talk about the college tours I have lined up this summer.

The last thing I wanted to do was spend time with Grant but I had agreed to co-parent, respectfully... for Ellis.

Ugh, fine. It was easier to talk face-to-face, and we did need to discuss the tours. Although, *I* was of the mindset that Ellis should be touring during the school year so she could get a student "vibe." Ellis needed to see how the students interacted at each school. While some summer school courses were in session, obliviously, more students would be present during the school year.

Fiiiiinnne I texted back. *I have a wedding tomorrow—will have to be an early lunch—like 11:00 AM—have to be on-site at 1:00 so just come over for take-out.*

I'll pick up something. How about Chipotle?

So now I really should be worried that Grant was taking this wooing me thing to a whole different level. He hated Chipotle. It had always been a thing with us. He just wouldn't compromise and sometimes agree to it. I sent back a smiley face emoji. Let's see if he remembered my favorite order. I had gotten it plenty during our marriage, but always as a single order since he never would agree to eat it, at least back then.

Kevin had gone home a little while ago. He had politely come into the kitchen to say goodbye. I'd have to text his mom, Rainey, and tell her how great he was.

"Elle," I hollered up to Ellis, "your dad's coming over with Chipotle tomorrow for lunch to discuss the college tours."

"Nooooooo," she moaned down the hallway and down the stairs. "I had plans tomorrow with Kevin."

Awww, young love. "Has to be done, Elle."

"UUUUUggggghhh," was the only response I got.

Ellis went off to bed, but I was restless. I decided to do a Google search on Rodney, the man from The Perk. My quick search showed that Rodney was a local boy, about five years younger than I. He lived bicoastally and had a house here and one in Los Angeles. He was a restauranteur and had several partnerships with well-known sports figures. Makes sense he would be involved with Jack. Is that how he knew Meghan? He seemed rather fond of her.

Chapter Ten

Saturday, June 28

If your wedding/reception is outside and you have any time for signage, stake those signs down! The wind is always stronger than you imagine.

Funny when you look forward to something, it seems to take forever for the event to arrive. When you dread something, it's upon you before you know it. Take this morning, for example. It was already time for old Grant and his Chipotle early lunch. At least I was ready for the wedding today. My trusty clipboard with the wedding timeline, vendor list, guest meals, table layout, procession, etc., was already in the car, along with my bride bag and lunch.

The door chimed with its deep 'bong.' Somehow, it pleased me a little too much that Grant was in the position to ring my doorbell. Okay...I loved it.

I answered the door to a smiling Grant. He was weighted down with Chipotle bags. I opened the door wide for him and relieved him of half the bags. "Come on in, Grant."

We settled into the Great Room and spread out our feast. No sooner had I taken an enormous bite of my steak burrito, yes, he remembered my order exactly (impressive) than my doorbell rang again. What?

Chloe, my wireless doorbell, announced with her very loud yapping that we had a visitor. Gotta love a dachshund.

This was never good. Friends and family went around to the side mudroom door. I clapped the crumbs off my hands into a brown paper Chipotle napkin and went to the door. I opened it with a little trepidation and revealed a frowning Brian.

"Brian!" I was surprised. He usually texted if he was coming over.

"Having a party?" he walked into the foyer around my half-open door.

"Brian!" Grant grinned when I led Brian into the Great Room and stood, extending his hand. Brian, frowning, took it, and they each held onto the other a bit too long. This was just the scenario Grant would love, and he showed it by inserting himself as host.

Grant grinned around his mouth, which was full of Chipotle. Here he was enjoying a meal with his family, he seemed to be saying.

"We're just having a little family lunch. I'm sure we can patch together some for you if you want to join us." Grant offered. I glared at him. What the heck?

Brian ignored him. "Kate, can I speak to you in the kitchen for a moment?" He had already started making his way to the kitchen. I followed.

"What's going on, Bri?"

Brian didn't meet my eyes, but the next moment, he did. "Having a nice little family meal?" His tone was syrupy with sarcasm.

"Whoa, whoa, what is happening here, Brian?" I put my hand on his arm. "You know Grant is a part of my life, that he will always be because of Ellis. I told you that from the get-go." I sat down on one of the kitchen barstools, ready for a sit-down, ready to sort this out. Brian remained standing. "Want to sit? Would you like a cup of coffee or something?"

"No, I don't want to sit, and I don't want a drink." His shortness stunned me.

"Brian," I reached out my hand to take his. He pulled his hand away before I could take it.

"I can't do this," he headed for the mudroom door, not the front where he had oddly entered. "I can't take Grant."

I grabbed his arm, stopping his progression. "Brian, this is out of nowhere. I know you're stressed with having the State Police in our town and having to take a backseat, with not being able to find Jen, grieving the loss of Jack, but it's unfair to take it out on me."

Brian scrubbed his face with his hand. I could see the fatigue in the way he was holding his body.

He removed his hand from his face. "Do you, Katie? Seems you're carrying on as usual, with the exception of enjoying a meal with your ex. I came over here for some support, to spend time with the woman I care about, but I see Grant's car here and no heads up from you." Brian wasn't keeping his voice down, and I was embarrassed. But why should I be?

"I didn't know I had to clear my calendar with you to do some college planning with my daughter and her father." Now, it was my turn to glare.

"I'm done. I've got a big day tomorrow." He continued, stomping off toward the mudroom and toward the door. I didn't like myself for it, but I followed him and caught the door before he closed it.

"What's happening tomorrow, Brian?" I tried to keep my voice level and the volume low. The jerk didn't even answer me, but just got into his car and left with more speed than was necessary.

I didn't even know what to think. This was so out of the blue. His reaction seemed too extreme. I could only assume tomorrow is more of the same as the investigation. I knew this was a beyond miserable situation, but I wasn't his punching bag. We should be a team.

I rejoined Grant and Ellis, and score one for Grant, he didn't give me a knowing smile or ask any questions. I almost think he felt bad for me. The three of us talked about schools, but the meal was ruined for me.

Chapter Eleven

Saturday, June 28

Religious ceremony location or ceremony at your venue? There are many compromises, think long and hard about your decision. If a religious ceremony is important, but you want the whole experience to be at your venue, how about a religious ceremony, just close family the week before, then either a 'vow renewal' or a 'reenactment ceremony on your big day?

I shooed Grant out of the house and gave a quick goodbye to Ellis. I had been looking forward to this wedding ever since I started planning it. The bride was Miss Connecticut, Sabrina McCall, and the groom, hot-shot attorney Roland Briggs. No cost was spared to create the perfect wedding. And what I loved about it was the wedding was tasteful. In part, thanks to yours truly. The ceremony was at St. Paul's Catholic Church on Main Street in Eastbury. St. Paul's was a white-columned building lending its regal beauty to the center of town. The reception was at the Tony River Club, right on the Connecticut River. The river was a decorating accent on its own. However, the Connecticut River Valley had more allergens than any other region in the country. I hoped guests had brought their inhalers! The view was to die for. What made this wedding so special, in my opinion, was the 'extra' of everything. The flowers were sublime—fresh and plentiful, with just the right shades of pink. The music was soul-inspiring. There was a string quartet for the ceremony, a small ensemble for the cocktail hour, a ten-piece band for the reception, and a mariachi band for the after-party. Yes, a mariachi band in Connecticut…no easy feat here in New England. I wasn't sure how this was going to go over. It was either going to be a huge hit, or a massive flop. But that's what I loved about Sabrina. She was up for the gamble, and that's what made an event exceptional.

The ceremony went flawlessly, as 99% of my ceremonies do. Post-ceremony photos were able to be held outside as the weather held. Rain had previously been in the forecast. Today, the timing was perfect. Sometimes, an event can't go perfectly, though. Try as you might, you can't control people. People will be late, and there's just nothing you can do about it. What to do? Put the fear of God into the Bridal Party and family at the Rehearsal the day before the wedding, (provided there is one), and make them a wee bit scared of you so they will do as they're told and arrive as instructed. Think I'm kidding…I'm not.

Cocktail Hour was now in play, all was humming along. The signature cocktail—"Sabrina's Swirl"—was a hit, made with mint lemonade and vodka, served in a vintage crystal saucer champagne glass. Mix music, delicious food, and alcohol, and people will have a good time.

I was weaving my way through the guests, taking a head count of the bridal party and family members to get a jump on rounding them all up for the big intro into the reception. Rounding these players up was about as easy as herding cats. Someone had to use the restroom, call the sitter, or get another drink just before they were all lined up to be introduced to the seated guests.

I squeezed in between a server and a young wedding guest who was dressed in the most beautiful pink floral maxi dress I had seen in a while. "It's just so horrible!" she said with horror to her equally dressed-up companion in a blue eyelet spaghetti strap sundress. "I can't believe he's dead! And poor Meg."

Okay, now I was interested. "I know, and with her expecting too!" Blue dress said.

"Well, I'm sure Meg and her baby will be taken care of. Jack had to have her and the baby in his will, didn't he?" Pink dress asked.

" I certainly hope so!" Blue Dress said with conviction.

"Did you ever wonder why Meg seems a little bigger than you thought she might be with a first baby? I remember when I had little Cade. No one knew I was PG until I was like, six months! Then, when I had Freddy Jr., I blew up like a blowfish!" Pink Dress smiled smugly.

I fiddled with a tray of used cocktail glasses, the only thing near that I could appear busy, and thus, stayed listening to the conversation. YUCK! There were lipstick stains on the brims, and several had smeared food. It always surprises me how messy people can be.

"Oh, but you're just so tiny, Taylor. Well, you were at least before you got PG with Avery." Wow...Blue Dress sure got a dig in.

Silence, then, "Thanks, Daisy!" Then, a giggle to show she wasn't holding a grudge.

Pink Dress, who I now knew as 'Taylor,' was not to be dissuaded from her gossiping. "I wouldn't be surprised if little Meg, and let's face it, she's even skinnier than I used to be, is further along that she claims. Makes one wonder. What do you think, working for an OB and all? And how *is* hunky Dr. Robbers, Daisy?" She said cryptically.

Pink Dress, Daisy, looked uncomfortable, as I glanced at her over my shoulder as I continued to appear to be arranging the used glasses. Why would someone do that? I hope no one was watching *me*!

"Taylor! We really should stop!" It appeared Daisy was trying to change the subject. "Meghan is my cousin, after all. I should stop being such a witch." She looked around to see if anyone was listening. I quickly averted my gaze. I don't *think* she realized I was eavesdropping. People don't always see 'The Help,' which is what some people saw me as. To other families of the Brides and Grooms, I was almost family. The two women wandered off.

"Kate!" The mother of the bride floated over in her billowing robes of a dress. She was in lavender, the most prominent color of the day. She was a big woman, but she dressed to her advantage and looked lovely. "Everything is just perfect. I love the cocktail music you found, but can we do something about these nasty trays with used glassware?" Awe, she is delightful in issuing a compliment with an 'ask.'

"Yes, of course, Linda. I'm on it. I'll find a server right away and get these taken to the kitchen. I love the lavender saucer glasses, by the way." I felt awful that I had neglected my duties to snoop. But it was for Jen, I thought, as I excused myself and went in search of one of the black-clad servers wearing a lavender bowtie.

I tried to keep busy and not think what tomorrow was…Jack's funeral. His family had handled it all, leaving little for Meghan to do, so I heard from the town grapevine. I would have to see Brian, obviously, and I dreaded it. I was still smarting from our fight this morning. But I knew it wasn't just a blow-up, but a deep-seated issue that would have to be resolved before we moved forward…if we *could* move forward.

Chapter Twelve

Sunday, June 29

Black is now an acceptable color for women's wedding guests. Although I think It's a poor choice, especially for a daytime wedding. A wedding is a time for celebration and one's clothing should reflect that.

I t was decided Ellis wouldn't go to the funeral. I think she had mixed emotions. It was sure to be an event that everyone was talking about, but it was depressing as all get out. I wanted to have a support system as I would be sitting with either Jen or Brian…and I didn't think Will and Rose would be offering me a seat next to them. I was at a loss where to sit.

I kissed the top of Ellis' head as I headed out to my Suburban. I was wearing a black silk/cotton 'A' line sleeveless dress with a black cardigan. Lucky for me, I wore a lot of black professionally. All invited guests were issued a card for entry to St. Paul's Catholic Church on Main Street (the same church where my last bride, Sabrina, had so recently been married). I know it seems weird to be given an invitation to a funeral, but with Jack's celebrity, it was necessary to keep the press and the lookie-loos out.

I showed my 'entrance card' to the security guard standing behind a barricade. He looked at it, then me. I thought he was going to ask for ID but didn't. He waved me inside the barricade, and I made my way to St. Paul's entrance.

"Manet, hold up." A female voice said, using my maiden name. I stopped, turned, and saw Sarah Deloro striding toward me. Of course, she looked chic. Tall, blond, and model thin… Uuuuggghhh.

"Come sit with me." She all but ordered. She didn't stop but passed by me on the way to the church entrance. I hated to admit it, but I was glad to sit with her. Everyone seemed to be in pairs.

As funerals go, it was awful. Yes, all the right words were spoken, but the grief was real. Meghan was pathetic. Her sadness, her tears were almost tangible. It was painful to watch. I couldn't get out of there fast enough when the Funeral Mass was over. The burial was to be private, thank God, but there was still the post-funeral luncheon.

"Are you going?" Sarah asked. We were walking to our cars in the parking lot; hers was a gorgeous navy Porsche Panamera, mind, of course, the Suburban. I knew she meant the luncheon.

While I was sure it could be a great sleuthing experience, I just couldn't… I just couldn't go. Jack's family was still a bunch of rough 'boys,' loud and heavy drinkers. Their wives were much the same. Jack's four brothers married local girls, and even back in high school, we all knew not to mess with those girls. No, I didn't want to go.

"No, you?" Sarah grinned when I answered.

"Is little Katie Manet scared of those mean old high school girls?" she cackled.

She hit the button on her car remote, it chimed. "A little, you?" I answered.

"A little." And she hot-footed it to her car, opened the door, and slid in, all cool and 'Sarah-like.'

"See ya around, Manet."

Chapter Thirteen

Monday, June 30

Food Truck Reception? Yes, you can serve your wedding guests a variety of Food Truck fare, and it is very much enjoyed by all. If you go this route, consider purchasing your own 'upmarket' disposable plates. Food trucks advertise "paper plates included in price per person." But we're talking one thin paper plate per guest—not enough, nor sturdy enough!

I made the decision this morning that I was going to stalk Daisy from Saturday's wedding, the OB nurse. She was Meghan's cousin, after all. Maybe she knew something that would be valuable. I did a quick google search and found the address of Dr. Robbin's office. I'd just go over there about noon and hang out at the Starbucks that was in the same complex. Maybe Daisy would come out.

Just then, I got an incoming email. Shoot! I had forgotten to approve the florals on the Smythe wedding yesterday. I'd do that as soon as I got back from 'The Doctor's,' haha. I really *did* need to make an appointment, I thought. I had neglected my overall health after my bike accident. I was totally focused on healing my broken leg, and then the extensive PT was a time thief after the move from southern California back home to New England.

I drove the two and a half mile to the medical complex and parked in front of the attached Starbucks. I jumped out and strode into the café, the lure of a cappuccino like a siren call. I ordered, then once my drink was ready, I sat at a table facing the parking lot. After only fifteen minutes, in walked Daisy, her pink scrubs attractive on her slim frame. She went right to the empty counter and ordered one of those fufu drinks I could never indulge in …unless I wanted to gain five pounds. She waited rather impatiently, tap tap tapping her pink nursing clogs. I was racking my brain trying to think of an into when she noticed me.

"Hey! You were the wedding planner from Saturday night, right?" Her smile was sunny. I love being recognized for my weddings… if they go well.

"Yep, that's me. Did you have a good time?" She was the reason I was here.

"One of the best weddings I've ever been to," Daisy claimed enthusiastically. "But believe me, I sure love not being a part of the wedding party. I've been in four weddings this year, and they are so expensive!" She contorted her face into a mock mask of horror. She came over, pulled out a chair at my table, and sat down. Could she have made this easier on me? I loved this girl.

Daisy took a delicate sip of her coffee, testing the temperature. She really was an attractive woman. She had medium-length auburn hair that flipped up just at her shoulders. And I was pretty sure the color was natural. You don't see that awesome shade very often. Her eyes were a sage green. Complemented her hair nicely.

"I bet you've seen some wild things at some of your weddings," Daisy said, fishing for gossip, I knew.

"Oh, yeah, I've seen a lot, but you have to remember it's the most important day in a woman's life until she has a child, that is. And you see a lot of *that*," and I chuckled.

"Oh my God," Daisy threw her head back and said, "You have no idea. Some of those women…"

I took a sip of my cappuccino. "How is your cousin, Meghan, doing?"

"I guess everyone knows she's my cousin, huh?" she didn't wait for an answer. "She seems fine, actually. I'd be a little more emotional, but that's just me." This time, she didn't meet my eyes.

Interesting. Where to go from here? How to ask about the ultrasound?

"Well, the baby is sure to be a blessing. Jack will live on." I smiled, trying to get her eye. She avoided mine.

Did I ever mention that people tend to unburden their souls to me? I don't know why, is a maternal air? Am I a good listener? But it happened again. There was silence for a full minute, which is a long time. That's the trick. Stay silent, and sometimes, sometimes, they'll talk.

"I should go." She started to get up. I put a gentle hand on her arm.

"Stay, Daisy. You seem…stressed." I didn't know what else to say. She really did seem stressed, though.

She sat back down and sighed. "I…I think I made a mistake."

I didn't say anything, just rubbed her forearm resting on the table. She looked up. "Can you keep a secret? I know I shouldn't say anything, but this is killing me."

"What?"

Daisy burst into tears. "I didn't want to do it, but she made it so I couldn't say no."

I reached over and covered her hand with mine. "Did what, Daisy?"

Daisy covered her face with her hands in embarrassment or grief, I didn't know. "Meghan said she'd tell if I didn't do it. And with Robbie married and all and *me* married, I just couldn't risk that she was bluffing." She said through the fingers covering her face.

I was shocked, not that I was surprised that Daisy had something to do with the doctored ultrasound, but that she confessed her transgression so easily. I guess it was weighing on her heart and mind, and I was the one benefiting from her release.

"What did you do, Daisy?" I asked again, more gently this time.

Daisy looked up, tears in those sage green eyes. I hoped we weren't attracting attention. She didn't need any more grief.

"Meghan said she'd tell my husband about my little thing with Robbie."

"Robbie?" Okay, it wasn't vital that I knew who 'Robbie' was, but I *was* curious. Okay, nosy.

"Dr. Roberts." Oooohhh, 'Robbie Roberts?' What a name.

"Anyway," she continued, then took a shaky gulp of her latte. "Meghan can be very single-minded when she wants something, and she hates to be told 'no.' So I thought she just might tell my husband and Dr. Robert's wife we were fooling around if I didn't help her. So, I did it. I changed the dates on her ultrasound."

Hum, this was interesting. My eyes fixed on the local paintings for sale on the wall behind Daisy as I thought this through.

"Do you know why she wanted you to do that?" I brilliantly asked Daisy as my gaze returned to hers.

Daisy was wringing her hands now. "Darned if I know, and she wouldn't tell me either." Now, she looked a little miffed.

"Was the baby Jack's?" My eyes shot to Daisy's to gauge her reaction.

"Of course, it was..." Daisy's eyes widened. "Oh... Oh my God. Do you, do you think..."

"I don't know, but it could be one explanation as to why she wanted the ultrasound dates changed, and I'm not sure I see another right now," I answered.

Now, Daisy was looking over *my* shoulder. "Oh, dang it all."

I did my best not to turn around. "What?" Just when it was getting good, too!

Daisy stood up, the chair behind her scraping noisily on the lacquered cement floor. "Hi, Mama!" Daisy walked a few steps to an older blond woman, but turned toward me and mouthed, 'I've got to go!" His eyebrows shot up into her bangs.

'Thank you,' I mouthed back. She had made me a solid, and I wasn't going to make the situation hard for her. I grabbed both our cups, pushed in my chair, and went to the exit at the opposite side of the room.

"Who's that?" I heard her mother ask sharply. Rude!

I didn't stick around to hear Daisy's reply but scooted out the coffee shop's door. Wowzah, wowzah! Who the heck is that baby's daddy?

* * *

On my way home from coffee with Daisy, I stopped by the Stop and Shop, our local market, and grabbed something for dinner. I hated to cook. Well, not so much the act of cooking, just the time it took away from getting other things done. I hope Ellis would be happy with rotisserie chicken and a premade salad. Yes, I felt guilty. I entered the house via the mudroom door. I sure did miss my attached garage in California. I had a garage here in Eastbury, but it was a separate structure from my historic home. It is not so bad in the summer, but miserable in the winter and the rainy early spring. I banged my way into the kitchen and slung the paper bags onto my kitchen island. I also missed plastic grocery bags. I understand that they're bad for the environment, so I had no qualms with stores that didn't use them anymore, but they were so easy to carry. Alas, progress isn't always convenient. I stowed the chicken and salad in the fridge…and yes, the ice cream that I splurged on, 'Drumstick.' It's to die for. I am so weak. I had a little time before Ellis would get home from her shift at the bed and breakfast. Time to do a little snooping. I grabbed my cell out of my pocketbook and opened the Instagram app. I went right to Meghan's account. It was open to the public, with no privacy securities in place. She had noted: "Public Figure" on her profile. I was jealous of her little verified "blue check." I guess she *was* a public figure, and now more than ever. I scrolled through the pictures of the beautiful girl. Although I knew the way a person looked in real life could vary vastly from how they looked in photos, that wasn't the case with Meghan. According to Ellis, most 'public figures' use photoshop and all kinds of filters and apps to look *perfect*. That was some of what was wrong with our world today. Poor young girls like Ellis thought they had to look perfect. Enough of the soapbox, I had work to do.

I went back four months, about the time Meghan's baby would have been conceived, according to the real ultrasound dates. And guess what? She wasn't with Jack yet. Or if she was, she wasn't acting like a very good girlfriend. There was a photo on the beach with a man whose face wasn't shown and even a video of the two of them. And it wasn't Jack. This man wasn't as tall as Jack and didn't move like him. But the photos and the video only showed the man from behind. The video was so cheesy. They were walking hand in hand on the beach into the sunset, and the mystery man reached over and kissed the top of Meghan's head. She looked back at the camera and smiled smugly. Come on, if she was all hot and heavy with Jack, why would she be walking hand-in-hand with another man? Did Jack not look at Instagram? Did none of her 'fans?' No one called her out on it, and most likely, her 'fans' didn't know about her pregnancy yet. AND who was taking this video? Did people not wonder that?

According to what Jack and Meghan told me at their planning interview, they would have met not long after this was taken. But, the nature of social media was to look at the current photos and move on. History was not the topic. This sure was suspicious. Oh, how I wanted to talk to Jen.

My phone buzzed with an incoming text; my Apple Watch thumped against my wrist with the same. I glanced at my watch, the messaging app informing me the text was from Brian with an "image" that could be "viewed on my phone." What the heck? He hadn't responded to MY last text, and now he sends a picture? It had better be a picture of roses that he had sent. I opened the green message app and went to Brian's name. The image was a screenshot of what appeared to be a Facebook page. I read the text first, so I'd know what I'd be looking for in the picture.

This doesn't help Jen—not at all. Has she said anything to you? I don't really think she killed Jack, but she's not helping herself. Please, Kate, if she said anything to you—tell me so I can help her.

Heck! I clicked on the photo and saw a neighbor of mine pointing excitedly at Jack and Meghan's arrival at Strawberry Moon the other night. Jack and Meghan were tiny in the upper left-hand corner of the picture. But to my neighbor's right was Jen, caught unaware in the photo. What was striking about the photo and the subjects was the look of hatred on Jen's face. And there was no question at whom she was looking, Jack. Oh my gosh, if this investigation went any farther, say to trial, and the prosecution saw this, Jen was doomed. Because as we all know from watching television, it was the perception of guilt, not always actual guilt. Couple that with the nasty words spoken at the little get-together we had at Lucky's Bar the night before Jack was killed, and we had some sort of motive for Jen. But why she was so angry, I didn't know.

I would try again to reach her. I needed to know what Jack had said to Jen that night at Lucky's. Would she respond to my text? Would she even tell me?

Hey Jen know you're for whatever reason off the grid, but really need to know what Jack said to you that night at Lucky's—plz Jen

Bubbles… then much to my surprise, a response and YES, answer to my questions.

He made a nasty comment about Jeff and how I probably wished my girls were his (Jack's) then he grinned. Why would he say that. I hated him then, but I didn't kill him.

Wow! This I did not expect. Not sure what surprised me more…Jen answering or this information. No wonder she was so incensed that night at Lucky's.

Dang it all. I need to talk to someone. I always did better when I could talk it out. But my two go-tos were not available to me. Jen was emotionally withdrawn, and Brian was playing a disappearing game, yet he had no problem asking me to help him now. He was being irrational and just plain mean. This wasn't a side of him I liked very much. If we were going to work things out—I hoped he wanted to work things out—he'd have to get past his jealousy of Grant. After all, as much as I wished Grant were still living in California, he wasn't. So until Ellis went away to college, Grant would be around. And of course, Brian wasn't happy about Jen. I know he thought I was withholding information about her, and now I guess I *did* have information I didn't want to share. There was nothing good about what Jack said to Jen. It sure made her look even guiltier. And then I knew whom to call. I'd call my old buddy Charlie Wentworth. Former high school friend and practicing attorney. He had always been a little sweet to me, and if truth be told, I think he'd be open to something more if Brian wasn't in the picture. He had helped me out gratis last spring when I had had a bit of legal trouble…if you called being a murder suspect a bit of legal trouble. I was very sensitive to not taking advantage of his residual feelings for me, but I needed a friend right now. 'You could always talk to Grant,' a little voice whispered. Yeah, right, I answered it.

73

I went into my iPhone's messages app and typed in "Charlie Wentworth." Before I could change my mind, I tapped a quick message that said,

Time for a coffee?

Sure! Came the quick reply.

I hoped he didn't read anything into this invitation. I'd have to set the record straight when I saw him.

Where?

How about my house? I answered.

It would be easier that way, we lived in such a small town. The tongues would be wagging if we went to a local spot, and I really didn't want to see anyone… especially Brian. Ugh, Brian. I needed to respond to him, but not right now. Now, I had to focus on this meeting with Charlie.

Time to get the good ole percolator going. No one, not even Jen, could hold a candle to my old-fashioned percolator. Okay…I exaggerate a little, but it *was* good coffee. Oh, jeez, did I have anything to serve? I thought quickly. Last time Ellis had a softball bake-sale fundraiser, I *think* I had frozen some extra chocolate chip cookies for an emergency. If this wasn't an emergency, I didn't know what was. Usually, my emergencies were me craving something sweet…I rooted around in my, okay, I'll admit it, unorganized freezer. And success! I found a Ziploc bag labeled 'chocolate chip cookies'—and I'd have to nuke them a little before Charlie got here. I set the frost-covered bag of cookies in the sink to defrost a mite. What would my mother say? Probably, it was better to serve nothing than to serve freezer-burn cookies. Well, I'd heed her advice. I'd just have to try one and see in advance if they were 'guest-worthy.' I grabbed a paper plate from the ever-full pile in my cupboard—I try to live 'green' but… The paper plates weren't as bad as plastic grocery bags…I tossed a frozen cookie on said plate and slid it into the microwave. Fifteen seconds should do it. I pulled it out and bit in. Thank God it wasn't too hot because I wasn't careful of potentially burning hot melted chocolate chips. It was…divine. Well, okay, then. I gobbled up the rest of the cookie and nuked the remaining six, that sounded

like a good round number, one at a time for the perfect fifteen seconds.

They were then placed on an antique plate I had found at Goodwill. I regularly found great china and glassware there. I was rather pleased with myself. I grabbed some sunny cocktail napkins, my carnival glass creamer, and sugar, also purchased at Goodwill and placed them all on the frantically cleared wicker coffee table in front of my cold kitchen fireplace. We would sit together on the matching wicker loveseat: too close? Now, I just had to grab some mugs and wait for the percolator to finish its sweet bubbling. And…Charlie.

I didn't have to wait long. My doorbell chimed. Charlie and I were not at the friend level where he came round to the mudroom door. I rushed to open the door. He was a handsome devil; tall, slim yet athletic build, and dreamy chocolate brown eyes. Charlie leaned in and kissed me innocently on the cheek.

I swung the door open wide and stepped back, welcoming him in. "Charlie," I couldn't help but grin. He had an infectious personality. "Thanks for coming on such short notice."

He came all the way into the foyer, and together, we made our way to my beloved kitchen. My house here in Connecticut wasn't as large and grand as my California home, but the kitchen was. Ellis and I did most of our living here. The fireplace with the accompanying seating area was my joy.

"Have a seat, Charlie," I indicated the wicker armchair adjacent to the loveseat. I had made a game time decision that sitting with him on the loveseat would be too close. I pivoted and went to the kitchen island where the stovetop was housed and grabbed my coffee pot.

"The famous percolator!" Charlie enthused as I poured both of us a mug that I had set out.

This surprised me. "I didn't know you knew about my mom's percolator!" I replaced the pot on the stovetop and sat down on the loveseat.

"Oh, yeah," Charlie confirmed with a grin, pouring cream in his coffee and adding two cubes of Demerara Cane Sugar from my sugar bowl, delicately using my antique silver sugar tongs. Glad I had last minute put out tiny spoons; never sure if your guest is going to dress up their coffee and needed a quick stir.

"Don't you remember the one time when the whole gang went skating on

Glastonbury Pond during that exceptionally cold winter in our junior year, and the pond was frozen enough for safe skating for once? The downside, it was exceptionally cold, and we all got super chilled. We trouped over to your house 'cause it was closest, and your mom already had the percolator on the stove, so she served coffee until she had the hot cocoa going. I don't think anyone wanted the coco after that delicious coffee. Of course, we dumped lots of sugar and plenty of cream in it. Why am I here, Katie?" The abrupt change of topic unnerved me. I bet he used that tactic in the courtroom.

I smiled sheepishly at Charlie. He smiled back. He was such a good guy. "Honestly, Charlie, I need someone to talk to…about Jack."

"About Jack, or about the missing Jen? Seems the police can't find her."

"I guess everyone knows about that, huh?" I sighed. "Not only am I super worried about her, but I usually would talk to Jen when I have a problem like this, but she's the topic of this conversation. Or Brian, but he's miffed with me and investigating Jen. Then, there's my ex. Did you hear he moved to the Hartford area for work?" Why did I even mention him? I wouldn't talk to Grant about any of this. Anyway, I didn't wait for an answer but continued. "So, to put it simply, I'm heartsick over the situation Jen finds herself in and the fact that she won't help herself. I'm not looking for legal advice for her; I just remember what a good sounding board you were for me last spring, and I guess I'm just looking for that again."

"I can be a sounding board," Charlie said as he reached for a chocolate chip cookie, bit into it, and smiled. He swallowed, "For you, Katie." He looked a little too intently at me, but I couldn't think about that now.

I smiled back. "Thanks, Charlie. I'm just so worried about her. She knows how it all looks, but she won't explain anything. Whatever it is, it can't be more important than her freedom." I felt myself tear up.

Charlie almost took my hand but seemed to think better of it. "So, ask yourself, Katie. What, or who would compel her to stay silent?"

"Well, her kids, for sure, or her husband, Jeff. But as far as I know, there isn't any situation surrounding them that makes her respond this way. And she tells me everything, or she used to." I sighed and took a sip of my almost lukewarm coffee. "Frankly, I'm hurt that Jen has kept me out of the loop."

"Has she been hanging with different people, going to unlikely places? Is *she* in trouble?"

"No," but then I paused. My memory shot back to Ellis talking about seeing Jen talking to her new friend's mom. Ellis had said the girl had dropped hints as to knowing a little too much about the women's "underground railroad" for women of domestic violence. Kevin, Ellis, and I had discussed Jen's involvement in this in any way. Is that what's going on?

"Katie?" You look as if you might have an idea.

"Actually, I do. Do you know anything about a, for lack of a better term, underground railroad system for victims of domestic violence? I heard there's quite the hub here in Hartford."

Charlie leaned back in his wicker seat. "I really can't say much about that. I have a client..."

Well, that tells me all I need to know. It was a real deal then. "I wonder," I began. At this point, I was so stressed out that all my personal self-control was out the window. I picked up a cookie, offered the plate to Charlie (which he greedily snatched one), and bit lustily into it. "If Jen is somehow involved, that would be just the kind of scenario where she would keep her mouth shut about all the comings and goings of these women. She'd never betray them."

Charlie was silent, but finally said, "Katie..."

The way he said it made me stop chewing my most delicious cookie and look at him. Wow...was this a moment? Had I somehow given him the idea that this was more than a fact-finding/'support a friend' mission? I'd have to be clear about my feelings after we hashed this thing with Jen out. Charlie opened his mouth to say something, and then...my phone buzzed a vibration with an incoming text. Thank God. I broke eye contact and reached for my phone. I heard an exasperated sigh escape Charlie's lips.

It was Rosemary, my client, for an anniversary party this weekend. Rain was projected, and she was FREAKING out.

Kate! I read. ***What are we going to do? The rain, oh God, the rain! Call me!!!!!!!!!!!***

"Charlie, I'm so sorry, I have to take this. It's my weekend client, and it's supposed to rain for her anniversary party."

He stood up, scooting the wicker noisily behind him in his haste. "I'll let you get to it, Kate. It rained at my little sister's wedding last year. All I can say is, I'm sorry." He genuinely looked it. "I'll just let myself out. You make your call." He met my eyes ruefully, then flitted away, almost in embarrassment. "And thanks for the coffee." His smile as he headed toward my front door, still not using the mudroom door, was...sad. I felt overall yucky. I shook it off and dialed Rosemary.

"Rosemary, hey!" My attempt at upbeat.

Silence, and then whimpers. Oh, jeez. She was going to cry. I had been monitoring the weather for the last ten days, as I always do, and this was no surprise. But it was a big disappointment to Rosemary. She was celebrating her ten-year anniversary and wanted everything to be perfect. And that just wasn't how life worked. The irony was that this anniversary party was a re-do because her wedding ten years ago was rained out.

"Rosemary, come on, Hon. It's going to be okay. We already have the tent ordered. We have ponchos for the brave guests and umbrellas for the less brave." I attempted a giggle but couldn't pull it off. "It's supposed to be good luck if it rains on your celebrations."

"Really?" She sniffed, yuck.

"Really." I coax. "And Rosemary, buck up." I hated to be a hard-nose, but someone had to tell this girl how the cow ate the cabbage. "We can do a lot, but we can't change the weather. It's life, and sometimes, you just have to accept it and move on." It was always a gamble using this tough love talk. Sometimes, clients went with it, and others... got mad. I waited, and finally, I heard a soft...

"Okay."

Chapter Fourteen

Tuesday, July 1

If you have volunteer decorators for your wedding/reception, make sure they are answerable to one person. This helps keep the volunteers on task, and the flow of the work moving forward.

Well, I sure do talk a good talk, but when it comes right down to it, I hate rainy events. Rosemary had chosen a weekday, as she was convinced it wouldn't rain on a weekday. Sure, it was life, and there was nothing I could do about it, but it made my life, my work life at least, miserable. I leaned out of my Suburban's driver's seat and popped up my umbrella. The anniversary party was on the grounds of the 'bride's' family home/hobby farm, and I had been instructed to park in the 'back forty.' I eased my feet into my trusty ancient L.L. Bean boots and heaved myself out of my Suburban, doing my best to tread softly and avoid puddles. I then opened the back door and hauled out my 'event bag.' Don't ask…okay, I'll share…it has everything in it, from florist tape to a steamer. And today, it housed a most delicious lunch (a turkey and cranberry sandwich on homemade sourdough, an orange, and a couple of cookies from my coffee with Charlie). I never know when or if I will eat, so I always pack a lunch and nibble when I can. I had one self-absorbed celebrity chef, (in her own mind), who held my dinner hostage because she was mad at me when a guest was a 'no-show.' I can do a lot, but I can't control when a guest is rude and breaks every etiquette rule in the book. I choose not to show with no notice to me or the bride and groom. At the end of the evening, about 11:00 PM, she offered me my dinner. I refused it politely. It was probably a bad career move. She was quite offended that I wouldn't partake of her creativity. Most vendors have it written in their contracts that they are served a hot meal. I probably should follow suit.

My cell phone, hanging over my chest on a strap, (always know where it is for a call or photo that way), swung wildly as I slammed the car door, locked 'er up and began my squish, squish, squishy way to the main house to set up control central. I heard a motor purr and looked up to see Rosemary's husband behind the wheel of a golf cart making his way to me. Ah, my knight in shining armor!

"Hey, Kate!" Tiger pulled up beside me and stopped. "Rosemary said you'd be here about now. How about a ride?" No wonder Rosemary loved this guy. I popped my event/bride bag in the back of the golf cart, hopped in, and we were off.

We rolled, with only a minimum of bumps and muddy splashes, to the back of the house, where a gorgeous tent had been erected. I looked around to see that the portable toilets, single-wide trailers, really, but quite nice, were set up. Way out here, the family had a septic system, not city water, for their property, and it wouldn't be in their best interest to have three hundred people using their facilities for twelve-plus hours. AND… who wants three hundred people traipsing through your house?

In addition to a full bar inside the tent, a cocktail hour would boast a "Bar Cart," a cute vintage truck that served drinks, in this case, the signature cocktail of "Lilac Lemonade," heavy on vodka. The bar cart would be located out on the back lawn close to the "Lawn Games." While the dinner would be a formal seated meal, a cocktail hour would be serviced by three food trucks: a pizza truck, a taco truck, and an espresso bar truck in case one needed a little pick-me-up. Yes, the guests were going to have a challenge navigating all these areas in the rain, and I really doubted there were going to be many lawn games played, but New Englanders were surprisingly resilient.

The morning and afternoon flew by with my attending to a needy

Rosemary, photography support, reading 'rounding up lots of family members who tended to wander off at inconvenient times,' and minor decorating adjustments. I also steamed several of the tablecloths that the caterer missed. Nothing puts my teeth on edge as much as wrinkled table linens. It ruins the whole tablescape.

All too soon, it was 'go time,' meaning the vow renewal was soon to begin. Rosemary had done a terrific job with the bridesmaids' dresses. Yes, she had bridesmaids for a vow renewal, thirteen in all! They were the most delicious shades of blue. Rosemary had sent a link to her chosen designer's website and told her attendants to pick the silhouette that best flattered that woman's figure. The shade of blue was up to them, too, as long as the provided color palate was used. This free-rein approach caused a little last-minute shuffling of where the bridesmaids would stand at the altar. Rosemary wanted them to stand by height, except for her maid of honor. But aestheticallyspeaking, we couldn't have three exact blue shades in a row and then pop in with one differing shade – or so I thought. I won out, and I think Rosemary will be glad she allowed me to place the ladies according to dress color vs. height when the professional photos come in.

The ceremony was concluded, and it was time to aid the 'bride' and 'groom' in making an escape before their guests descended on them to wish them well. If the bridal couple and the guests meet immediately after the ceremony, forget your timeline. You will never get back on track. Guests will embrace the couple and talk their ears off. It is imperative that the couple scoot out for photos and the guests begin Cocktail Hour, in the opposite direction; thank you very much. I was in the process of shooing the guests (sometimes it's like herding cats!) toward cocktail hour under the reception tent when I saw someone out of the corner of my eye who made me pause. I turned and looked at him, but his back was to me. That was actually for the best, because whoever he was, he looked exactly like the mystery man from Meghan's Insta. It was more than just his body type; it was the same way he moved in the video. I had to get a look at him. Was I going to stalk him? Yeah, I kinda was. I smiled at an elderly couple, concerned about obtaining a cocktail and the 'facilities' and assured them the bar was 'open,' and that the restrooms really were quite nice, and not 'like an outhouse' at all. Then I dashed after the mystery man as discretely as I could. Dang! Where had he gone to? There he was, in the tent bar line, of course. I sauntered over to the bar and smiled at the bartender, Jerry. He was a good guy, and I had worked with him quite a bit as he was with my best caterer.

"Hey, Jer," I said as I picked up some of the couple's cute heart-entwined cocktail napkins and rearranged them.

"Hey, Kate. Everything is perfect as always." He was a handsome young man with model-worthy chiseled cheekbones and wavy chestnut hair.

I gave him a genuine smile back. Who didn't like praise? "Thanks, Jerry. Keep up the great work." I turned to face the bar line and zeroed in on the mystery man. I tried to keep my expression neutral, and thank goodness MM, (Mystery Man), wasn't looking my way, because I recognized him. He was none other than Jack's angry business partner, Rodney. Whoa! Was Meghan involved with Jack's ex-partner? He was talking to a curvy blond in a, alright, I'll say it, inappropriate short WHITE dress. Who wears a white dress to the wedding if you're not the bride? Who raised these people? This wasn't the first time I had seen a guest in a white dress at a wedding. If I were going to be catty, I'd say her hair was a very poor blond dye job, and the polish on her nails was chipped. But I won't be catty. It was the couple's turn at the bar, and he ordered a cosmo for the lady and a scotch on the rocks for himself. He didn't go anywhere near the tip jar. Shame. This was a huge part of the servers' compensation. They left the line, his hand on her back, sliding a little lower than it should in public. Dang! That hand wasn't too far from the hem of her too-short dress. That's how short it was. Did I mention it was white?

I followed at what I hoped was a discrete distance, stopping only briefly to smile and answer questions from guests. Yes, the table assignments really were written on the beautiful antique mirror at the tent entrance, and no, they didn't have assigned seats at their assigned tables. And no...they couldn't change their meal choice. Why in heaven's name would they think they could? But they probably would.

With answering those few questions, the couple had gotten farther away from me than I wished they had. I spotted them grabbing an umbrella from the holder at one of the tent entrances and heading out into the rain. Dang! I really didn't want to go out, but if I wanted to possibly glean any intel from them, I'd have to. Luckily, they were probably only going as far as the barn, which was only about thirty yards away. I use the word 'barn' very loosely. It was basically a party structure and was even air-conditioned. Other guests had gathered here to escape the tent and the rain. The barn boasted another bar. Rosemary had a playlist going, and the vibe was festive. If I had to guess, there were about 65 people in the barn. Enough for me to blend in, or shall I say, eavesdrop without being detected…I hoped. Our couple joined another man and woman, and they appeared to know each other. Rodney greeted the other woman with a kiss on the cheek and the man with a fist bump. He appeared to be introducing his 'date' to the couple. I fielded more questions from guests. Yes, we were on time, and yes, there would be a wedding cake. I, too, agreed that was the best part of a celebration. I actually *did* agree with that.

Soon, the two men peeled off from the women toward the open back door of the barn. Hum…I thought. Maybe I should go outside the barn and listen right next to the door, out of sight, of course. I know, I'm shameless.

I exited quickly, pulling my rain hood up, only being stopped once to assure a guest that, yes, there would be a champagne toast. I sincerely hoped that no one was watching me as I crept outside the barn and made my way to the back barn door in question. Please, God, don't let them change direction. I did my best to tune out the music pouring out of the doors. It really wasn't too loud, just too loud for my nosy purposes. I stopped just inches from the door opening and listened. I had to have a plan to explain my presence in case I was caught out. Think, think! I looked up, I looked down. There really was nothing out there that would need my attention. Then I saw the pretty peach tree not ten yards from me, loaded with fruit. Luckily, I had my trusty carry all hung over my shoulder. I always carried it as I trudged through the party jungle. If anyone asks what I'm doing out here, I'll just say I saw the peach trees, and as the peaches were ripe, I thought they'd be a nice addition to the bar. Can anyone say peach daiquiri? Weak, well, yes.

But it was the best I could do on short notice.

"Has she said anymore?" Rodney's friend asked him. At least I think that's who was speaking, I couldn't see the men. But I was pretty sure I remembered Rodney's voice, and the speaker wasn't he.

"No, but it really made me wonder. The dates don't add up. I loved her." I heard despair in Rodney's voice.

"Man, how did you get caught like this? Love? That's something from high school." The speaker's voice was a cross between humor and scorn.

"Shut up, Gavin. I remember you mooning about Becky Harris not too long ago."

Gavin was quiet, apparently chastened with an unpleasant memory, but then said softly, "You really go for the jugular, don't you, Rodney."

Yes! Confirmation that this was indeed Rodney.

"Did Jack know? Did that have anything to do with…"

"NO!" Rodney answered quietly. "How can you even suggest such a thing?" He hissed. I could hear the anger emanating from him. Was it such a stretch to think he maybe had something to do with Jack's death? Looked like he may have a motive.

I heard other voices, and they appeared to be coming from around the other side of the barn. Dang! If I didn't move fast, I was going to get caught eavesdropping. And I had been negligent with my duties as it was. I ran over to the peach trees and frantically began picking peaches. They were wet from the rain, and so would I be if I carried them against my dress. Better use my bag. I hoped they were ripe. What the heck? The guests had plenty to eat and drink; a couple more minutes wouldn't matter either way. I glanced over my shoulder, continuing my sporadic picking and flinging of peaches in my carry-all bag, surely soaking my bag, but I didn't see anyone yet.

"Gavin, Rodney," a female voice said jovially. Was that Meghan's mom? How had I not noticed her on the guest list?

"Hey, Aunt Lois!" Gavin said. Whoa….Meghan's mom was Gavin's aunt? Yikes. But that explained why Jack's business partner was here at this wedding. He, too, has a hometown boy, or so it seemed, but I didn't know him. He was probably a few years behind me in high school.

I saw Julie, Rosemary's mother, peek her head out the barn door. "Kate! There you are! I've been looking everywhere. I have a quick question about the 'Introductions.'"

Busted. "Oh, oh, hi, Julie," I stumbled over my words and a couple of rotten peaches on the ground. Yikes, I'm glad I have my Bean boots on, and I'm glad the rain decided to hold off for a little while. "I was just picking a few peaches for the bar. Doesn't a peach daiquiri sound fun?"

Julie's hand flew to her heart, and she beamed to Meghan's mom, "Kate just thinks of everything, doesn't she?" Oh jeez.

I answered Julie's questions. Really, I don't know *why* she had any questions. We had been over all this, and it was committed to a Word document. But I guess some people are just anxious. But now I was interested in Lois, Meghan's mom. How much did she know about her daughter and Rodney?

I dropped my peaches off at the bar. Jerry gave me a puzzled look. "Don't ask," I told him. He shrugged and went back to cutting lemon and lime wedges. I kept silent, but Jerry knew I liked that prep work done before he arrived on site—but I wasn't going to mention it now. I had other fish to fry. Now, I was going to stalk Meghan's mom. She had more to tell me. She just didn't know it yet.

She and her daughter, Meghan's sister, Marjorie, left the barn on the way to the main tent. It was almost time for the introductions and the anniversary couple's first dance. I'd have to hurry.

The mother/daughter team made fast work of using the trailer facilities, and then headed to the tent. They stopped abruptly, and Lois grabbed her daughter's arm roughly. I didn't see that coming. They were speaking in hushed tones, and I couldn't hear them, but they were angry. Okay. I was going to have to get closer and hear what they were saying. I walked briskly along behind them as if I were on a mission. I wasn't sure how I was going to get close enough to listen in without being noticed, and then the angels smiled on me in the form of the Rosemary's nervous mother. She came sloshing up to me at a canter, much like the horses she loved and kept on property, wheezing my name. I guess she wasn't in the best of physical shape.

"Kate," wheeze. "Thank God I caught you." Julie bent over at the waist and took a few deep breaths. "I guess I'd better get back on that Peloton." She grinned and stood up. "Rosemary

has completely changed her introduction order. I love the girl, but this is beyond." For a moment, her face was stormy, but then it cleared. She began reciting the new order, and I mindlessly wrote it down while listening to Lois and Marjorie. I'd say I have a knack for multitasking. Call it 'mom mode.' Julie went on and on, I smiled vacantly, nodded, and continued to scribble on my clip board, all the while listening in.

"But the will! Can we wait until it's read?" Hissed Marjorie. Marjorie was wearing quite the amazing dress. It was a lovely rose color, but it was made of the tiniest knit type fabric. And then I remembered. She was a knitter. She had been even in high school—quite the lost art, but she was really a gifted artist in this field.

"Keep your voice down, Marjorie." I took a quick glance back at the women and saw Lois relax. All she saw was the mother of the bride and her wedding planner in an intense discussion a few feet away. She dismissed us.

"We have time. It's her first baby, and she's hardly showing, even though she's further along than she's supposed to be. No one will question the timing of the baby's birth. We can always say she was 'under undue' stress, which is actually true. Your job is to keep Meghan quiet. She has a mouth on her and could possibly blow the whole thing for us."

"I'm trying, Mom, but she isn't making it easy." Meghan was a pill about not coming to this anniversary party.

I glanced over my shoulder; I couldn't help myself. Lois had her hands over her face, shaking her head. "That girl is her own worst enemy. She gets herself pregnant and then has a sweet way to deal with it, and she won't wait a little while to enjoy the fruits of our plan. I could wring her neck." This last was said with great drama.

"But Mom, what about Rodney." I could barely hear her; her voice had dropped. "I think he really loved Meg."

"He doesn't want to know. None of us want to know."

"I think you're wrong, Mom. I think he would be happy. And he does very well. Meghan would do well with him," Marjorie argued.

"Now listen, Marjorie. We are not deviating from the plan. 'Doing well' is not the goal here. Hundreds of million from Jack's estate is."

Marjorie nodded. I saw as I turned to take a peek. I shouldn't have, as she caught me, and our eyes locked. Dang. There was a definite question in her yes. I didn't dare another look, but she was silent.

"Kate, Kate!" Julie brought me back to our conversation with a wee bit of irritation.

I guess I wasn't as good at listening to two conversations at the same time as I thought. But I smiled my best smile and smoothed things over. "Got it all, Julie. We're good to go. I'm going to go line everyone up. Did I tell you how much I love your dress?"

Julie beamed. It really was a gorgeous dress. She scurried off, and I just stood there thinking about all I had heard. I'm sure that Rodney, Jack's disgruntled business partner, had been involved with Meghan, how involved? Did Rodney question the baby's paternity? Was the baby his? Not only was he infuriated with Jack over their business dealings, but maybe he wanted Meghan and his baby…and what does all this say about Meghan? Should I tell Brian what I've learned? Would it help Jen?

Chapter Fifteen

Wednesday, July 2

Make sure your caterer requests guests' food allergies well in advance of your wedding. Nothing worse than trying to scramble to find safe fare for a guest on the spot. I suggest a place on the response card for guests to note food allergies. Then, have your planner double-check with the caterer for allergies on the response cards before the event.

Wednesday morning, my feet ached. They always did after a full day of event coordination. I found that my feet *and* my back benefited from a change of shoes halfway through the day. I'm not sure why, but maybe it's the change in heel height. I only know that I recommend this to anyone who has to be on their feet for many hours.

I limped downstairs and made my way to the kitchen. It was only eight in the morning, and the house was silent. Ellis had the day off from the B&B, so I knew she'd sleep as long as she could. Coffee. I needed coffee. My eyes burned, and my mouth was dry, the side effects of too little sleep the night before. I never slept well the night after a party. I was just too keyed up. But I would pay for the next couple of days, yes, days. It took me a few to get over an event. I put the percolator on the stovetop on auto-pilot. I stared at the coffee pot in a stupor, as if that would make it perk faster. It didn't. I took Chloe out while the coffee brewed. Finally, the sweet bubbles hit the top of the clear dome. I let it perk for the seven required minutes, then turned off the gas as soon as they were up. I poured the magical brew into my favorite 'Best Mom' mug, cream already poured in, and was taking my first sip when there was a soft knock on the mudroom door. Huh?

I took another big gulp of my coffee and burnt my tongue. Ahhh the sting! Who would be at my door this early on a Wednesday morning? You know what they say, one way to find out. I went to the door and gingerly moved the curtain covering the rectangular window next to the mudroom door. Brian.

What the heck? I opened the door with trepidation. I wasn't sure of my emotions. Was I happy, mad, both? I hadn't heard from him since that day he texted the photo of Jen.

"Brian? Is everything okay?" I opened the door wider so he could come in. He removed his very muddy boots, which were no easy task, and tiptoed in his stocking feet. His socks were pristine, by the way.

He entered the kitchen without a word and nodded at the mug I held aloft, silently asking if he wanted coffee. He nodded, and I filled the cup. He took it black and passed it to him. Oh, how I wished I had put on a cute skirt or nice slacks instead of my comfy, but warm joggers.

He took a sip and said, "Kate, we need to talk." I guess we did. Last time he was here he left in quite the huff.

This situation was like a cat in a bath. We were both miserably uncomfortable. We sat down on my kitchen loveseat. I took another sip of coffee, he squirmed.

"Well, just spit it out, Brian. You're making me nervous." I gripped my coffee mug so tightly that my knuckles were white. I spoke the truth. I was nervous.

Was this about Jen, or about us?

"Auugggg!" Brian ran his hand through his hair. He wasn't at ease, or happy. I took one of his hands and held it. I was furious with him, but he was in emotional turmoil, and my empathy overruled my anger.

"Brian, you can talk to me."

Brian met my eyes. "Kate, we need a break."

This floored me. "What the heck, Bri?" I dropped his hand more abruptly than I meant to. I knew this was a miserable, trying, taxing, stressful situation. But to 'take a break' over it?

He tried to regain my hand, but I wouldn't let him. I even stood so I could put more space between us.

"I told you at the very beginning that Grant was part of the package. You knew this, Brian. He's Ellis' dad, and as much as I wish it were different, it will never change. It's in Ellis' best interest that I maintain a good working, more than civil relationship with him. It's nothing more than that." This was really coming out of nowhere. What had he interrupted, one family lunch? But then my mind went back to last week when I ran into Grant at the dry cleaners, and Brian was next door at the UPS store. He saw us laughing together over what I can't even remember, or the time at Panera last week when we had lunch to discuss Ellis's senior year plan. I didn't see Brian that day, but I did see a couple of members of the force stop by to pick up carry out. Okay, I can see how this stuff might irk Brian, but to 'take a break' over it? Ridiculous and hurtful. Not to mention, no effort was attempted to work the hard things...together.

"Kate, it's more than that, and if you don't realize it, you're deceiving yourself. I think..." and he stopped.

I was angry now. Super angry. How could he even think that? He couldn't be more wrong, or could he? Was there any truth to what he was saying? No, NO! I told myself. I rounded on him, furious.

"Do you think so little of me, Brian, that I would allow myself to have *feelings* for someone who left me for my California next-door neighbor? Really? I can't help that they broke up, and Grant got a promotion to move to New England..."

Brian didn't say anything. He just looked at me. Finally, he said, "Did you just hear what you said, Katie? 'Allow myself to have feelings.' It's as if you do but won't let yourself. If we're going to be together, I want to be your one and only."

I couldn't believe this. "Of *course*, you're my one and only, Brian. You always have been." I tried to soften my features, but I am not sure I was successful. I was plenty mad at him.

"Any good relationship is based on complete honesty both with your partner and, even more importantly, with yourself. And I don't think you're being honest with yourself about your feelings for Grant. And that's not surprising. You didn't have time to get over it. You had no say in how it ended, but you do now, and I don't think you've taken that into consideration."

I saw red. I took a couple of yoga breaths. I didn't trust myself to answer him right away. One more deep breath. "Where is this coming from Brian, and by the way, what makes you such an expert on long-term relationships? When have you ever had one?"

The look on Brian's face broke my heart. Me and my ugly temper. I never really knew I had one, but apparently, I do when it comes to matters of the heart. Now it was his turn to be quiet.

Brian stood slowly and with what seemed regret. Finally, he spoke. "You're right, Katie. I've never had a long-term, successful relationship. I've been too busy waiting for you for twenty years." He headed for the door and slipped on his boots way too easily and quickly.

I put my hand on his arm and tugged gently, trying to turn him around. "Brian, I'm sorry. I didn't mean that."

"Yeah, you did, Katie," he said without turning around. "Look, you never got a chance to get over Grant. You separated, divorced, and high-tailed it back here. Make your peace with Grant, get back together, or don't. When you have your act together, let me know. I've waited twenty years, a guess a little while longer won't matter. But then life's funny. You never know." He turned around then and leaned down to gently kiss my cheek. He left without another word. What had just happened? I couldn't stand Grant. I tolerated him for Ellis, but was there any truth to what Brian was saying? Was it too soon? I already felt Brian's absence. I felt so...alone now.

I didn't even have the chance to tell Brian what I learned yesterday about Meghan and Rodney. Not that I wanted to now, but I should because it could help Jen. I looked out the window to the side of the door, and I could see his car pull away. Too late now, I thought.

Chapter Sixteen

Thursday, July 3

Is a wedding planner too far out of your budget? Consider a 'Day of Event Coordinator.' Remember, though, any good "Day Of" staff will need to invest time in planning the day, timeline, etc. This will cost. You do get what you pay for. A 'Day Of Coordinator' differs from a 'Full-Service Wedding Planner' in that the Full-Service Planner has her hand in every detail and decision the wedding couple makes.

I had to keep my chin up. I wouldn't let another man rule my emotions. If Brian wanted to let me go, so be it. I had a life to live, a job to do...and a wedding to run. I love barn weddings. New England has 'barn venues' in abundance. Contrary to what may be in vogue for wedding venues country-wide, barn weddings are still very popular in New England. Today's wedding, another weekday event, was a small affair, just sixty-five people. This was the only date available, so she grabbed it. And I can't say I blame her. This site had it all: real restrooms, not the kind that had to be trucked in as trailers, air-conditioning in the main barn space, and lush lawns ready for guests to enjoy yard games. What I appreciated about this site was that it wasn't so spread out. I didn't have to go on a manhunt just to gather guests for wedding events.

Dinner was complete, the cake was cut, and I was getting ready to make my escape. I decided to stay for one more song. I really liked the DJ. We had never worked together, but he was high-energy and got the guests hoppin'. We had had dinner together and I had never seen anyone eat as quickly as he. I was in awe.

I was enjoying this last song, a slow one that made me think of Brian. I saw the DJ grab one of the beams on the low-hanging loft where he was stationed. He hit at it with great purpose, keeping time to the music, I figured. Then, without warning, he fell flat on his face. It wasn't a stumbling fall or a gradual one. It was 'boom,' and he was down. The few that saw gasped in horror, the rest of the crowd kept dancing as the music was still playing. I knew there was a doctor among the guests and saw him make his way over. I ran outside and placed a 911 call in

a quieter environment. I was told the EMTs, as well as the police, would be there in minutes. Not soon enough for me. I went back inside, turned off the music, and let Dr. Collins know that help was on the way. He had loosened our DJ's shirt and was assessing him. I heard the sirens and asked the crowded guests to make way for help. Once the music stopped, everyone knew there was a crisis, and they all wanted to see it and clustered around. Dr. Collins spoke briefly to the EMTs, and then they carted our fallen friend out and into the ambulance. The bride was wringing her hands in distress, both for her event and the DJ. She was a lovely, thoughtful woman who taught special needs children. Her father was on the phone, I'm assuming, calling the entertainment company to find a replacement. That was my job, really, but at this point, I'd take all the help I could get. Then, a thought occurred to me, and I ran to the ambulance before they closed the door. What was I doing? Well, as the DJ had regained consciousness, I was obtaining his password for his computer, which ran the whole show. That's what it was. Am I embarrassed at my insensitive behavior? A little, but it had to be done.

The maid of honor said she could fill in as DJ until the entertainment company sent a replacement, thank God, and I wiped the bride's tears and encouraged the guests back onto the dance floor. Things were just getting back to the level they had been before the DJ's collapse when Brian walked in.

I met him at the barn entrance and asked, "What are you doing here?" I wasn't friendly.

He didn't smile, or even made direct eye contact, his tone was business, but hesitant. "We always send out an officer when the EMTs are called." He pulled out a little notebook from his sports coat pocket. "Name of the patient?"

"George," I answered curtly.

"What happened?"

I really don't know. He just collapsed."

"The force sends out detectives for something like this?" I eyed him suspiciously.

He shifted awkwardly. Brian was usually never awkward. "Most of the department's out with the flu. Believe me, Katie, I don't want to be here."

Gee, thanks, I thought. "George Crane," I said, remembering his last name. "I have his contact info on my clipboard." What the heck did I do with my hot pink clipboard? It was my lifeline to all the wedding events for that particular day. I looked around frantically, not sure if my panic was over the lost clipboard, or the unexpected visit from Brian.

"Kate," Brian gently put his hand on my forearm. "Take a breath." And I did, in and out, in and out. I did feel better.

"Kate!" The mother of the bride came sliding over in her stocking feet, executing quite the slick move. I guess she was ready for dancing. "Robert has a new DJ coming! Whoo Hoo!" Then her face fell. I'm so sorry. How is the DJ? Is he going to be okay?"

"I sure hope so. He's in good hands." I did my best to reassure her, but how could I make promises? I had never worked with him before, but I felt awful for him, and I imagine now that he was being stabilized, he was embarrassed.

And she ran off again to join a group of women, duplicating the same slide, much to the enjoyment of her whooping pals. Okay, maybe all wasn't lost. Sadly, the sensationalism of the DJ's collapse created an almost festive air.

I met Brian's eyes again, and he smiled at me. "Looks like 'Kate the Great' has things back under control. His eyes softened. He had a hard time staying mad at me. But I wasn't feeling in a forgiving mood.

"Kate," screamed a female voice from the crowd. Oh, jeez. "I have to go, "I said curtly.

I looked over my shoulder, trying to find the screecher. Then looked back at Brian. "See ya."

"Kate," I heard again as I turned away from Brian. "The women's toilet's backed up!"

Crap, I thought. Great choice of words, I laughed to myself. Glad there was a maintenance person on site because I didn't mess with that side of an event…ever. I remember a week before one wedding when the mother of the bride emailed me over the 'Day Of' To Do list. KEEP AN EYE ON RESTROOM TRAILERS, TIDY UP FLOORS, TOILETS, SINKS, TRASH. Ah, no. I got right on the phone, and she wasn't happy when I gently, but firmly refused. I had told her in the beginning planning stages that if she wanted that type of help, she should hire a restroom attendant. She chose not to. Sorry, not sorry.

I followed the facility custodian into the ladies' room with an attempt to gently remove any stragglers so the poor man could set the restroom to rights. We were met with female bickering. And it appeared to be escalating. Well, this was going to be awkward, but they were just going to have to take their argument somewhere else. But I didn't expect to see Meghan and her mother as the offending parties.

"I don't care, Meghan. You are just going to have to suck it up for a little while longer. Don't blow this." This last was said with Lois grabbing Meghan's arm. Both women looked up when they saw the maintenance man and me in the restroom doorway. Can you say awkward? Oh, my stars. I'm glad Lois quickly released Meghan as soon as she saw she had an audience. I really didn't want to step in and break up a cat fight between a mother and her daughter, her pregnant daughter! But I would have if the situation demanded. I had done worse. Wow these ladies were really on the wedding circuit, weren't they? But then this was wedding season in a small town. I frequently saw the same group of people at multiple weddings in a season. It seemed the younger set's friends got married around the same time, and their parents were all invited as they knew the kids and their parents, too.

But...I *was* surprised to see Meghan. It seemed not only inappropriate, but not somewhere she'd want to be after the sad, dramatic loss of her own fiancé. But we all grieve differently.

"Kate!" Lois recovered quickly, putting her arm around an increasingly uncomfortable Meghan. "Poor little Meghan is having a moment. This was probably an ill-advised event to attend so soon after...Jack." She smiled with saccharine sweetness, as artificial a smile as I've ever seen. Meghan looked miserable. Why had she come tonight?

"How are you feeling, Meghan?" She had taken on a green tinge, uh, oh. I didn't want to be an opportunist, but it *was* my duty as the wedding planner to make sure all guests were feeling their best—to look after their comfort, right?

"Let's find you a seat and a glass of water, Meg," I took her arm gently as and led her away from her mother and toward a small grouping of chairs near the air conditioning. I flagged down a passing server and asked for a glass of ginger ale. The sugar and bubbles would help, at least they always did when I was expecting Ellis.

Lois didn't join us. Something told me she was tired of playing babysitter to her daughter. Once Meghan had a couple of sips of the soda, her color began to return to normal.

"Thanks, Kate. I was starting to feel a little faint and nauseous."

"What have you had to eat today, Meghan?"

She looked down at her hands, which shook slightly. "Nothing really, I just, just don't feel well." I think she was waiting for a scolding, but she already knew she needed to eat. She needed a little kindness. I put my arm around her and squeezed. "Let's get you something to eat. I'll round up something fun." She smiled, and so did I.

I came back with a grilled cheese and some potato chips (my personal favorite), courtesy of the more than kind chef of the catering company. "When I was expecting, I l-o-v-e-d potato chips. And I hope you're not lactose intolerant," I held up the grilled cheese.

Meghan smiled the first real smile I'd seen from her since before Jack was murdered. "Oh my GOD!"

I thought she was going to drool. She greedily grabbed the plate and rather indelicately shoved half the sandwich into her mouth. She rolled her eyes and groaned. "Viz is soooo goot!" Meghan managed to get out around munching her sandwich. There was something so satisfying about feeding someone who was in need of a good meal.

"I love this, thanks, Kate. I never know what I can keep down these days, but this works." She said all this with her mouth full. I tried to look at her nose, and not her open mouth. "What, do I have something on my nose?" Meghan rubbed frantically on her nose.

"Ah, no, no, of course not." My gaze went to her cute little baby bump, well, not so little anymore. She was dressed in a figure-hugging pink dress. I wish I had the courage to wear these body-revealing numbers when I was pregnant with Ellis. They actually make the mother-to-be look good.

"I'm sorry about my mom. I know it may not seem like it, but she grew up with nothing, and then after she had Marjorie and me, my dad took off, and we super struggled. She just wants us to have security, which she never did. Marjorie tried to help out when we were growing up. She made some really awesome clothes for us. Have you ever seen her knitting?" Meghan glowed with pride at her sister's accomplishments.

"Yes, I have to seen Marjorie's knitting successes. She has a real talent." Meghan smiled, then her face clouded over.

"I really should be over this morning sickness thing at this point…" Meghan cut herself off abruptly and flushed a pink as bright as her dress. "I mean, I, I…" and she burst into tears. I don't blame her; she was going through a lot, but was there something a little forced about those tears? No matter, I gave her a rather awkward hug around her belly.

She sniffed indelicately, a little too wetly for my taste. I pulled a tissue out of my cross-body, ever-present wedding planner bag. "Here, Hon."

Meghan blew her nose, and I made an excuse to make my getaway. I was in charge of this wedding, after all. But I did glean from this little chat that she was most definitely further along than she had told everyone else. But I already knew this, didn't I?

A text came in from Brian:

Good to see you tonight—things feel unfinished. I have a few questions about Jen. Can we talk?

Did he care, or did he just want info? I didn't know what to think, but I sure wanted some information from him.

I'm still at the wedding, but I can text. I think Rodney is the father of Meghan's baby. Your turn...

Everyone's alibi has cleared, except Jen's. And by the way, why are you just telling me this now? I could tell he was angry. How can you tell someone's angry via text? You just can.

What about Meghan and her mom and sister? I asked. They looked guilty to me, but it would take a strong person to kill Jack, and I didn't really see a woman do it.

Footage at the B&B confirmed Lois entering the building for the night, and not exiting well before Jack was killed, which was estimated 11:00 PM to 1:00 AM, and Marjorie's husband alibis her. Huh. I didn't think of the B&B video footage, and before this, I didn't know the time of Jack's death. Good intel convo!

I'm so very worried about Jen, Bri—you know she didn't kill Jack. I'm going to check in with Jeff tomorrow.

And he was gone, no response. Was this what we had become, only connecting about a case?

Chapter Seventeen

Friday, July 4

Do not assign wedding day prep tasks to your wedding party. They are looking to celebrate you and just...celebrate. Enlist a paid employee. There are often high school students in your community who may be interested in earning a small fee on a weekend day.

"Kate, I am beside myself. My wedding is in two weeks, and I *still* can't get in touch with Logan!" I was meeting today with a bride whose wedding was, well, in two weeks. We were enjoying a cappuccino at The Perk...okay, I was. I was doing my best to stay off Main Street until the Fourth of July parade was complete. It was adorable; anyone who wanted to ride their bikes in the parade was welcome to—as long as you decorated your bike in red, white, and blue. The high school cheerleaders made an appearance, as did the Boy and Girl Scouts. I loved the tradition, but not this year. I had too much going on.

Caprice was too agitated to even sit down. She paced around our tiny table, and she was making me nervous. I reached up and took her cold, bird-like arm in mine. When were brides going to get over the idea that they had to starve themselves before their wedding to look good?

"Caprice, sit down, please; you're making me nervous." I tugged gently on her arm. She sighed heavily but complied. She buried her head in her hands.

"I'm just so worried, Kate. This isn't like her at all. It's as if she's fallen off the face of the earth."

Now, I was beginning to worry. This brought my mind right back to Jen. Where was she? And was it a coincidence that another woman was unaccounted for? "How long has she been gone?"

My mind started to drift to the world of weddings. Sad but true, it was beginning to whirl and problem-solve, and it wasn't related to finding Logan. It revolved around replacing the missing bridesmaid…should I do that, or just have one of the groomsmen be escorted by *two* of the bridesmaids down the aisle during the recession?

"Kate, Kate!" Caprice shook my arm slightly. "Are you listening to me?"

I brought myself back to the moment and smiled. I hoped my 'Katie smile.' "Oh, course!"

Caprice didn't call me out on it, but she looked at me as if she wanted to. "It's been a day and a half, and I think her phone's dead 'cause it goes straight to voicemail."

"Have you contacted her family, a boyfriend, friends?"

Now, Caprice looked at me with what I can only call disdain. "Yes, Kate." She sounded tired.

"What about the police? Did you file a missing person's report?"

She looked down at her hands, "No."

"Does she have a partner?"

Caprice didn't answer right away, or even at all. Caprice played with the giant emerald-cut diamond set in platinum.

"There's more to this than you're telling me. What's going on, Caprice?"

She grabbed a paper napkin embossed with 'The Perk' and rubbed her eyes, getting tiny flecks of scone icing on her face. I reached over and brushed them off with my own napkin. This just made her cry harder.

"I think I really messed up, Kate. I should have taken her more seriously, but I didn't want to make things uncomfortable for my wedding."

I didn't even know what to ask, so I stayed silent. I caught Tally's eye from behind the counter. She raised her eyebrows at me. I ever so slightly shook my head no. I'm not quite sure what she was asking, but I didn't want any interruptions.

"Is she safe?" I didn't know how to approach this. What were we talking about?

"She has this boyfriend, and he's a real jerk. I, I think he may be hurting her." At this statement, Caprice looked ashamed.

"Do you know where he is right now? And how do you know he may have been hurting her? Did she tell you?"

"No, but I saw bruises, and she didn't want to explain them. He was always touching her in public, in a nice way, but she didn't seem to like it. I knew they were having problems; I just didn't want to deal with it."

Not the most supportive friend, but at least she was doing something about it now

"Kate!" Caprice's tone and volume told me I hadn't been listening to her again.

My gaze flew to hers. "Sorry, Caprice. Just thinking about how to best proceed. You should go to the police. I imagine that you suspect domestic abuse will encourage them to start an investigation sooner than usual."

She nodded... "Go now, tell Det. McAllister, you're one of my brides."

Caprice gathered up her sweater and pocketbook and touched my arm in a gentle gesture. "Thank you, Kate; I'll let you know how it goes."

I felt eyes on me and turned to find Charlie. Oh no. I never called him again after he came over for coffee. He didn't smile but raised a ceramic mug to me in salute. He walked over and leaned down to me, and whispered softly.

"Let it go, Katie, and try to get your bride to stop filing a formal report." Then he left the shop. What the heck?

I put a reminder in my phone to call Carice and check on Logan. Not just because of the wedding, but because I was genuinely concerned.

Chapter Eighteen

Saturday, July 5

If you have a ring bearer, do not give him the real rings for his walk down the aisle. If you want a visual, you can sew on copies of the rings so he can't lose them? The real rings should remain safely in the pocket of the best man. Yes, both the bride's and the groom's rings. The Maid of Honor will probably not have pockets to keep the groom's ring safe for the bride to give the groom.

I had a wedding today, and it was necessary that I be on site first thing in the morning. I thought I'd treat myself to a scone and a strong cup of coffee, so off to 'The Perk' I went. Of course, I turned my mind to Jen. There was something going on here in our little burg, and I didn't know what to think about it. Jen and Sarah seemed to be in on the secret, and I wasn't. I didn't like that, no, I didn't like that at all. It kind of hurt, to be honest. I was going to text Jen again. I thought it had something to do with the domestic abuse 'underground railroad.' But one thing I've learned is that it's never wise to assume. While it looked to be the case, it wasn't certain until it was.

* * *

It was the one of the few lulls in the day at 'The Perk.' The super early morning rush was over. It wasn't yet time for the lunch rush, where locals grabbed a prepackaged sandwich or salad and a caffeine pick-me-up. Believe it or not, the afternoon crush was even more harried than the morning. How else would Eastbury get through the remainder of the day without their stop at 'The Perk'?

When I walked into The Perk, it was Tally who was once again in front of the refrigerated display case stocking the aforementioned salads and sandwiches in preparation for the lunch crush. I walked to Tally and placed a gentle hand on her shoulder. She almost jumped out of her skin.

I felt awful. "Sorry! Any messages from Jen?" I asked. Maybe she was texting Tally with instructions for the coffee shop?

Tally flushed, then stood up to hug me. "Just a couple, marching orders for the shop," She brushed nonexistent crumbs from her lavender apron.

I rubbed her arm after we broke our embrace. I accepted the coffee. Tally went around the bar and poured it for me with a smile. I placed a hefty donation into the tip jar, but decided to skip the scone.

If I couldn't talk to Jen, I was going to sit at her table and try to text with her. Hopefully, she'd respond. I was happy at least to see Jen's girls here today. They were lovely, wholesome girls, but not in the same grade as my Ellis. One was a year older, and one a year younger. They got along like a house on fire when our families gathered but didn't hang otherwise.

I changed my mind and decided to settle in a cozy chair by the bay window. It didn't seem right to sit at Jen's table without her. The Perk was decorated in a very eclectic style. Nothing matched, but everything did. It just…worked. It was cozy without being cramped, warm but not too hot in the winter, cool in the summer but not freezing with the chill of refrigerated air. She had a bounty of gourmet items for purchase lining two walls of the shop and if I was ever waiting on her to join me for a cup, I busied myself salivating over those luxury items. Did I mention they were heavy on the chocolate?

I unlocked my phone and fired off a text to Jen.

You there, Jen?

"What's up Katie?

I was thrilled to have reached her, and how cavalier of her, acting as if nothing was going on.

Jen, please come home. Why would you stay away? We can talk to Brian, if that's what you're worried about. But you have to defend yourself. If you don't it looks so bad. You have to know that.

Bubbles, then nothing.

You won't come to your own defense and alibi yourself for Jack's murder, how serious could your secret possibly be? Does it have something to do with the domestic abuse support thing?

Also, there is something going on with Sarah Deloro and her assistant. Sarah is just being too nice.

Weirdly, Jen and Sarah Deloro had become friends while I had been living in California.

She finally answered. *Sarah isn't so bad, and I know I can trust you, "* Jen typed, *but I just didn't want to involve you, worry you with yet another problem. And in all reality, it's safer for you, and Ellis to not know anything.*

Now, she was scaring me. Whatever she was involved in, was she and her family in danger?

Does this have anything to do with Jack's murder?

No, NO! Look, I'm glad you're pushing for answers. This has been weighing on me and I want to tell you everything. I don't like how things have been weird between us. I know I can trust you. I'll be in contact soon and clear this up, I promise.

I certainly hoped so, I wasn't exactly in a position to get the information any sooner.

Chapter Nineteen

Saturday, July 5

Are you sad because it's raining on your wedding day? Yes, I understand that, but did you know that a cloudy day is better for photos? Maybe it will clear for a little while, and you can get some great wedding pictures. If your venue site has lots of trees, they can provide a natural and beautiful canopy from the rain.

Time to stop procrastinating and get to my venue, I thought as I dropped my paper coffee cup in the bin. My job would be such a dream if I didn't have to go to those nasty weddings, kidding, not kidding. Actually, I got very close to my couple, and I loved seeing them get married. It was the rare wedding when I didn't get misty-eyed.

Today's wedding was at the bride's father's best friend's home. Yes, New England home prices are hefty, almost in line with California's, but in New England, you get a lot more land for your money. Today's venue is going to be in the back garden of the friend's home with the cocktail hour around the pool. The reception would be under a tent erected for the wedding. We had to truck in restrooms, which were really nice and clean. But if I had trouble with something, and we trucked in restrooms, it was usually with them. One time, one of the caterer's employees turned off the water source to the restrooms, as they had used that spigot to wash a pot. There was no running water out in the field. There was panic among vendors and early-arriving family members alike. It didn't take me long to troubleshoot the issue, but I have to admit, I had a couple of perspiration stains on my prep shirt when I was done. Disaster averted.

The ceremony was beautiful. It wasn't a religious ceremony, but it was very heartfelt. The bride and groom planted a tree in a large wood tub that they planned to transplant at their new home in West Hartford. I'm glad I put in my contracts that I didn't lift things over ten pounds because dollars to donuts, they would have asked me to carry it to someone's car. But I liked the idea.

Finally, the post-wedding family and bridal party photos were finished, and it was almost time to line the VIPs up for the 'Introduction into the Reception.' The last thing to do before I was to bustle Bethany's dress. Her dress was a gorgeous, fitted lace affair, but the train was long, and we couldn't get away without busting it. A dress with a train must be "bustled" so the bride doesn't trip over it (or others don't!) during the reception. Bustles proved to be a thorn in my side. Every one of them was different. I don't go to dress fittings, so I ask the bride to have someone video the seamstress bustling the dress. Quite often, this is forgotten, so I have to wing it on the wedding day. I'm pretty good at it, but I sure do need my reading glasses for the process.

I walked over to Bethany and gently interrupted her conversation with the Maid of Honor.

"Bethany, we need to bustle your dress before the 'Intro.'

Her smile was exquisite. Her hair and makeup team had done a fantastic job. Bethany's hair was a warm shade of brown, and she had it arranged in a half up/half down style, her hair falling halfway down her back. Her makeup was so natural that it didn't really look like she had any on, but I had seen her without, and it sure flattered her.

"Kate!" Bethany gave me a big smile. "It's all been so perfect, I'm so happy!" She hugged me tightly.

I broke the hug but kept my hands on her forearms. "I'm so happy *you're* happy, Bethany." And I was. She had been a dream to work with, and her new husband was equally lovely.

"Didn't I tell you, Kate? Maria forgot to put in the buttons, hooks, and snaps to create a bustle, and I said to never mind." My life flashed before my eyes. OH, MY, GOD. This was a disaster. Someone would end up flat on their face, having tripped over yards of delicate lace trailing on the floor if this dress wasn't bustled. Think, Kate, think.

I picked up Bethany's train, put my arm around her tiny waist, and almost dragged her into the uncle's lavish home. We went immediately into what I knew to be the master suite. I used my head to swish a movement to direct the maid of honor to join us. Bless her heart, she complied and scurried after us. That Bethany could move quickly when someone was pulling her!

"What's going on, Kate?" Ruthie, the Maid of Honor, asked as she took quick little baby steps in her oh-so-high heels. Not the best idea for footwear for the bridesmaids, I had told Bethany, but she insisted, and no one had fallen...yet.

"Ruthie, would you please grab my Bride Bag?" My prize possession, which contained everything I could possibly need for a wedding emergency, except, in this case, a bustle.

"Sure!" She said enthusiastically as she quick-stepped in those ridiculous heels.

Ruthie came back with the bag with incredible speed. Think, Kate, think, I told myself. Luckily, Bethany's dress was super lightweight. I could do this.

"Kate," Bethany finally questioned me. "What's going on? Isn't it time for the 'Intros'?"

"It is, yes, but we have to do something about your train. We have to create a bustle to bundle it up so you can walk around during the reception easily, and your guests won't trip over you."

I'll give this to Bethany. She didn't argue. I think she knew it was a lost cause. I don't over-rule my clients on much, but when I do, they know I'm serious. I rooted around in my bag and pulled out a giant safety pin and a face mask. I gently removed one white ear loop from the mask and attached the pin to it. I then picked the train in the middle and fashioned a bustle by pinning the dress right below Bethany's derriere. If the dress had been made of heavier fabric, it never would have worked. I tied the remaining ear loop around the safety pin to hide it. I stood up and admired my handiwork. It looked pretty good. It looked great. I took a quick photo and showed it to Bethany.

She wrinkled her pug nose a little, but then smiled. "Well, I guess it will have to do. Maria would have done better, but…" Well, of course, Maria would have done better. She was a professional bridal seamstress. I had just fashioned this bustle in under five minutes with a safety pin and an ear loop from a face mask. Was I annoyed, well duh, yeah… but I put a smile on my face then rolled my eyes when I turned away. If she wanted a professional bustle, she should have made sure Maria did what he had been paid for! Let it go, Kate, I cautioned myself.

My smile was plastered sincerely back on my face. "Let's get this show on the road… Intro time!" I was trying to get the energy back up. My version of the bustle had taken much less time than a proper one would take to get buttoned, snapped, and hooked into place. They can be wicked hard to 'do up,' especially if no one videoed it. I had a moment to breathe, and that's when I noticed a little alcove off the master. It was decorated, in of all things, as a nursery. Weird.

"Hey, Bethany," okay…I'm nosy. We all know this. "I thought your dad's friend was single, but is that kind of a nursery of his master?" In fact, that was why he wasn't present at the wedding, he was off on a boys' trip that had been planned for forever but had graciously offered up his home as a wedding venue to Bethany. If that wild boys' trip didn't scream single, I don't know what did.

"I know, right? That's what I was telling my mom, weird. He's an old college friend of my dad's, so my mom knows him too and all Mom would say was that he had been in a relationship, and it looked like he was going to be a dad. I guess he was pretty stoked about it, but she didn't give me any more details."

"You mean you didn't ask," chimed in our maid of honor, giving Bethany an indulgent smile. "You were a little preoccupied with the wedding." That's a kind way of saying it.

Bethany blushed sweetly. "Yeah," she agreed.

And just like that, I wasn't miffed anymore. This was Bethany's big day, after all. We were talking as we walked through the house, making our way to the outside pool area, when I glanced into what I assumed was the family friend's office/study. There was a large photo of a man hanging on the wall over his desk. It was Rodney! Jack's disgruntled, okay, very angry ex-business partner...and maybe father to Meghan's baby.

"Bethany," I stopped dead in my tracks. Is that your dad's friend?" I motioned with my head toward the photo as my hands were full of her veil.

She glanced over where I indicated. "Um, yeah." She kept up her steady trek to the French doors leading to the pool area.

Wow, wow, wow. What an interesting turn of events. I was going to have to get in that office. There had to be something incriminating in there. Luckily, I was staying to assist in the restoration of the house, post-wedding. I was going to get a look in that office if it was the last thing I did.

The rest of the event went off seamlessly, with the culmination of Bethany and her single friends enjoying the old-fashioned custom of 'tossing the bouquet.' There were no knock-down-drag-out fights we all love to enjoy on social media, but there were a few ladies who really wanted that bouquet. I think the lucky winner, who snatched it right out of her neighbor's hand, thought her boyfriend might drop on one knee and propose on the spot. She looked around greedily after acquiring her prize, and her eyes lit up when they landed on a tall young man. He stared back blankly at her. Oh well, maybe another time.

The end of the evening finally arrived. I was chomping at the bit to get back in Rodney's office. It was going to be tricky. I couldn't be known as the planner who snooped.

Bethany and her new husband, Philip, had already departed in a flurry of pink and cherry-colored streamers. I was thankful to the young flower girl and ringbearer for embracing my idea that picking them up as some sort of contest. I was going to have to provide a prize, I imagine. I'm sure I have a spare chocolate bar in my lunch bag. I always do.

"Kate!" I heard the mother of the bride call for me. That woman was a workhorse. She was amazing. I just may have to ask her if she'd like a part-time job.

"In here, Lydia." I was in the kitchen.

"My generous family friend, Rodney, requested that we lock the sterling cake server and knife in the china cabinet. I swear, that man is more of a fussy old lady than I am. Would you mind taking care of that, Kate? I brought them in from outside. They just need a quick wash and rinse."

"You bet ya, where's the cabinet key?"

"Hum..." Lydia mused, shutting the French door from outside with her hip. "I think in the front desk drawer...in his office."

Shazam! Just the break I needed to get in that office to snoop around!

"Got it," I replied with as little emotion in my voice as possible. I sedately walked to the office, doing my best not to skip. Could I shut the door as I snooped? No...but oh, how I wanted to. I grabbed the china cabinet keys lickety-split from the desk drawer. I peered out the office door to see if anyone was waiting on me. Nope. Everyone was going about their own exhausting task of the last stage of a wedding, the dreaded clean-up. The few family and friends entrusted with helping me were tired and had had a cocktail or two. I never indulge when I'm working, so I was a wee bit clearer than my fellow worker-bees. I had a few minutes; I could do a quick search of the desk drawers. Why was I doing this? Well, I would do just about anything juuuuust this side of legal to help Jen. She was like a sister to me. I knew she didn't kill Jack, I had to help everyone else to see that. So far, Jen was the only person of interest who hasn't had a police interview...or an alibi—because she wouldn't provide one, I told myself with chagrin. So, was I going to go against my personal code of decency and snoop like my life depended on it? Yeah, I was because Jen's, in fact, did.

The second desk drawer down had a locked drawer. I grabbed a paperclip, from a little souvenir espresso cup from Mystic, Connecticut. Huh. I quickly unbent it and slip the wire into the lock. Come on, these locks weren't intended to secure the crown jewels, but to keep a snoopy wedding planner out. I twisted right, I twisted left, and then I felt it give. Ta-da! The thrill of success was a little out of context, but I thought I'd take the win when I could. I glanced at the open doorway to see if anyone was missing me, but saw no one. I heard tired laughter from the kitchen, I think, but no troubled shouts for 'Kate.' I slid the drawer open slowly, wasn't sure if it was a creaky one or not, and saw…a cell phone. I picked it up, wondering if it was an older, replaced model or if Rodney had two phones. Many people did; their company issued them a phone, and they had a personal phone, too. I had trouble keeping track of one phone, much less two. I picked it up and tapped the screen. It lit up. The phone was obviously not a personal one; the screen was blank blue with just the date and time and no personal photos. I tapped the screen again and got a lock screen. Okay, can't get in. I'd never guess the password; it was probably secured with Face ID anyway. Face ID…no, the security was better than that, wasn't it? I grabbed a framed photo off the desk. Rodney's face was about the size of a person's head, and they held the phone to the photos. Boom! I unlocked the phone. OH MY GOD. I was going to disable the face ID function on my own phone when I got home. This was too easy. I snapped a photo of the desk photo with my phone, I never know when I may need it. And then opened the messaging app, fingers crossed for something that could point the police from Jen to Rodney. Not that I had anything against Rodney, but he might have killed Jack, so if there was proof of it…my eyes widened. There was a string of messages between Rodney and someone called Meg-Meg. Bingo.

Roddy, we need to talk—said Meg-Meg. This message was dated a couple of months ago.

I asked you not to contact me on this phone you know this is my work cell—(Rodney)

Forget it then—(Meg-Meg)

Come on, Meg, don't be that way—you're right we do need to talk—(Rodney).

No, I've changed my mind. Shouldn't have texted. You know there's nothing to say I've made my decision—(Meg-Meg)

You don't love him—(Rodney)

I love you!—(Rodney)

The baby's mine, isn't it?—(Rodney) It seemed he still wasn't sure.

I *knew* it! Meghan's baby isn't Jack's. The dates didn't add up, but even after what I heard Rodney tell Gavin a few weeks ago, I wasn't positive he was Meghan's baby daddy. Until now.

"Kate!" The mother of the bride called out to me. She didn't sound happy. Had I been gone too long? Okay...I'm not going to make excuses for my next action. I pure and simply panicked. I shoved the cell phone into the pocket of my vendor's apron. And a good thing, too, as Lydia poked her head in the office door just after I bounced up my seat in Rodney's desk chair, where I had been gleefully scrolling through his cell phone. I held up the china cabinet keys.

"Finally found the china cabinet keys. They were pushed back into the bottom drawer." Could I somehow slip the cell into one of the desk drawers? Not with Lydia's glaring at me. I hope she was just tired and not suspicious. I trotted out of the room and went straight to the dining room to put the beautiful sterling cake server and knife back into their velvet-lined cases. I locked the cabinet doors back up and before I could make my way to return the key to Rodney's office, there was Lydia with her hand extended.

"I'll return the key for you, Kate," but this was said with a smile, so I don't think she was suspicious of my over-long stay in the office. "Sorry I was a wee bit of a cranky before. It was a lovely, but long day. Thanks so much for everything." She hugged me. "I really don't even know *how* to say thank you. We couldn't have done it without you." She squeezed my forearms and let me go, spinning quickly on her heel and heading toward the office. *Now*, what was I going to do? Should I just leave the cell on a counter somewhere? I couldn't take it home with me, but I certainly couldn't go back into the office. That would be a major red flag. I was immobile with indecision when a text came through from Ellis.

MOM *we have a flat tire!*

I knew Ellis was out with her beau Kevin, so she wasn't stranded alone, but I hated to be in this position—having to finish a job and having a child needing me. I was getting ready to tell Ellis to call Triple A, my fingers flying across the keyboard.

But my face must have betrayed me, because Lydia suddenly said, "Kate! What is it?"

I smiled, hoping it didn't look too strained. "No problem. Ellis and her boyfriend have a flat tire. I'm going to call the road service for her."

Lydia actually shooed me. "GO!! Are you even kidding me right now? You have gone above and beyond" I blushed here, as I wasn't still on site due to my exemplary work ethic but because I wanted to snoop.

"Look at your blush." Now I really did feel like a jerk. "Go to your Ellis. We're really done anyway." She hugged me again. I hugged her back.

"Thank you, Lydia. I'll call you tomorrow, and we'll gloat over the lovely day."

I made my getaway before I could think better of it, only realizing as I climbed in my Suburban that I had Rodney's cell phone still tucked in my apron pocket. Crap.

Chapter Twenty

Sunday, July 6

It's not uncommon to see the bride and groom's dog make an appearance at the wedding or reception, or both. It's pretty darn cute! If you go this route, consider having someone come and pick your dog up after you have your photographer snap a few pictures. The whole event would be too long for any dog.

I awoke the next morning with a scratchy throat and a headache. Did I think I was coming down with something? Not really. I didn't sleep well or long enough last night. It took forever to get Kevin's car set to rights. Luckily, Kevin's dad came out and changed the tire. But like many things in life, there is one setback after another.

Thank God today was Sunday. I loved Sundays as long as I didn't have an event, and I didn't today. I think this morning necessitated a trip to The Perk,' but Jen wouldn't be there, and I didn't want to have coffee alone. I needed a sounding board. I couldn't talk to Brian, we were still on rocky turf (his breaking up with me and all—I'd laugh if I didn't feel like crying). Grant? Ah, no. He'd take it the wrong way and think I was making moves on him. My ex was such a self-centered jerk. Charlie was an option, but when I had him over for coffee not long ago, it wasn't the best situation. I knew there were feels there, and as annoyed as I was at Brian, I didn't want to muddy any waters. I guess I knew a lot of people but didn't have that many close friends. There was my mom...ah no.

There was always...no, no, my mind didn't just go there. Was I really considering asking Sarah Deloro for coffee? Sarah and I were getting along pretty well, planning the baby shower she was having for her friend. I had hated Sarah Delorgo in high school, the reason, well, Brian McAllister, of course. Because he was Sarah's before, he was mine. Did I steal him, well, kind of, but not really...maybe the old news of my stealing, kind of, Brian from her was old news. Did I like Sarah Deloro? No, but I didn't hate her anymore either, and she had a good head on her shoulders. Besides, I think she already knew something about the domestic underground railroad thing. I needed help, and I guess it was going to be from Sarah Deloro.

I made my way downstairs, careful to let little Chloe out as quietly as possible so as to not wake the sleeping Ellis. I needn't have bothered. She slept like the dead. I was so jealous.

I put my favorite 'Save a Life (the bride's) and Hire a Wedding Planner' mug under the Keurig and hit start. Ah, the nectar of the gods would be ready soon, even if it was crummy old-brand K-cup coffee. I was putting it off long enough. I was going to do it; I was going to invite Sarah Deloro for coffee.

Hey Sarah, want to grab a coffee in a few? I texted. Would she think it was weird? Would she come? I saw the little bubbles.

Well, this is weird—Yep, I thought she'd think it was weird.

Did I respond to that?

JK, sure Kate. I have some stuff I'd like to talk to you about too. Guess this is about Jen?

Radio silence, Sarah

Check. The Perk in 20? I know for a fact she's not there—already had my first cup

Check

Now, what the heck was I going to wear for coffee with Sarah Deloro? It was harder than it should have been—but I finally settled on lightweight 'A' line dress and a short cardigan in case the air conditioning at the 'Perk' was up too high, although it never was. I was putting on my brave face by wearing a 'resort wear' dress. The scar from my bike accident, yup still self-conscience. The fact that I was baring it for Sarah's scrutiny was my own brand of bravado.

When I entered the cool confines of 'The Perk,' Sarah had already grabbed us a primo table, one that was against the wall but where we could watch all the townsfolk coming and going. She tipped her head at the cup sitting across the empty seat from her. Maybe she did have a heart. It appeared she again had ordered my favorite beverage, a 'half-caf, non-fat, extra hot cappuccino was in the cup...*and* a biscotti rested on the saucer like a fat cat in the sun. Be still my heart.

Sarah's eyes went to my leg, and she winced. "Well, that had to hurt."

And we're back...I hated her again. Maybe it wouldn't have bothered me if she hadn't said it in a snarky tone. I slid into my chair and pushed the delicious-looking coffee and biscotti away.

"Don't be a baby, Katie. It had to hurt, didn't it? I heard about your accident, and I've never been one to pretend." She cocked a brow at me. "True?"

"True," I said.

Sarah pulled up the cuff of her gorgeous berry-hued raw silk joggers, revealing a nasty scar. "Check this out. I fell on a run right out front here a few weeks ago. I think about, oh, fifteen people witnessed it. But within a few hours, it went viral. Robin Chester was taking a video of her daughter practicing her book report and caught it." And then Sarah laughed. As I remembered from our 'moment' last spring, it was a light tinkling sound.

And then I was laughing, too. "I would have liked to have seen that." Heck, maybe I could when I got home and went online.

"I bet you would have. I still haven't forgiven you or Brian, Katie." I wasn't sure if she was kidding—it did happen twenty years ago. "But we can come together, for Jen. We've done okay with planning the shower, right?" I am still not sure why Jen and Sarah had become friendly in the years since high school, and my return home hadn't come in between that relationship.

"I think we should try to get our hands on some sort of footage and try to pin down where certain suspects were at the time of the murder." The idea popped into my mind.

Sarah frowned at me. "Footage, like CCTV, or doorbell video?"

"Well, both, if we can."

"Don't you think the police have thought of this?" She queried.

I looked over my shoulder. Why did I feel as if I was being watched? Was this the best place to have this discussion? "I think the police think they have their murderer and aren't going to look further. Scott Bennett, the statie who's running the investigation, is known for being a 'fast closer.'"

I saw something I rarely have seen, Sarah Deloro shocked. "But it's Jen! Brian couldn't believe…"

"He's not the lead detective, and part of being a cop is to look at the evidence and keep your personal feelings to yourself. It's a hard job, but he's good at it."

"I know." Sarah looked wistful and then…mean. "I heard that the food at Saturday night's wedding was barely mediocre."

"Good thing I didn't cook it." I glared right back at her.

Sarah scooted her chair back with a loud scrape. "Meet me at your office at 9:00 tonight. It should be dark by then and wear black." Another glare and then a smile.

I gave her a look and then a smile. She was okay.

Chapter Twenty-One

Sunday, July 6

Even if it's not raining, if your wedding is outdoors and you hear thunder, you must move the event inside. Always have a rain plan, a 'Plan B.' The last thing you want to do is be out in a field under a tent with a metals frame in a lightning storm.

I really didn't want to tell Ellis that her mother was again trying to catch a killer, so I rushed dinner (pork chops, green beans, and potatoes in the slow cooker, thank you very much).

"Are you trying to get rid of me?" Ellis asked, one foot on the bottom stair as I encouraged her to go upstairs and 'start on her homework.' "Usually, you beg for me to stay and watch a movie with you." She was not easily fooled, that daughter of mine.

I patted her back and smiled.

"Oh," she nodded her head knowingly. "Brian's coming over. You could have just told me, Mom. I'm cool with him, you know that." She spoke like an indulgent mother who was trying to use the appropriate lingo. I wanted to laugh but didn't. She was a dear girl. I didn't bother to correct her, to tell her that her mother was going on yet another sleuthing expedition. I'd text her when I was out of the driveway, so she'd know I wasn't in the house. She'd be okay for an hour or so. She could always call Brian, ha!

I met Sarah outside The Perk. My office, where she had dictated, we meet, was upstairs. I was close to a point where I could pay Jen the fair market value of the office space I was leasing. I wanted to fix that soon. Business was business and friendship – well, friendship. The two didn't mix well.

Sarah had black paint like the football players wear smeared on her face. Pleeeeze!

"Nice look, Sarah," I scoffed at her. I couldn't get too chummy with the spawn of Satan.

"Want some?" She held out a little pot of what I could only assume was the face paint.

"Sure, I held out my hand, "what the heck." I smeared a glob on my cheekbones. What was happening? Yeah, I felt silly. The whole thing was silly.

"Let's go up to my office before we make our game plan. There is something I want to show you." For once, Sarah didn't mouth off and followed me to the stairs leading to the outside entrance to my office. I could enter via The Perk too, but not at this hour. I was still on the fence whether I should share the cell phone I had 'accidentally' stolen from Rodney's house. I recognized that if I shared this information with Sarah and she used it, it would be career suicide. I knew this, but somehow, I didn't think she'd betray me. I knew about a shady transaction she had been a part in her real estate dealings. She was an innocent player but it wouldn't look good for her if it came out. Would I really ruin her business and reputation? No. But she didn't have to know that. Did my feelings about Sarah seem all over the place? Yeah, they were. She had been my hated enemy in high school, and a very close ally last spring. I guess our fragile friendship would remain delicate for a while.

I unlocked my office door, and then we entered the little reception area. The moonlight was flooding in, illuminating my desk and the two little blue visitor chairs I had so lovingly selected last year. I gestured for her to take a seat. She sunk into the right one with a grace and elegance I envied. My bum leg was improving, but its stiffness prevented any type of gracefulness. I pulled the black backpack I carried off my back and removed the cellphone. Sarah leaned in.

"A map, an email?" she queried. Then she saw the phone and looked up at me. "This doesn't look like your phone, Katie." I'm assuming she thought my phone would be filled with pictures of Ellis, or weddings. She would be right.

"Whose phone is it?" She snatched it out of my hands in an impressive cat-like move. She went right to the phone's photos. I had disabled the password function. Waaaaait a minute. This is that guy who has been lurking around, wasn't he Jack's ex business partner?"

I tapped my nose, indicating an affirmative. I really didn't trust my voice right now.

Sarah raised two perfectly arched brows at me. I hated her. Do you know how hard I tried for perfect brows? One time, in high school, I plucked more and more until my eyebrows started over the center of my eye. That was a long year. I doubt I'll ever have those perfect brows. I've discovered a good eyebrow pencil does wonders, though.

"Kate," Sarah was all business now. "Where did you get this phone? *How* did you get it?"

I could deny everything. Now was the moment of truth. Did I trust her...or not? I took a gulp of air.

"Funny thing...I was doing a wedding, and he had offered up his home for the venue as he's a friend of the father of the bride. I came across it, and somehow it ended up in my apron pocket. I forgot to return it..." I was rambling. Even in the dark, I couldn't look at Sarah. My guilty conscience was so great, I was even confessing to Sarah Deloro.

"Slow down, Katie," she placed her hand on my forearm. "You know how serious this is, right? You have to get this phone back as soon as possible."

I stood up. "I know," I began pacing in the small space. "But there is some really good intel on it. Did you know Jack wasn't the father of Meghan's baby?!?"

Sarah was silent. "I didn't even know Jack had gotten this girl knocked up."

A little rough around the edges, was our Sarah.

"But you're right. This does make for interesting fodder. Show me this interesting evidence."

I sat back down and showed Sarah the texts between Rodney and Meghan.

"Interesting, yes, but you have to get this phone back. Do you realize how catastrophic it could be for your business if people found out you took things from their homes? And what's our goal here tonight? You said something about looking at doorbell footage. How are we going to do that? I was looking for a bit of fun, Kate, but this is crazy."

"I know, I know." I thought my heart was going to explode out of my chest.

"Take a breath," Sarah said calmly. "you know I don't have a maternal bone in my body. I don't want to have to coddle you." She wasn't smiling.

It was just what I needed. Leave it to Sarah Deloro to shake me out of it.

"Okay," I was getting my mojo back and began pacing in my minuscule space. "Let's head over to the Bed and Breakfast where Meghan and her mom are staying. I'm sure they have some sort of security system, and we can look to see if and when she left the building the night of the murder."

"Not bad, not bad," Sarah nodded. "But you are making me so dang nervous. Sit down!" She grabbed my arm and manhandled me into a chair. She was rough!

"What is your big plan, Miss Snoop?"

"So, we go in together to the front desk, and as it's late, hopefully, they won't be well staffed."

"Try staffed at all. It's not a Four Seasons, Katie. Everyone may have gone to bed."

"Even better!" I was getting ramped up now.

"And the phone?"

"It's one town over; we'll return it after. Sarah," I paused. She cocked a brow. "Why are you helping me?"

Now she stood up, went to my office window, and looked out. "I had a good time last spring, Katie. I," and here she paused. "I like you. I think we could have been pretty good friends except for Brian, 'our mutual beau. ' And as you've pointed out, on more than one occasion, I don't have a wealth of friends or family, and I've always liked Jen...a lot. And she's in trouble."

I really didn't expect all that, but respected it, and her. Just as I was getting ready to respond, she continued.

"But don't think I've forgotten what a little snake you were in high school." She turned, pointed two fingers to her own eyes, and then at me. "I'm watching you. Let's go."

She was at the front door of my office in a few steps, opened it with more strength than it needed. "LET'S GO!"

Okay, I guess I knew who the team leader in this mission was going to be. I was okay with that. It was a short walk down Main Street to the B&B. Would Ellis kill me if she knew what I was up to? Oh, crap! I forgot to text Ellis that I had 'taken a walk.' I stopped and whipped out my phone.

'You have to text *now*?" The snark was back.

"My daughter. Forgot to tell her I was out."

"Yeah, doesn't your kid work here? Couldn't she review the footage?"

"She does, and ah, no. I can't involve her in any more of this than I already have. Feeling some big guilt feels over this. I doubt she'd help me anymore anyway."

"Smart girl."

By this time, we were at the B&B. Good news, the lights were still on downstairs. I pointed to the ridiculous face paint on Sarah's face, and we both scrubbed it off with a wet wipe provided by yours truly.

We reached the door, and, whoo hoo, the door was unlocked. A bell tinkled merrily as I opened the door. Sarah was less aggressive as we entered. She also had a professional persona to protect. She didn't back out, though.

Maisie, the ever-patient assistant to the rather prickly owner, Isabel, walked from behind the desk from an apartment I knew to be hers. I had been back there once when I had been waiting for Ellis to complete her shift. Maisie had graciously invited me back for a cup of tea. It was all of six hundred square feet, complete with an efficiency kitchen, sitting area, a full-sized bath with shower, a private bedroom, although only large enough for a double bed, no dresser or nightstand. She had gotten creative with basket shelving on the walls. The sitting area was cozy, not cramped. The plums and burgundy colors she used to decorate were warm and inviting. I felt guilty interrupting her off-time. I could hear the low voices of a cable or streaming show coming from her apartment.

"Hey, Maisie! How's it going?" Okay, not the best start, but I really hadn't thought it through. How in the heck was I going to get her out from behind this desk, out of the reception room, and look at her security footage without her knowing what I as up to?

"Hey, Maisie," Sarah chimed in. "How's your mom liking Arizona?"

Maisie beamed. "She loves it. Thank you so much for lowering your commission on the sale of her home so she could have a little more time to get that condo in Phoenix."

My head swiveled at rapid speed to look at Sarah, what?

"My pleasure; your mom was always one of my favorite teachers. Ah, Maisie... we need a little favor." Oh, this was so much easier.

"Sure, Sarah," Maisie tried to stifle a yawn.

"We need to look at your security footage for the night Jack O'Malley was killed.

Maisie's face blanched, her fingers gripped the desktop. Her eyes darted upstairs where I knew Isabelle, the owner, kept a suite of rooms. I'm guessing this was a big no-no. She cocked her ear to the stairs and was apparently happy with the silence. She grinned with a mix of glee and mischievousness. "Follow me."

Sarah and I followed Maisie to an office adjacent to her little apartment. She opened the door quickly. "If you open it fast, it doesn't squeak." She waved her hand for us to sit in the two folding chairs. "The police already asked to see the footage, but let's be frank, Isabelle would be ticked if she knew I was showing you—privacy of guests and all that. So, let's keep this between us." And she winked. Yes, she did. Huh, there was another side to the reliable Maisie than I knew. I liked the little round woman.

We took the footage back until we found the night in question, the night Jack was killed. I wasn't sure what I was looking for. We skipped over Jack bringing Meghan home and Jack going back out. When we got to Lois coming back to the Bed and Breakfast at 10:01 PM (Lois had elected to stay in the luxurious Bed and Breakfast instead of with her daughter, Marjorie, in town. And why not? Jack had been paying the tab, or so I imagine). As Jack's time of death was somewhere around 11:00 PM to 1:00 AM (the next morning), and I saw no one leaving again, it looked as if Meghan and Lois were in for the night.

"Maisie, is there another way in and out of the Inn beside the entrance in this footage? Yeah, there is the mudroom door, but we don't have cameras there, and it sticks, so it's rarely used." Drat, but then I was familiar with sticky doors. Progress, I guess? Did I want the murder to be Meghan or her mother? No, I just didn't want it to be Jen, or look like she was the killer.

We thanked Maisie nicely. Sarah promised to alert Maisie if any small houses in town came under contract before they went on the MLS, and all were happy.

We exited the quaint little B&B as quietly as we came. I think no one was the wiser unless they reviewed security. But we had every right to stop by, albeit a little late in the night.

"You know it hurts me to say it, Sarah Deloro, but that was impressive. And who knew you had a heart." The last was said with not a little snark. She responded in kind.

"Who knew you could run a successful business, Katie." She only called me 'Katie' when she was feeling friendly.

We had reached my office. "Game to do something about this phone?" I waived my pocketbook where the phone was encased.

"Sure, someone has to save you from yourself. Did you walk?"

I nodded.

"I drove. Let's take my car then. You have directions?" She didn't wait for an answer, just guided me into the side alleyway where a few cars fit in the tight space that was Main Street. She beeped her car open, a beauty of the newest Range Rover, black, of course. What a dream car. Yep, still hated her.

We settled into the soft leather seats. They could be heated or cooled, depending on the weather. Wish I had time for a nap, these seats called out for that. Not a great selling point in a car in my book.

Sarah turned toward me, her big golden hoop earrings bouncing on her neck as she did so. "Before we return it, and you *know* we have to return it, Katie. You, in your tiny little mind might think it's a good idea to hang onto it in case we need it, but *it's not a good idea!*

CHAPTER TWENTY-ONE

I held my hands up in a surrender position. "Okay, okay."

"Hey! How did you get into Rodney's phone anyway? You can't have his password." A statement, not a question.

I pulled up the photo I took of the photo of Rodney and showed her. "Then I went into settings and disabled the passcode function."

"You're insane, you know that right, Katie?" Then she laughed. "So, before we return this phone, we have to check his socials. You never know what might be in a person's DMs."

"He wouldn't have his socials on his work phone!"

"Oh, Katie. And you call yourself a mother of a teen. Of *course,* he has his socials on all and every device."

She grabbed the phone from me and began scrolling through the pages, until she stopped on the Instagram app. She clicked and turned the phone to me to show me. "See!"

I leaned in. Sure enough, he had his account up and running on this phone. Sarah went to what I can only assume was his Direct Messages.

Meg, I'm not letting this go—the kid is mine. Jack isn't going to win this time. I'll do whatever it takes WHATEVER IT TAKES

If that wasn't ominous, I don't know what was. Did 'whatever it takes' include murder? I could tell Sarah was as unnerved as I was at this chain of messages.

"We are not dealing with a boy scout here, Kate. We have to be careful, very careful."

I took a picture of Rodney's phone screen with the messages just in case we ever needed it. Did you hear that? "We"

* * *

It took us forty-five minutes to arrive at Rodney's house, one town over. It should have taken us twenty-five, but Sarah and I argued about the best route and neither one of us listened to the car's GPS, and neither of us gave Siri the time of day. Both would have gotten us there a lot faster. We did a drive-by and confirmed there was a dark house. But if I have learned one thing tonight, you were probably always on camera. If your house didn't have a doorbell camera, your neighbor did. Sarah parked five houses up the street and turned off the engine.

"Thoughts?"

"Actually, no."

We sat quietly, each with our own musings. "Okay," I turned to Sarah. "here's what we're going to do. We've got to go in through the back. Not all homes have the doorbell cameras on the back unless they have a full-blown security system, and I don't think I saw a panel for that at the wedding last weekend."

"And how are we going to do that, Einstein?" Sarah looked bored or angry, or both in the blue of the dashboard light. "And even if we do get to the backyard undetected, what are we going to do with the phone then? Toss it on a patio table? He'd know for sure he didn't leave it there."

I thought some more. She was right. If the phone showed up in the wrong place, it would point directly to my event and dereliction of my duty. But wait…Lydia said she was going to lock the side door of the garage, but did she? The caterers had been using the garage all night to stage the bar service. If it was still unlocked, I had a duty to lock it, right? And no one locked the garage to inside the house door.

"I have an idea," I told Sarah as I opened the passenger door of the giant SUV and jumped out.

Sarah got out on her side and silently locked up the car. "I go into this caper with little confidence. I want you to know that in advance." This was said dryly, but she was still following me to the end of the block, where we entered the backyard of the last house on the block. We creeped along the edge of the natural woods, luckily in this neighborhood, like many in New England, there were no fences. We were able to go from one neighbor's yard to another until we were in Rodney's yard. We both paused, reflecting, I think on the magnitude of what we were about to do.

"Okay, walk with your back to the house, as if there's a camera back here. I'm fairly confident there isn't, so just in case." Sarah rolled her eyes at me but followed my lead. I sincerely hoped we weren't going to trip over anything.

It was a cloudy, moonless night, thank God. And no motion detector lights popped on. We made our slow progress until we arrived at the door that opened from the outside into the garage. Not all garages have this feature. We were lucky this one did…and the fact that it might be left unlocked was my greatest wish. I was the first to reach the door. I didn't bother with gloves for myself, as I had recently been on the property, and my fingerprints would be expected to be all over the place. Sarah, not so much. I silently handed her a pair of disposable gloves. They are something I always carry in my backpack/purse. She wordlessly slipped them on.

I hesitantly put my hand on the doorknob and twisted. It opened! We crept in, and no alarm sounded, at least that we could hear. I prayed there wasn't a silent monitoring system. The next hurdle was the entry door and garage to house. Was it open? Could be. Who would lock it and not the outside garage door? Sarah took this one and opened the door. We grinned at each other. I went in first, not at all spooked by the light on over the kitchen sink. People did that when they weren't home, right? What I hadn't thought about/made provision for was if Lydia had set the house alarm after the wedding. As I didn't hear a warning beep, I'm guessing not. Sometimes, people don't like to share their passwords with others and don't want to go into trouble by over-riding the system with a temporary password. It appeared this was the case. The security panel by the garage door was dark and silent. I breathed a sigh of relief for a worry I didn't know I had.

I wasn't messing around now that I was in the house. I went straight to the office and opened the unlocked desk drawer. I placed the cell phone in the drawer exactly as I found it. I even made sure the phone was on the same "home" page where I originally found it. I gently close the door.

"Are you going to lock the drawer?" Sarah asked, leaning over me.

Drats. There was a flaw in my plan. I had no key. I'd used a paperclip to open the drawer but didn't think I could lock it, too.

"What do you think we should do?"

"We? I'm just along for the ride, Katie." But she smiled a smile.

"Come on, Sarah, don't be a jerk."

"Did you *look* for a key?" I felt like an idiot.

"No," I confessed.

"Well, it won't hurt to look a little," she began opening drawers and rooting around. In less than thirty seconds, she pulled out a small gold key with a gold satin ribbon attached. She held it aloft with something approaching glee on her face. I didn't care.

"Genius," I whispered. She swiftly locked up the drawer, and we retreated, retracing our steps both in the house and in the yard exactly as we had entered. We finally made it to the last house on the block and onto public domain when a devil dog came barreling out of the last yard we had just exited. We looked at each other and ran as if our lives depended on it, and I guess it kind of did. We determined that I was a faster runner than Sarah, if you could believe it. I think she delayed unlocking the car door just a little to give me a bit of a fright, as the dog chose to come after me rather than her at that moment. But she finally beep-beeped the lock, and I leapt into her car. Sarah threw something away from us, and the dog went after it like it was going to be his last meal.

As soon as we were both in the car with the doors locked, I let her have it. "Gee, thanks for unlocking the car door with such speed, Sarah!" I glared at her in the darkness of the car.

"She shrugged. "Sorry, Kate, I was a little preoccupied."

"What did you throw for the dog?"

"A stray newspaper. He seemed to like it." And we both burst into giggles. She dropped me off at my house twenty minutes later. This time, we listened to Siri.

"Sarah, thank you." I didn't know what else to say.

She bobbed her head once. "I'm here, Kate. Let me know if you need me." And she roared off.

Chapter Twenty-Two

Monday, July 7

If you have an outdoor wedding under a tent, consider getting flooring. If it rains, you will be dry under the tent, and won't be standing in possible mud.

oday saw me at a posh retirement party located in a boutique hotel in Hartford. No expense had been spared, but the wife of the retiree surprised me. She had doled out small projects to her children—five sons in all, as if they were gifts. The hotel staff or I could and *should* do those things. I had to create a chart of what each family member was supposed to do, and if they didn't do it, I'd have to. This necessitated me arriving on site much earlier than I should need to be just in case people didn't do their jobs and I had to. Sigh. Enough of the pity party. I was feeling sorry for myself. It didn't help that I saw Brian pulling away from the front as I was having my car valeted. What was he doing here? Was he talking to Will, whom I knew to be the food and beverage manager here, someone else, following me? I wish…

Okay, problem number one, I thought to myself, as I pulled open the beautifully carved wooden door of the hotel. No welcome sign. As soon as I got settled, I'd review who was in charge of that task. The small foyer of the hotel was luxury itself. The carpet was scarlet and so plush I was happy I had flats on, otherwise I would have wobbled on the thick pile. It had a dark wood, 'Boys Club' air, but it wasn't shabby the way some old clubs could be.

There was a huge round table in the center of the space, and the sun came in to make it gleam. There wasn't a speck of dust on it. How often did they have to dust that table throughout the day to ensure that? The most gorgeous floral arrangement of peonies was displayed on the pristine table, all pinks and lavenders. The water was clear in the enormous vase, the blooms fresh, I loved it. If you keep floral water fresh, your arrangement will last much longer.

"Welcome," a young red-headed woman with a perfect French twist and a burgundy blazer said brightly.

I smiled back, trying to balance my magic bride bag and clipboard. "Good morning," I tried to add some enthusiasm into my voice. "I'm Kate Ludlow, here for the retirement party."

"Of course! I'm Remy. We've spoken a few times."

Remy was a delight. She looked familiar, but I couldn't place her. She scurried around the front desk in her high heels, a supple calf-skin pair that looked to have cost a fortune. The navy was just the right hue of blue. Yup, jealous!

"Hey, Remy, have you seen a welcome sign for our party?"

Remy took my overly heavy bridal /event bag and placed it gently behind the desk, at the same time she pulled out a shiny lacquered sign.

"That's the one." I felt a sense of calm at seeing it. I wasn't going to have to track it down. "Is the easel back there too?" I had been promised by the wife there would be an easel. And I wasn't disappointed when Remy whipped one out from behind the desk. "Great, I'll just set it up."

Remy pulled the sign back from my outstretched hands. "Oh, no, Kate! There are specific instructions on Skyler's 'Details Page. The oldest son is slated to put out the sign."

I looked hard at Remy. Was she for real? She wouldn't let me set the welcome sign on the easel. I know people can be particular, but here's a secret...the wife would never know. I wasn't happy and didn't do a good job hiding it.

"Are you kidding me right now, Remy? You are insistent that the oldest son set up the sign? Vendors are coming, and there's no sign up."

Remy's eyes widened. "Skyler was very clear," she looked behind her. "And so was her husband." Weird!

Ah, yes, I had met the very discerning 'Retiree.'

I sighed dramatically. "Where is the 'oldest son,' Remy?"

Remy smiled at me with relief as she smoothed her immaculate French twist, her many bangle bracelets jangling merrily. "He's in the bar with the other early-arriving family." And just then, I heard them, the rowdy barks of men who were drinking. Oh boy.

I gave Remy a look, and it wasn't altogether friendly. She looked down at her neatly painted nails, a nice pale pink and avoided my eyes. Really, I was being hard on her. It wasn't her job to keep the men sober. And really, it wasn't mine either.

"Hey, guys!" I smiled my brightest smile at the frat boys/sons of the honoree, lounging all over the cozy pub-type bar. The lights were low, the laughter high. "I'm Kate Ludlow, the Planner."

"Kate! Nice to meet you. We're here to help, right guys?" And here I thought that was my job. Be nice, Kate, I scolded myself. Well, he seemed friendly, but with a few beers in him, I wasn't surprised. I gave another smile all around. "I'm looking for the 'oldest son.'"

My new friend stood up and bowed. "Sloan Withers at your service."

"Nice to meet you, Sloan, men," I included them all. "I have a party task of my own for you right now, Sloan, well, a task from your mom." The boys all laughed.

"Yeah, she's big on including everyone. Come on, Kate, let's go."

Sloan walked just fine; maybe they were just happy about their dad's retirement. I steered him into the charming little lobby. Sloan rubbed his hands together in anticipation. "So, what's my 'task'? He started laughing. Not good.

"You're to put the welcome sign onto the easel." I tried not to roll my eyes. Remy walked over to the bubble-wrapped welcome sign and handed it to Sloan. He accepted it, and promptly dropped it. Remy went white and scurried back behind the reception desk, refusing to make eye contact with me. I took two deep yoga breaths. I could see through the bubble wrap the sign was in at least two pieces. OH MY GOD.

Sloan looked down at me, his face as white as Remy's. "Mom is going to kill me. I'm not speaking figuratively here. She's going to kill me dead."

"Yeah, she really is, Kate." Remy piped in from behind the safety of her desk. I glared at her. She was *not* helping.

I unwrapped the beautiful acrylic sign. I handed the bubble wrap to Sloan. Please stow this behind the desk." I didn't smile. Sloan was shame-faced and complied quickly. Then he tried to escape into the bar.

"Uh-un." I stopped him. "Back here, Sloan." He spun on his heel and walked back to me, but he didn't want to. He looked like a little boy who was being forced to eat his vegetables. 'I don't want to.' I could almost hear him whine.

"Remy, Magic Bride Bag," I called out like a surgeon demanding instruments. Remy was quick and seemed just happy to be helping in some manner to right this terrible wrong. "Sloan, hold both pieces of the sign." Remy had handed me the bag. "Remy, position the easel." People liked to be told what to do in a crisis. It helped them feel things were under control. My orders were to keep them out of my hair while I wracked my brain on what to do. Too late to get another sign made, even a different one from an office supply print shop. The key was to try to fix it to such a level that no one would notice. I rooted around in my bag until my fingers closed around the black gorilla tape. The sign was black acrylic with gold lettering. None of the lettering had been impacted. In fact, only the right corner had been broken off and cleanly, at that. "Remy, are there any extra blooms around the hotel?"

She brightened, happy to actually contribute in a real way. "I'll be right back," she promised as she scampered off and went in the direction of one of the small reception rooms.

I tore off six small pieces of the black tape and applied them to the back of the sign securing the broken corner. It looked okay but would look rather festive when I attached flowers to the damaged corner and the one opposite. "Now put that sign on the easel, Sloan, so I can tell your mom that you did your duty." He did, and at the same time, Remy slid into our space with some beautiful pink roses. I grabbed some ribbon and wire from my bag and hooked up those flowers. It looked even better than without, I tried to tell myself. One disaster averted.

"This stays between us," I threatened Sloan and Remy. Remy nodded once, and Sloan put up his hands in a surrendering position.

"I'll never tell," and he grinned. He did have a particular charm.

I was tweaking the flowers, rather pleased with myself, when in walked Will, my old high school friend, and Jack's sparring partner the night he was killed. I knew he worked here as the Food and Beverage Director. A big job, but I'm sure not a career choice he wished for in high school before his injury.

"Hey, Will," I welcomed him.

He appeared lost in his own thoughts. He turned and smiled. "Hey Katie, ready for tonight?"

He had been emailing me frequently this past week regarding the party. Will was efficient and thoughtful; was he also a murderer? I had so many questions for him. Where was he when Jack died, why did he feel he need to punch Jack for saying something to Jen. She wasn't *his* wife...and *why* did he go to spring training where he *knew* Jack would be...?

"All set; thanks so much for all your help this week."

He continued his progress toward the kitchen and dining areas. "No problem, Katie, it's my job. Hey, Remy," he said by way of greeting to her." She just followed him with her eyes. With longing? I looked at his retreating back. He wasn't a happy man. I heard an audible sigh as he walked past.

I started putting the escort cards—table seating cards—out on the round table in the foyer, I had requested they be alphabetized, and our party planning wife had complied. It made the rather tedious task so much easier. One of the cards didn't have the little color-coded sticker to indicate the 'chicken, fish, or beef' entrée choice, so I was headed to the kitchen to check the master list when I heard Will and another man talking.

"Come on, Sergio, if anyone asks, can't you do me a solid and say I was on the schedule? I was here; we just didn't cross paths." I was surprised at the pleading in Will's voice.

"Will, I heard again from that police detective. He was here today. They don't seem to believe me that you were here the night that baseball player died. When I agreed to help you, I wasn't expecting so much drama." A heavily accented voice stated.

"I took care of you, Sergio, both with scheduling and a little something extra."

There was silence at first, then the man I now knew as Sergio asked, "Is this a wife thing or a police thing?"

"Forget it." Nothing more was said, and I heard what I could only assume was the kitchen door slam against the back wall. Not a safe or smart thing to do in a professional kitchen. Will must be angry, assuming Will the was door banger, and I'm guessing he was.

Was Will trying to cement an alibi for the day Jack was killed? We had all been at the bar together. But the evening had broken up about 8:00 PM, and as the Food and Beverage Manager, Will could have a reason to go to work here at the hotel. He might be one of those people who are efficient late at night, so he could've come in to do paperwork and now feared that since no one saw him, he had no alibi. Or he might be a big fat liar. He looked as guilty of the murder as Rodney. How was I going to find out if he worked that night or not? Was he an hourly worker, or did he earn a salary? I looked at the front desk computer. I'm sure there was a master employee scheduling system on the hotel computers. But also, I was sure the computer was password protected. Would I be that bold as to try to get in? For Jen, I would. I had to get Remy away from the desk, but I also had to have her log in with her password and then walk away.

Could I ask Ellis to call and request the check-in status of a party guest? She would balk. Who could I ask who wouldn't grill me about the 'why'? Well, Sarah…

I sent her a text and asked if she'd call the hotel and ask if some extended family had checked in yet for the retirement party. I knew Remy wasn't supposed to share the information but if Sarah posed as someone close to the family, I think she'd at least open the computer. That's all I needed. Then I'd have to do something to get her quickly away from the desk.

Can you call the front desk at the 'Lavender House'? I texted Sarah

CHAPTER TWENTY-TWO

And say what? she responded.

Say you're a cousin looking to see if the guest of honor at the retirement party has checked in.

They won't tell me that

You're Sarah Deloro

True

The hotel's house phone rang. "Thank you for calling The Lavender House," Remy sing-songed. "How may I direct your call?" She listened. "I'm sorry, ma'am, I can't share any information about guests." She was silent again. I could faintly hear a raised female voice. And still Remy remained silent. I could see the wheels turning in her head. I tried to look busy with my little escort cards while still cocking an ear to her conversation.

Click, click. I heard the computer keys being struck. "Well, in that case, ma'am... No," she answered. "She hasn't checked in yet." Apparently, the call ended abruptly, because Remy held the phone receiver away from her ear, looked at it, shrugged. And then replaced it.

I quick walked to the desk. "Remy!" I got her attention then lowered my voice discretely, 'I'm not positive, but I think I saw a... mouse..." I looked around to make sure no one heard me, at least that's what I hoped she thought. "in the side parlor."

Remy's face flamed and then went white. "Oh my God! Not again!" She flew from behind the desk and went in the direction of the front parlor. Oh, jeez, was this a thing?

"Better close the door, just in case," I counseled. She looked over her shoulder at me and nodded, running the entire time into the front parlor, and shut the door quickly.

I flew behind the desk. Yes! The computer was still unlocked. I looked at the icons on the home page. "Security," one said. I double-clicked on it, and it opened. I scrolled quickly, not sure how this was organized. Time was ticking. I'd email it to myself and look at it later. I knew Will wasn't on the employee schedule, as he was just now trying to convince Sergio to alibi him again. I'm guessing Will wasn't at the hotel at the time Jack was killed. But where was he? Should I tell Brian? Surely, the police had dug deep. Did they request the employee schedule of the day in question? Did they ask for the security footage. I only cared as far as this information could help Jen. I'd have to tell Brian. But first, I wanted to see if I could find out myself where Will was.

Maybe I could pump Remy for information. Was she on the schedule that night? I heard the door of the small parlor begin to open; thank God it was sticky. Remy had a bit of trouble opening it. I scurried around the desk and threw myself under the round table.

"Kate, whatever are you doing under the table?" Remy's voice was filled with genuine concern, as she leaned down and looked under the table at me. Why did I throw myself under the table? Well, in my frenzy to look like I hadn't been snooping through her company computer, I thought I'd put myself in an awkward physical position. Brilliant, I know.

"I think I dropped some of the escort cards..." I faded off. Just as Remy started to straighten back up, a beautiful green St. Christopher metal escaped from beneath her dress collar. Ah, ha! I knew I had seen her before.

Chapter Twenty-Three

Monday, July 7

If you have a wedding planner, you should be honest with them. If you plan on two hundred guests, give your planner the accurate head count. They will know at some point, but be upfront about it, even if it costs more for them to hire an assistant to accommodate the number.

Guests were starting to arrive, and I was swept away with smiling graciously and tending to their needs. But my mind kept going back to Will and Remy. Remy was the woman I saw in the ladies' room the night of our reunion at Lucky's. She of the red hair and beautiful green enamel St. Christopher metal. She, who was dating a married man. Her glorious red hair had been down that night, she looked different, I thought excusing myself for not recognizing her. I don't know why she'd ever wear it up. It was just gorgeous. Wait! A thought flitted in and out of my mind.

"Miss, Miss," a sweet blue-haired lady interrupted my musings. I don't have one of those name card thingies. And I sent in my meal selection the very first day, too!" Her ire was real. I need to squash this firecracker immediately.

"I'm so very sorry, ma'am. A mistake, for sure. I'll get right to finding it. What is your name?"

"Humph. Olive Peters." She crossed her arms in disdain. "Oh, *here* it is!"

She exclaimed joyfully as she gave the table one more glance. I looked over her shoulder to view the card, as I surely didn't remember an 'Olive Peters." And there's a reason for that. There *was* no 'Olive Peters.' The card read 'Minnie' Just 'Minnie.' I remember that card and meant to check up on it, but time got in my way…okay eavesdropping on Will and Sergio got in my way. Wedding Tip: Put formal names on your seating card/or 'escort' cards. The guest will be looking for their name, and so will your staff if they're called upon to help.

Immediate problem resolved, I went back to my thoughts about Will and Remy.

Was she the woman who was in the corner of Will's Instagram photo of Spring Break? More and more, I think there is something going on with Will and Remy. That's probably why he didn't want to tell Rose where he was really going. I think Remy would be the weakest link, so I'd confront her tonight.

I didn't get my chance until the very end of the night. I tried to make it casual, not so sure I did. Remy was once again behind the reception desk, slipping out of her sky-high heels, I could tell because she suddenly became much shorter. Hey, Remy, can you please hand me my bride/event bag?"

"Sure," she said with just a wee bit of fatigue in her voice. As she leaned down, her St. Christopher once again bounced against her cheek.

"Gorgeous metal, Remy. Hey, I think we've run into each other. You were at the Lucky Charm a couple weeks ago, right?"

Remy flushed, scarlet. 'Uh, I'm not sure." She didn't meet my eyes.

"I am, Remy. You were talking about a married man…" Still nothing. "Is it Will?" I didn't have all that much time. If I was going to do this, I'd have to cut to the chase.

Her head bounced up. Her face paled, and she straightened her body. "Ah, no, no. Why would you think that?" But her body language told me all I needed to know.

Chapter Twenty-Four

Tuesday, July 8

When planning your flowers for the wedding, make sure you choose blooms that are in season. This will help your flower budget stay on track.

I t was 8:00 AM Tuesday morning, and I was sitting across from Meghan and her mother in my office downtown. How was I? Well, I was appalled. So appalled I didn't know what to say, which *never* happened to me. If anything, I talk too much when I'm uncomfortable. And I was plenty uncomfortable.

At least Meghan had the decency to look shamefaced. It was just too soon to be celebrating after Jack's murder.

"And since we know it's a boy, there will be no pinks or lavenders, but I don't want everything to be all in blue. What do you think, Meg?"

Meghan and her mother, Lois, were here to discuss Meghan's...Meghan's *blowout* baby shower, with Jack's money, I'm sure. I wonder if she still had his credit card and if he had been reported as deceased yet.

'I, I'm not feeling great, Mom." Meghan's face did look a little green. I felt sorry for her, and I didn't...all at the same time.

"Powder room is out by the reception area." I said, smiling. I felt sorry for her, really. She was under Jack's thumb when he was alive, case in point, he was paying all the bills for the wedding, so even though he had made it seem at our wedding planning session that it was Meghan's show, we both knew it was his. And now it appeared that her mother wanted to pull the strings, although I was pretty certain Rodney wanted to.

Lois continued planning, or should I say scheming, as if her daughter had not just gone to the powder room, either sick or distraught. "I want one of those giant balloon bunches that are all the rage now, maybe in some greens?" Her face glowed. I bet she was planning all the ways to spend Jack's money. Meghan's baby was her ticket to a sweet life. Would she want her own condo, or a granny flat on Meghan and the baby's estate? Luxury sedan or SUV? Why not both? Travel would be first class, of course, They'd have to get the travel in before the baby started school, as after that Meghan probably wouldn't want to go except on school vacations. I could hear Lois' thoughts as she rambled on about games, finger sandwiches, and favors.

Now I was all about parties and the planning of them. That was how I supported my little family of two. Okay, Grant was starting to pitch in again, but still…but I just couldn't get behind a baby shower, no matter how deserving, so soon after Jack's death, especially since Meghan isn't poor. She doesn't need her friends and family to give her the things she'll need for the baby. She can easily buy everything she needs herself.

"Lois, perhaps," Perhaps was a good word. It said a lot without saying anything. "Perhaps it would be better to wait until after the police investigation has concluded.

Lois crossed her arms over her ample chest and twisted in her seat as if to dig in. She squirmed a little more, but not in an embarrassed way. "I didn't know Jack long, or well," here she paused and gave me a stern look, "but I know he loved his Meghan and the little one and would want them to be celebrated." She glared at me over the top of her bifocals.

What a spot I was in. I didn't want to offend her by suggesting that she was potentially committing social suicide for herself *and* her daughter, but I also didn't want her to make such a faux pas. And on a selfish level, I didn't want to be associated with such an event.

I heard the toilet flush in the powder room in the entryway. The sink ran, and then Meghan rejoined us.

Lois turned in her chair. "Well, Meg, green or blue for the balloons?"

Meghan met my eyes; then she skidded over to her mother. "Mom..."

"No, no backing out now, Meghan!" Lois' face turned red. "It's important that it's established that this baby boy is Jack's heir. It has to be done now, not later. I know it may be a little 'unorthodox' to have a baby shower now, under these circumstances, but the times are unusual. We don't want anyone questioning 'anything.' " She cocked a brow at Meghan and looked at her baby bump.

"Mom!" Meghan looked mortified.

"Kate, may we have a moment?'

I stood and walked into the kitchen area. It felt odd to be kicked out of my own office. This didn't offer them much privacy, but at least I was out of their vision.

"Quit being a drama queen, Meghan Spring. I haven't gone to this much trouble for you to blow the whole deal to smithereens. Get with the program, Meg, Kate..." Lois beckoned me back,

I stood. "I'm so sorry, Meghan, Lois. But as you may or may not know, Jack was a personal friend, and I don't think I'm up to planning a baby shower so soon after his death."

"Well, you were okay with it when you booked this consultation." Lois steamed, standing up, too.

"That was before I knew you wanted to plan the shower for next week!" I tried not to let any emotion in my voice, but I'm not sure I was successful.

Meghan pulled on her mother's arm. "Mom, I told you this wasn't a good idea. I'm sure Kate will help us later in the year. Let's go."

I tried to smile but was very uncomfortable under the wrathful gaze of Lois.

The duo grabbed their pocketbooks and made their way to the outer door of my office suite. Meghan threw me an apologetic glance over her shoulder.

Lois wasn't going quietly, literally, which was good for nosy old me. "Meghan, you can't let all my plans go up in smoke," she said as they descended the stairs. "Have you talked to Jack's attorney again to find out when the money will be transferred? You have a shelf life on this thing. You don't want them asking for a paternity test. You know that, right?"

Nothing from Meghan, but oh my stars! Lois was most definitely the one pulling all the strings.

Chapter Twenty-Five

Tuesday, July 8

As a bride, if you're lucky enough to still have your mother in your life, make sure you give her the option of walking in the procession ahead of the bridesmaids and after the groom's mother. Plan ahead and have an escort chosen either by her or for her. Some mothers like to walk their daughters down the aisle with the father of the bride. That is a lovely option, too.

Later that afternoon, I was in my kitchen with Brian, believe it or not.

"Thanks for being such a good sport about this barbeque, Katie. I know going with me the way we left things the last time we talked is probably the last thing you want to do. But I don't feel like explaining what's going on with us to my partner." We both knew there was more to it that, and maybe now was a good time to tell him about Will and Remy. Neither one of us wanted to let 'us' go, but neither one of us wanted to say we were sorry. Brian leaned down and gave me a gentle peck on the cheek. And why *was* I being such a good sport? He didn't deserve it.

We were in my kitchen getting ready to head out to a barbeque at his partner, Gregory's home. Gregory wasn't his first name, but his last. No one seemed to know what his first name was or care. Truth be told, I wasn't looking forward to this get-together. Not just because, for all practical purposes, Brian and I were broken up, but I didn't like Gregory. I hoped there would be other officers and their wives/significant others there. I don't think I could handle an entire afternoon with just Gregory and his wife. His wife was nice enough, I just didn't have anything in common with her. I know I'm sounding a little snobby...

I picked up the baked brie and fig jam dip I had made, one of my favorites, and the bottle of chardonnay we were taking.

The Gregory home was close enough that we could walk it from my house. It was a beautiful Tuesday afternoon. We were finally getting some warm weather, but that came with some humidity. The humidity was what always wore me down. Brian carried the wine and crackers in a cloth bag, and I carried the brie dip. Even though we were in crisis, romantically, I still had that butterfly in the belly feeling. I hoped it would never end...but maybe it needed to if we were really going to end things.

Just two blocks down, and we were at the Gregory home. I had been here once before and was very impressed at the pristine caretaking of the yard and the house. There was not a weed in the yard, or even a dead flower in the garden. Did they have a full-time gardener? I know Claire worked part-time at a law firm, in fact, my bride, Jane's firm, and that they had two young children. It was a lot.

The inside of her home was every bit as clean, orderly, and well-maintained. I would hate for Claire to see the inside of my drawers and cupboards. And I was looking inside Claire's right now, at her request, when she asked me to grab fondue forks.

"Hey Kate," Claire didn't know me from high school, so she didn't call me 'Katie.' The fondue forks should be right next to the butter knives." Yep, there they were. I'm sure I didn't even have fondue forks, much less know where they were or have them in the general rotation in my kitchen drawers. And if I were going to be perfectly honest here, you just *might* find a crumb or two in said drawers...

I placed the fondue forks in front of her with a little smile, proud of myself. Hey, if I couldn't have a perfect kitchen myself, I could help navigate hers with a happy attitude.

"Thanks, Kate. Can you please grab a new bottle of ketchup from the cupboard? Gregory hates it when the bottle looks half full. I should have refilled the old one."

'Usually she refilled them'? Wow, if that wasn't overkill, I wouldn't know what it was. 'Whoa,' I thought as I opened that pantry door. Everything from spices to canned goods had labels facing forward and were alphabetized. Yes, alphabetized. It was easy to grab the ketchup under 'K.' I handed it to her with an uncomfortable smile. She didn't seem to notice, to her this was normal.

I was more uncomfortable than I expected to be at the barbeque. Two other couples joined us, but I just couldn't relax. I kept thinking about those drawers, the cupboards, and, more importantly, the way Claire was around Gregory. She was like a little mouse when he was near. Trying to please, but to stay out of his radar as much as possible. Maybe it was just that I was feeling inadequate about my own yard, kitchen, and house and nothing more. I shrugged it off and accepted a cold beer from Gregory and a beautiful burger from Claire.

* * *

Our walk from the Gregory home back to mine was magical. The breeze was soft with just a little touch of cool, which felt like a mother's cool hand on a feverish child's brow. We didn't have anything to carry. I had left my brie dip bowl at the Gregory's (Brian would get it from Gregory and bring it to me), as well, of course, the wine and crackers.

I hated to ruin a nice moment, but I had two things I wanted to address with Brian. Will, Remy, and I wanted to get his take on the Gregory situation. First Gregory. What did I mean? The vibe was just off in that marriage. I hadn't had a good marriage. Well, in all honesty, it wasn't bad until the end, but there was never abuse, either physical or emotional. I think, and I hope, that I would have had the strength to leave had that been the case. But it's never good to judge. No one knows how you'll deal with a situation until you are in it. But I was very worried about Claire. Things weren't normal in the Gregory household. One had just to look at how Claire acted around her husband to see it, much less take a look at her house. It was a classic abuser's scenario. She was terrified there would be fault found somewhere in her home or yard. She did all she could to prevent that.

I thought I'd ease into the discussion. I didn't want to make Brian feel guilty that he hadn't picked up on it, or that I was criticizing him in any way. But it had to be addressed. "Hey, Bri, how long have you known the Gregorys?"

"Eight, nine years, I think. They'd just gotten married when he joined the force."

"They've been together that long? They're so lovey-dovey, you'd think the marriage was newer. There's something off there, Brian."

"No one knows what goes on behind closed doors. We can't judge their marriage, Katie."

I turned to him. "I'm not *judging* them. I'm worried."

Brian stopped walking, right there in the middle of the sidewalk. "Worried?" he said, turning to face me directly. "Gregory's my partner, and a great cop."

"You can be an abuser and a good cop. They are not mutually exclusive."

"Whoaaa abuser?" Brian almost, but not quite, yelled.

"All the classic signs are there; have you never suspected anything? Brian looked down at his feet.

"Brian?" Silence.

"Once. Once, she said he had hit her, and I confronted him. Gregory swore it would never happen again."

"And that was it. You went on as if nothing had happened? If he had hit her once, he had done it before. Most certainly more than once. You're supposed to protect. This is in your job description. You had to know that."

I started walking back to my house again quickly. He followed. "Katie, Kate!"

I had reached the mudroom door and wrenched it open. I had apparently forgotten to lock it. I entered, threw off my shoes, so did he. Then I turned.

"Brian, did you even talk to Claire? Did you follow up? Did you make sure it hadn't happened again?"

146

He followed me into the kitchen where I busied myself with putting the percolator on the stovetop. I gave the delighted Chloe a treat and sent her out on her own to do her business, something I usually didn't do. I banged open the cupboard where my coffee cups were housed in a most disorderly fashion. And slammed two mugs down on the counter.

Brian gently touched my arm. "He's my partner, Katie. I have to trust him. I have to believe him; I have to trust him with my own life."

Point taken.

"You know Kate, does this have anything to do with your lousy marriage to Grant? Cause it's not fair that you attack Gregory just because you had a loser for a husband." Wow.

I turned to Brian then, surprised at the angry red face that I saw. "Unfair, Brian. Grant was a cheater, but never abusive physically or psychologically. We were okay until his big transgression. Not perfect, but okay."

"I knew it!" He exploded. "I knew you still loved him, that you've never gotten over him!"

What? "What in the heck are you talking about, Brian? I don't love Grant. I love you! How can you not know that?"

"Because you rarely say it, that's why. I've said it to you plenty, but you hardly say it back. There can be only one reason for that: you are still in love with Grant."

Brian had made me good and mad. But was what he was saying true? Had I rarely said, 'I love you.' He noticed my pause.

"See! You're thinking about your feelings and realize I'm right. You are still in love with that complete jerk. Admit it!" He bellowed. I didn't like the yelling, not at all.

"I'm not in love with him. I'm not sure I ever was."

"My heart has always belonged to you, Brian, and I love you. I'm sorry I haven't said it more. But if you can't believe that, if you can't stop your jealousy and temper from boiling over so often, if you can't stop yelling at me all the time, then I don't see a future for us. You were right about that 'break' for a while." I put the mugs away. "I don't think either of us needs coffee."

"Yeah, I better go."

"And I think we should reschedule dinner for tomorrow." It was our four-month anniversary, and we were supposed to drive to Mystic for dinner. I wished things were different.

"Yeah, we're going to have to reschedule that. For sure." I've got to pull a double anyway." My feelings were inordinately hurt, even though I canceled first. I knew he was lying to me. I don't think I could be with someone who lied to me.

"I'm sure that's for the best."

He looked me in the eye, shook his head, and left without a word.

It wasn't until he left that I realized I never mentioned Will and Remy.

Chapter Twenty-Six

Wednesday, July 9

Guest books are no longer the padded white books of our parents' generation. They are whatever you want them to be. Just make certain it is something that will last. Guest books I have seen in the last five years: a wooden propeller, a canoe, a beautiful painting of the couple's home, which the guests signed, Jenga blocks, and a tiny wooden heart that guests signed and then inserted into a glass box; all lovely.

I awoke the next morning heartsick. My fight, if that's what we were calling it, with Brian last night was just so ridiculous, or was it? How long had he been carrying all that insecurity and worry inside of him? He was obviously miserable, and now so was I. In some ways, it was kind of nice to think about something other than Jen and her problems—but what a personal cost.

I didn't know how to help us. I was worried that there was no help to be had. Were we too broken? I certainly hoped not. But I needed to stand up for myself. I'd have to give this a lot of thought.

I was miserable but still had a day to get through. The fact that I was exhausted from tossing and turning in my anguish over Brian couldn't be helped.

Today, I was doing a bridal shower. I usually stick to weddings, rehearsal dinners, and engagement parties, but this shower was for the sister of a bride I had worked with—five years ago in California. While they still live in California, they had family out in West Hartford, and a bridal shower was on the docket of events for their visit 'back east.'

I had worked almost exclusively with DeeDee, the mother of the bride-to-be.

I arrived at the Boat House Community Center room where the shower was to be held, and DeeDee was already there fluffing the decorations I had ordered. There was a blue and white balloon arch and more blue and white flowers than I had ever seen. They were on every available surface. The whole room had been transformed into a secret garden. The room pre-decoration had been a generic white, but no longer. DeeDee was giddy with delight over the transformation.

"Welcome to our wonderland," DeeDee gushed. I saw a lot of beautiful decorations in my work life, and I was impressed. No cost had been spared. And the cake, it could have served two hundred, but DeeDee wanted BIG. I had to agree, it made a statement. I loved the gentle chamber music I heard being played over the room's sound speakers.

"It all looks fabulous, DeeDee. Guests arrived in thirty-five minutes?" I said, looking at my Apple watch. I had been here earlier to supervise the décor set-up but had run home to shower and change.

DeeDee got serious. "I know this day is all about Rudy and Clark, and it will be. But you know me, I worry about everyone." I knew this to be true. DeeDee was the most giving, generous, kind woman I knew. And I'm not talking only financially here. Although she was that too. She cared and invested in all who crossed her path. So, it could be any of a hundred people we both knew that she could be worried about. But somehow, I wasn't surprised when she mentioned Claire.

"I know it's none of my business," DeeDee said, moving the ladies' nametags, shaped like

teacups and teapots around absently, "but I know things aren't right, and I just can't let it go."

"I think Gregory's abusing her. I saw her last week, and she was wearing a turtleneck, but she reached up to adjust the neck, and I saw a nasty bruise.

Your Brian is Gregory's partner, right? Maybe he can help?" She looked so hopeful; I didn't know what to say.

"Correct, Brian is Gregory's partner." I would not gossip; I would not gossip. I told myself. "But I don't know what he could or *would* do. When you're someone's police partner, there are certain 'codes' shall we call them. I don't think I can broach this with Brian, DeeDee, as much as I'd like to." I wouldn't mention that I already had.

"I knew I was being too interfering, but I'm just so worried about her. Her mom died of breast cancer last year, and I promised her I'd look after Claire. I don't feel like I'm doing a very good job." See, I wasn't crazy, but what a thing to be happy about! I wasn't the only one who thought Gregory was a threat. Maybe I'd have an ally?

"Well, helllooooo?" An older lady with pink hair and a walker said as she hobbled in.

"Auntie Hilda!" Pronounced 'Awntie.'

And we were off to the races. The shower had begun, twenty minutes early, but we were ready.

Chapter Twenty-Seven

Wednesday, July 9

When you start looking for your wedding dress, take into consideration the season of the wedding, not the season you're shopping in. Remember, it may take up to six months to acquire your dress. When you order your dress, plan for your headpiece and veil if you choose to wear one. What about a little shrug if the weather is cool? Will you wear gloves? They are making a comeback. Will your jewelry be borrowed or new? Plan now, you don't want the pressure of a last-minute decision.

After the baby shower, Brian had texted and asked me to meet him at Cotton Hollow. I was fed up with him, but decided to go as it was our anniversary. Cotton Hallow was an Eastbury town tradition. It had a beautiful public pool for residents during the summer months, walking trails for the spring through fall, and an unsupervised swimming hole that was the bane of every mother in the town's existence. Cotton Hollow was also the town's 'Lovers' Lane' for the teen set and for cheating adults. Brian and I didn't fit into either category today, but we had our history here. Is that why he wanted this venue?

Kate, he had texted *meet me at Cotton Hollow*.

I got that butterfly feeling in my belly, but it was coupled with hesitation and anger. Were we going to solve anything with a nostalgic make-out session?

I pulled my Suburban into the empty parking lot. Mid-afternoon was when the humidity was the worst, and my air conditioner had trouble keeping up with it. The condensation formed on the vents. Cotton Hallow was beautiful, though. All the surrounding trees were lush with the deep green of early summer. Brian wasn't here yet. I had time to make a run for it and stand him up. I was so mad I could do that. But I wouldn't.

Brian pulled into the lot, right next to me in his department-issued Bronco. Those SUVs had more power than the department would ever need in our little burg. He leaned over and opened the passenger door. I got out of the Suburban and climbed into the Bronco. The SUV was immaculately clean. Brian was a stickler about that. I shut the door softly; the radio played soft jazz. Brian smelled good, like he always did. He smelled like Dial soap, shaving cream, and the outdoors. I hoped I smelled as good. Hard telling, I had had quite a day. I couldn't wait until Ellis moved on from her learner's permit and got her driver's license. I was a non-stop Uber for that girl. Of course, getting her license would mean we would need a second car, something else Grant and I'd have to hash out. I stole a look at Brian. I don't think he'd be happy if he knew Grant had just crossed my thoughts.

"Katie," Brian reached over to take my hand, "I'm sorry about how we ended things after the barbeque at the Gregory's. You're right. I should have followed up with Claire. Just because Gregory's my partner doesn't mean he gets a free pass." It was a start.

I felt warm and tingly. Okay then, okay. I leaned in for a kiss, which Brian gladly provided. But then the real world came crashing in via the nifty little devices we called a cell phone. It wasn't mine this time. It was Brian's.

"Don't." I hated the pleading tone I heard in my voice. I had a bad feeling.

Brian leaned back in his seat, away from me. "Sorry, Katie, I have to. I'm on call tonight.

"Hey," he said into the phone. Silence.

"Gregory, I can't. You know I can't." Brian listened some more. "I'll be right there, don't do anything else. It will only make it worse." Brian ended the call without saying goodbye.

I looked at Brian questioningly. "What's up?"

Brian sighed and said, "They need me to come in. Guy ran a stop sign, hit another car. It's a mess."

"Really?"

"I have to get back." He looked pointedly at me. Well, I guess that was my hint to exit the car. I got out, all the good feelings and good will going with me.

Chapter Twenty-Eight

Thursday, July 10

This is for wedding guests: when making a specific request, don't always direct your first inquiry to the wedding planner. If your question is about food, ask the caterer. If you'd like a photo taken with the bride and groom, ask the photographer, if you desire the air conditioning turned down, look for the building facilitator. If all questions were directed to the planner, she wouldn't be able to do her own job.

I was up early this morning, took Chloe for a quick walk, showered, and made my wedding planner meal for the day. I had found this great cloth lunch bag that had inserts you could freeze, so instant refrigeration!

Ellis was already at the B&B. I hadn't slept well again last night. So much on my mind, mainly that I hadn't uncovered anything to help Jen. I still hadn't told Brian about Will and Remy. I had to get back to Jen's and try to talk to Jeff again, I couldn't believe he was okay with Jen being gone. Then there was Gregory's wife, Claire. I had such a bad feeling about her safety, and always, there was Brian. Where were we in our relationship, and did we even have one?

To compound matters, I had a rehearsal at noon today for a weekend wedding. The venue wasn't available the night before, so the family decided to have the rehearsal mid-week. This was the most nervous I had ever been for any event. It was being held at the newly built 'barn-type' structure built on a family's working farm in North Eastbury. It was lovely, boasting a restroom, (a big deal where renting restroom trailers can go into the thousands of dollars), and heat and air conditioning. With today's weather changes, one never knew if they were going to have a heat wave, or a chilly day in June. So nice to have coverage for either.

The bride was heck on wheels. I don't think she was stable. Her fiancé had the patience of a saint, and I think that encouraged her bad behavior. He was an average-looking guy, of average stature, with an average job.

But the bride, Marsha, was otherworldly beautiful. She was tall, about five foot nine, model thin, with hair black as a raven's wing, that shown blue in sunlight. Her eyes were the color of new spring leaves in New England. Her features were the classic ones that Instagram and other social media platforms told us we desired. There, her perfection ended. I'm guessing the groom thought it was a fair trade to deal with her moods and have the beauty on his arm. And she seemed to enjoy keeping the groom on his toes.

I never knew who I was going to find from one day to another with this bride. She was sweet as pie one day and angry and cantankerous the next. The mother of the groom asked me if she could provide me with a sedative if I would slip into one of Marsha's beverages on the wedding day. That was a hard NO!" That wouldn't even be legal, much less the duties of a wedding planner. I should probably report her, but she'd just say she was kidding. But that showcased the difficulties I faced with this bride.

We were all waiting on the bride, everyone else required for the rehearsal was present. Even the food truck contracted to provide the post-rehearsal late lunch had arrived and was humming along in their prep. I am a fan of food trucks for casual events. They arrived when promised and had their food prep planned down to the minute, so they are always on time.

I lined up the procession, we did a walk through a few times. Everyone was on their best behavior, feeling compassion for the worried, distracted groom who was over in a corner frantically texting and making calls to his bride.

Twenty minutes later, the bride finally arrived in her Prius in a cloud of dust as she pulled into the area reserved for parking—way too fast. The groom ran out to meet her, embracing her as soon as she emerged from the car. She hugged him back. Had he been afraid she wouldn't show? Not likely, not if she wanted to get married. Not too many people would put up with her antics.

They joined our unusually silent group with big smiles. I had heard rumblings from the bridal party that David, the groom, was 'making the biggest mistake of his life' and from others who said, 'they gave the marriage six months *if* it happened.'

"Let's get this party started," Marsha whooped. So, we were getting a manic Marsha today. Who would we have tomorrow?

I walked over to the couple. "Would you like to do a walk-through, Marsha" I gently asked. I didn't want to spook her.

"Do all these nice people know what to do?" She waved her hand around at the bridal party.

I smiled at the hesitant, uneasy bridal party. Like me, they were waiting for the other shoe to drop. It was only a matter of time before Marsha would morph into her other self. The only question…would she make it until the wedding was over or would it be part of the 'Big Day.'

"I think we're good to go," I responded when no one else did.

"Well, let's PAR-TAY!" Marsha whooped. I don't think I've ever seen Marcia happy before. Wait, was *that* her happy?

"Well, everyone can grab a beer or a wine cooler from the buckets," I looked around; everyone had something; it was that type of day, I guess. I laughed uncomfortably. "Well, looks like we have that covered. I'll just check with the food truck.," It as a pizza truck that served a coffee espresso bar after the pizza. "and see if they're ready."

I walked over to the truck. "Hey, Frank," I said to the owner. "I think the party is ready to begin. How are you on time? I queried.

"About ten minutes, Kate. Hey, you knew that guy who got whacked, that pro baseball star, right?" Kinda odd he'd bring Jack up, but whatever.

"Yeah, I knew Jack." It made me sad all over again. And to my utter embarrassment, my eyes welled up with tears.

Frank didn't seem to notice, thank God, just kept working at a rapid-fire pace. I guess the stout guy didn't know any other way.

He kept going. "I didn't know him, but I knew someone who knew someone," isn't that always the way! "who did a deal with 'Jack,' and he said, he was squirrely. Just wanted to get your take on it, if you thought it was true, but…" he paused, uncomfortable, finally. "But sorry for bringing up a sensitive topic." He bent his head and focused on his placement of pepperoni on an uncooked pizza. I could let it go, or I could quiz him.

I decided to quiz him. "So Frank, how does one 'get squirrely' in the restaurant industry?"

Frank shook his head. "So many ways. So…many….ways. You can ask for funding from a bank for more than you need for a build, get someone in your pocket who will do the appraisal, pocket the rest. Or do events off the books. If you have a partner and you want to cut him out, keep some of the events off the books, give a discount for cash, and pocket the difference between wholesale food you needed for the event and staff payment for the night. Anyway, I heard Jack was into the scamming the bank part. That he had a partner he was cheating, who was a pretty stand-up guy, and it turned into a real mess. The money had to be repaid plus interest, but Jack and the partner shared that burden, so even after Jack repaid his share, he ended up making a killing." Interesting word choice. "Then the partner found out." I held in a sigh over the man Jack had become. Then, another question sprang to mind.

"Why are you so invested, Frank?" That seemed like an important question. It seemed a little weird that Frank was talking about this at a wedding and that he knew about this at all.

"He, Jack, was going to use his dirty money, and open a chain of pizza restaurants and undercut me. I wasn't the only one who would be affected, of course, so I thought maybe…"

Wow…did Frank just admit to having a motive to killing Jack? I guess, but why would he bring him up if he did? I don't think he'd want to draw attention to himself. What the heck? I'd try to find out if he had any sort of alibi the night Jack was killed. What did I have to lose?

"Wish I could help more, Frank. Hey, how's the season going? Been busy?

Lots of weekend events?"

Frank gave a big belly laugh. "Ah, Katie. I can see right through you. I was at a christening in Rhode Island the night Jack was killed. So wasn't me." And he continued laughing as he started pulling pies out of the truck's brick oven.

I had to laugh with him. " I can't tell you if any of those rumors are true. Frank. I can't even guess." Not exactly true. The more I knew of Jack, the more I believed he was capable of. "Wish I knew more to share." And I really did. It was hard to pump someone for info when you had none to share. "So, there is probably someone out there who was in cahoots with Jack over-inflating the bank loan thing? Like someone who approved a bigger loan than he should have in exchange for a kickback?"

"That would be my guess." If you're interested, check out the Middleview Bank. Frank shrugged. "Pizza will be ready soon." And that was it. Food for thought.

Chapter Twenty-Nine

Friday, July 11

This is for wedding guests: if you are assigned to a table at a 'plated' event, meaning you have chosen an entrée, do not change tables. This creates a nightmare for the catering staff. They have organized dinner and know which guest is at which table and what their entrée will be. If you move, they will be frustrated, dinner will be delayed, and you just may not get what you ordered.

I spent the daytime hours today working at my office downtown. While at times I preferred to work at home, I felt closer to Jen to be here in my office above her shop.

I busied myself with a vision board for the tablescape of a wedding I had this December. The bride wanted red and silver for colors but didn't want anything to look 'Christmassy', especially as the couple was Jewish. It was a challenge, but I decided to present her with more of a seasonal theme, read: winter, than a holiday one. It was working out nicely, and I think she'd like it. Next up was a string of emails to alert vendors that I was the wedding planner for several new couples. They needed my point of contact so they didn't bug the bride and groom.

I finished up at the office and concluded that I needed to do something about the sad state of Jen. Everyone has an alibi that checkout out, but Jen. She was the main suspect for the simple reason she was in hiding. I wish I could tell them about the underground domestic abuse thing, but I couldn't throw vulnerable women under the bus. It was ultimately Jen's decision how she handled her life, not mine. That is why I so conveniently avoided sharing info with Brian. I felt the info wasn't really mine to share.

Jen had texted me that she was safe but still wouldn't turn herself in for questioning. We had never had secrets. If I were being honest, I was kind of hurt that she wasn't telling me all. I had to remind myself, though, that it wasn't about me.

So, where was I right now? I was lurking outside Jen's Cape Cod-style home. It was everything Jen had wished for as a young girl. It was on a good-sized lot right on Main Street, with a wrap-around porch circling the entire first floor. She had created several small seating groups around the porch. I think I enjoyed every one of them. There was one to watch the sunrise, one to watch the sunset. I loved Jen's home. She did too, but more than the structure, she loved those housed in it, her husband and two daughters. She wouldn't go long without seeing them. I was going to confront her tonight.

I was dressed in my standard sleuthing attire of black leggings and a black long-sleeved t-shirt. I was lurking behind a maple tree, its leaves, the mature green of summer, full and lush. It was a good cover, and I reconciled myself to a good long wait. I may even have to come back tomorrow night. But I knew she'd make an appearance at some point, and it would likely be at night, when she could more easily go inside without someone seeing her—unless that person was hiding behind a tree, that is, like me. Why weren't the police doing the same? I think it all came down to staff issues and knowing that she'd turn up sooner rather than later. She had too much to lose.

The damp was getting to me. While the day had been hot, it had also been humid. With the temperature beginning to drop overnight, the dampness was settling into my bones. With my inactivity, I was getting chilled. I wasn't used to being still.

I was ready to pack it in, I guess Jen didn't come home every night and tonight wasn't that night. I was tempted to go in and badger Jeff, Jen's husband. Surely, he knew what was going on. I felt confident I could make him talk. But did I want to get that aggressive? The answer was 'No.' I could be a bully, but that would be to Jen, not her poor husband. Moreover, he'd probably already been pressured by the police. I didn't want to add to that.

The muggy breeze I had felt shifted, then stilled. Something had changed. I knew then, I wasn't alone. Run or hide, that was always the question. My gut said I'd been seen, and hiding wouldn't fly. And who was I kidding, I could *maybe* outrun a second grader, or Sarah Deloro, as it turned out. My thoughts ran through my mind at lightning speed. Maybe it was Jen, of course it was Jen! I spun around, and there…was Brian. And it wasn't a happy Brian. Is he following me?

"What the hell, Katie? I've been watching you for ten minutes." Ten minutes! "You're not here for a family visit. Do you have a rendezvous set up with Jen? Is she meeting you here?" he was angry. I could see a vessel pulsing in his temple. Yes, I was that close to him. Was Brian mad at me or Jen? Probably both. I knew Jen's absence was driving him crazy, when I saw him, that is. I hadn't seen him since Cotton Hollow. It hurt almost as much as the first time we were estranged in high school. It seemed our relationship was still very immature, almost stunted in time from twenty years ago. Neither one of us had grown in the communication department, apparently. Maybe there was a reason my marriage had failed, and Brian was still single. It's never just one person. Maybe realizing these things was a kind of growth on my part. One could hope…

"No, I don't have a meeting set with Jen, Brian. I wish I did. I have so many questions."

"You have questions? Oh, my God, Katie. When are you going to start keeping your nose out of police business? As if last spring wasn't bad enough. You could have been killed." Brian rubbed his hand over his face in an exhausted fashion. "God, Katie." His voice broke at my name, and my heart broke, too.

I flew into his arms. He lifted me off my feet and buried his face in my neck. He hugged me so tightly I almost couldn't breathe.

"Brian," I got out. He released me, then cupped my face in his hands, gently this time.

"What am I going to do with you?" He kissed me then, it didn't start tenderly like it often did, but with pent up passion. I wove my arms around his middle and pulled him closer.

Then, a light on the porch switched on. "Hello?" We heard Jeff call out as he opened the front door. Brian broke our embrace and gave me a little nudge to respond to Jeff. I guess he didn't want his presence known.

"Hey, Jeff," I called out. "It's Katie. I just was out on a walk and was going to ring the bell and see if Jen was home yet."

Brian slowly backed away from me. I felt a chill from where our bodies had been warmed by our embrace and a chill in my heart by his withdrawal. Jeff was still silent. I imagine he didn't know what to say.

Finally, "Katie, come on in. Jen's not home yet, but let's have a cup of coffee. House is quiet, the girls are upstairs doing their homework." The door opened wider, and golden light spilled out onto Jen's prized porch. I went inside, and Brian faded into the night.

* * *

I was going to do what I said I wouldn't. I was going to grill poor Jeff. It was almost as if the universe was begging me to. 'Oh, alright,' I said to the universe. 'I'll interrogate my best friend's sweet, shy husband.'

I followed Jeff into Jen's gourmet kitchen. Yes, she was every bit as good a cook and baker at home as she was at 'The Perk.' I sat down on one of the kitchen island barstools, and Jeff had a cup of coffee with cream in front of me in no time. There was always coffee, hot coffee, at Jen's house, just like at The Perk.

No one ever accused me of beating around the bush. "Where is she, Jeff?"

Jeff put down his coffee cup that he was raising to take a sip. "Right now, I don't know, Katie. I know what she's up to, but that's not my story to tell, and I won't." Jeff looked me dead in the eye. He wasn't kidding.

"But you have to know she had nothing to do with Jack's death." He stopped his movements. "She loved him." He said this softly, and I knew how much it cost him to utter this. "Jen didn't know, but Jack and I had connected through a couple of business deals – real estate development mainly, a little bit in restaurants."

Now it was my turn to stop and put *my* coffee cup down. Whoa! Was Jeff the partner Frank had been talking about? Of course, he wasn't, Jeff was a dentist, what did he know about bank loans and scams? And even if he did, Jeff was as straight an arrow as they come.

"Wow, I didn't know that. I didn't even know Jack was back in town frequently enough to connect for business deals with locals." I was trying to think of ways to root out info from Jeff about his business relationship with Jack without being obvious. Was that even possible?

"We never really worked in person. Rodney Liverwell connected us. I had had a few good years at the practice and wanted to invest. I met Rodney at the club, and we got to talking one day on the course. He said he had a sweetheart deal with a local celebrity. I almost said 'No' when he told me who it was. I had no interest in doing business with Jen's ex. But in the end, it seemed like too good a deal to pass on." His face became stormy. "The one time we met to sign some papers, I was prepared for awkwardness. But apparently not enough. I didn't think Jack would give Jen and me two thoughts, but he was relentless in questioning me and our lives. He asked about my practice, The Perk,the girls, our house. It was weird." He shook his head, then looked off over my shoulder, focused on what I don't know.

"I think I hated him about then." Jeff continued. "I never have hated anyone. But this man, who Jen had loved, well, he wasn't making it easy for me. Pure and simple, I was jealous."

"Dad!" I heard Larkin, Jen and Jeff's daughter who was a year older than my Ellis.

"What," he bellowed back. He stood up and shook his head as if to say 'kids.' I realized my moment was gone. Jeff wasn't going to say anymore, and even if he continued, I think he would have stopped before he said what he had been thinking. It seemed too monumental. What was he hiding? Could he be the killer? My heart said 'No,' but my head had a lot of questions. After all, Rodney said Jack died owing him millions. How much money had Jack owed Jeff? Had he scammed Jeff, too? And did Jen know about it? If she did, that's a big motive for her. For both of them. And if the police knew... Wow,

I really had to find the real killer before they found Jen.

I went home and crawled into bed. An early night would do me good. I had big plans for the weekend. But then morning came, and I didn't even get dressed all day or Sunday either. I just floated around the house and, to be honest, slept most of the weekend away. I think Ellis was a little worried. It's rare that I had a weekend off in 'The Season,' so I made the most of it...or the least, depending on how you look at it.

Chapter Thirty

Monday, July 13

Do you want a candlelit reception? Check with your venue point person to make sure you can have open flames. Some venues prohibit open flames to prevent a fire hazard. You can purchase or rent cute votive or larger style LED candles that look very similar to the real thing. The advantage of a "fake" candle? They may be brighter than the real thing, they will stay lit all night, (with the real thing, you may have to relight them...several times!), and no discoloring smoke will blight your candle holders.

When Monday rolled around, I was recharged. What I had considered a wasted day Sunday had actually been good for me. I was ready to take on the world again.

Even though the impromptu meeting with Jeff Saturday night was dissatisfying, I got just enough info to spark my interest, but I had more questions than when I started speaking with him. I had no idea how to help her or move my snooping forward. I refused to call it an investigation; I didn't think *that* much of myself. I decided to go to the bank this morning. Frank had mentioned that Jack, Rodney, possibly some person I didn't know, and...possibly...Jeff used.

Frank had said the bank was located in Westwood, Connecticut, a couple towns over. It would be about a twenty-minute drive.

Middleview Bank had four local branches, and the Westwood branch was the largest. I had never been to the bank, but today....I was going to apply for a small business loan. I dressed in my best 'business attire,' which was actually a very nice suit I had purchased a couple of years ago when I was still a corporate wife. Grant had had a conference in New York where spouses were invited. Men were to wear a suit and tie to all events. We women had more flexibility. We could wear skirts and jackets, pantsuits, or dresses. I had several of each type, but my favorite was a chambray blue knit dress with a matching jacket. It was slimming, and I felt like a million bucks were in it. How many outfits in a woman's life can she say that about? I can only think of a few others, one being my wedding dress, but that was a whole other story.

It took longer to get to the bank than Google said it would, I think, because I was going at a turtle's speed. I really hated what I was about to do. I was going to pretend to be someone I wasn't. I'm not saying I wasn't going in as Kate Ludlow; I was. But I was going in as a person applying for a small business loan and maybe getting something a little unethical on the side. I just hoped it wouldn't come back to haunt me.

I pulled into the surprisingly full parking lot and drug my very prettily dressed self to the bank door, which was opened by a security guard. Did all banks have them? Seemed like a little overkill for a tiny bank like this one, but whatever.

There was a greeter who smiled warmly and asked if she could help me.

"Sure!" Okay, I was a little too enthusiastic. I'd better tone it down a bit. "I'm here to apply for a small business loan."

Ms. Greeter's smile brightened if that were possible. "Terrrrrific!" She enthused. "I'll set you up at Gabriel's desk; he'll be over in a minute; he's in a staff meeting. Would you like a coffee or tea?"

While I was more than tempted to ask for the coffee (and I noticed donuts next to the coffee tray!), I decided to keep it clean. Better to talk about what I needed to without donuts in my mouth. That same mouth watered at the sight of the donuts, though.

'Gabriel' was taking his own sweet time to get back to his desk. I had memorized all the goofy sayings on his coffee mug collection housed on a shelf behind his desk, felt I knew his family rather well, knew that sports the kids played, where they vacationed by staring stupidly at their photos located on every available surface of his office.

Then a male voice behind me said as he knocked on his own office door, "Knock knock!" He was overly bright. Must be Gabriel.

"Hello, there, you must be," he looked down at the clipboard where I had so recently printed my name. "Kate. I'm Gabriel." He looked up from the paperwork and smiled at me, his brown eyes twinkling at me behind his horn-rimmed glasses. He was a nice-looking man, not handsome, not plain, just nice-looking. He was tall, I'd say six foot three. I rose to extend my hand, and he grasped it with just the right amount of pressure. I always cringe when a man squeezes my hand and makes my rings dig painfully into my other fingers. But I may hate a limp handshake even more.

"Nice to meet you," I smiled, and so did he. I hoped this guy wasn't one of the dirty ones. I liked him already.

"Sit, please," he said as he circled round to his desk chair. "Did anyone offer coffee?"

"They sure did, but I already had my quota for today. Thanks, though."

"All righty then. So, you want a small business loan. How long have you been in business?"

"Full time?" I asked.

Just a slight eyeroll on his part, 'of course full-time,' I could see him thinking. "Ah... yes," he said politely.

"Well, I worked part-time as a wedding planner in California, but I moved here a year and a half ago, so I've only been working full-time for that period of time."

"Gosh, Kate, I wish I could help you. But the bare minimum to be eligible to apply for a small business loan is two years. And even then..." His voice trailed off.

That was okay. I didn't want a loan anyway. I was doing pretty well, but I did get my foot in the door. Now the work started, I needed to see if he had any pertinent knowledge about the...well, I'd call it what it was, bank fraud.

"That's what I was afraid of," I said, making my voice soft and gentle. I hated myself just a little. I never liked it when women played those games. But if it served my purposes today, so be it.

"Are there really no options? I mean, I have so much experience even though I haven't been in business full-time all that long..." I let my voice trail off. "I mean, I'm even open to something unconventional..."

Gabriel frowned, then stood up. Yikes. "Kate, I really wish I could help you. But banks are conventional. We have no other options. I'd be happy to help you in six months or so. Maybe a friend or family member could be a short-term help?"

Now I felt dirty. I hoped he didn't think I was an awful or shady person. My goal today was to catch *him* in a shady deal.

"Gabriel, it was lovely meeting you. I'll be okay, no worries, and when my two-year business probationary period ends, and if I still need a loan, I'll come back. Thank you for your time." I couldn't get out of that office fast enough. Can you say, 'Failure'? Although I had hoped he wasn't a bad guy, and it seemed he wasn't, which was a positive. But now what?

I was walking with the purpose of getting out of the bank. I didn't want to look like I was hurrying, but I was. I was almost at the door, and ready to breathe a sigh of relief, when a perky blond bounced in front of me.

"Kate, right?" She smacked her gum at me.

"Yeaaaah." I had weird vibes.

"I'm Suz. I'm a teller, and I couldn't help but overhear your chat with Gabriel. Grabbing Lunch!" She yelled over her shoulder as she walked me out of the bank. How did she 'overhear'?

"I know how hard it is to manage money these days. If you want to move into a little more 'unconventional' relationship, give this person a call. Works miracles."

I took the card. Was this what I hoped it was? Was this the connection to the person who Frank was referring to, the one who fixes loans to be funded that were more than a person would normally be qualified for? I glanced at the card. It was printed on a Middlebrook Bank card. So, they must really be a bank employee.

"Thanks," I finally got out. Suz smiled, waved, and made her way to a cute little mini Cooper and roared off.

Would I call the name on the card? You bet ya. Did the name on the card surprise me? You bet ya again.

Chapter Thirty-One

Are you getting married soon? Do the smart thing and build a 'Wedding Website.' On it, you can post fun things, such as 'How we met' as well as photos, your gift registry, wedding weekend events, directions, and 'fun things to do' in your geographical area. The 'fun things to do' is especially important if you have guests traveling in for your wedding. This may be the first time they have been in your region of the country. May it be a good time!

"Mom," Ellis said as she walked into my home office that afternoon. I looked up from the computer, where I had taped the name on the card Suz had given me against my palm. Would it be too obvious if I sent a query letter? I didn't want to alert anyone since we knew each other. And to add to my distress, there was rain in the forecast for my wedding Sunday. To compound matters, the family wasn't open to a rain plan 'B.' I was worried.

"Yeah, Hon?" Ellis sunk into the chaise lounge that I kept in my office. I'll be honest here: I, too, frequently, took a nap in the afternoons, right…there.

"I have to tell you something." Uh, oh. She looked worried and guilty, and all rolled into one. Fear gripped my heart.

"Shoot, kid." I waited while she looked everywhere but at me. "You know you can tell me anything, right, Ellis?" She was worrying me a little more.

This wasn't like her. Usually, I have to pull info from her, and even then, she wasn't remorseful. I had never met a more confident person.

"I know you've been worried about Jen. So, Kevin and I started to do something about it."

"Ellis..." my heart was pounding. "what did you two do?"

Ellis stood and started pacing. "Well, I thought it was pretty cool how you investigated last year and found out who killed Lori-Sue. You saved your own skin, didn't wait for some man to save you. Way to be a strong woman, Mom."

I beamed; I couldn't help myself, but now wasn't the time. "But we're talking about what you and Kevin did."

"Well, back to Jen. I know how close you always were, since all the way back in high school."

"Yeah, waaaaay back," I joked. "So enough with the compliments, although I appreciate them."

"Well, you know I hate it, but you know how when I'm just a couple minutes late for curfew, you can track me on Apple's 'Find My'? You follow me. I follow you. Get it.?

"Yes, I do, but how does this relate to Jen?"

"Moooommmm," Ellis stopped pacing and smiled at me. "Don't you think Jen tracks her girls?"

I stood too. "So, if Jen tracks their girls, they probably track her too! If we can just get a hold of one of the girls' phones, we can see Jen's location. I can track her down and get some answers. I was jubilant. "Let's go!"

"Mom, whoa, no need."

"What do you mean, 'no need.'?"

"I have Drivers' Ed with Larkin, even though she graduated, she waited to get her license." Here in Connecticut, kids, and their parent had to pay a private company to get the hours for kids to qualify for their drivers' licenses, they usually took the course in summer...anyway...Larkin is Jen's middle daughter, the one who is a year older than Ellis.

"So, I had Kevin send her a text. I knew she wouldn't be able to resist opening a text from him while I was sitting right next to her. Larkin would probably think he was trying to get info about me. She loved to mess with him.

"As soon as she got the text and opened it, I texted Kevin, and he called the driving school's main office and said he was her dad and he was on the way to meet her in the office. Now, the tricky part. How was I getting to get her to leave her phone? No teenage girl leaves her phone ANYWHERE. Well, no teen guy, either, but we're discussing Larkin here. The driving school secretary announced in our classroom, 'Larkin Cooper, come to the office.' The class, as usual, ooohhhhed, but Larkin, being Larkin, Ms. Self-Confidence, shrugged it off. She picked up her phone. Of course, she did. I whispered to her frantically, 'Hey Larkin, leave your phone. You know we're having a quiz today, Your phone is probably out of juice, (I hoped it was, it usually was), I'll charge it while you're in the office so you can use it for notes during the quiz." Thank God for open-book quizzes. "You're a lifesaver, Elle, thank you!' Larkin even handed me her phone. I plugged into my external charger, thanks for that Mom, I think my friends use it more than I do! She left for the office, and I slyly swiped to her 'find my app.' I went right to Jen's info. She's at an address in Hartford. I'll send it to you if you want."

If I want... OF COURSE, I WANTED!! So many conflicting emotions. I was proud of Elle. I was horrified, but I was happy mostly. I could find Jen, confront her, and help her get this all sorted.

Chapter Thirty-Two

Tuesday, July 14

Ms. Bride... are you looking for a gift to give your father and grandfathers? How about a pocket square/handkerchief made from remnants from your wedding dress alterations? Easy to make, and I bet your wedding seamstress/alterations lady will be happy to make them for a small fee.

I sat on the address until the next morning. I didn't want to do this at night. I didn't want Ellis worrying about me, not when she had provided me with the information.

Jen, I know where you are; I've tracked you on 'Find My.' I want to see you, I texted.

I'd know 'what was what' soon. If Jen didn't respond, I'd just go to the address in Hartford. Yeah, I'd given up the element of surprise by texting her, but this was Jen. I didn't think she'd run from me. I felt a sense of relief. I wouldn't have to speculate any longer. I'd know.

The apple bubbles were moving on my message screen. ***Meet me in two hours at the back of The Perk***

I wish I could say I passed those two hours putting the final touches on my nearest wedding or cleaning my entire refrigerator, but the truth was, I did laundry. We had enough of it! And the simple act always soothed me. So much so that I was almost late. When I finally looked at my Apple watch, I realized I had only seven minutes to meet Jen. 'The Perk' backed up to the

Connecticut River. I made short work of grabbing a hoodie and my sneakers and ran out my mudroom door.

Jen was waiting for me in her own hoodie and sneakers. I loved that woman. She had a hot cup of coffee for each of us. Okay. So, it was going to be a stroll, which was fine by me. There were a few people hiking on the trail along the river, but they didn't pay us any attention. I didn't recognize them, so I doubt they recognized us.

"Don't keep me waiting, Jen. What's going on?" Even though I thought I knew. But I wanted to hear it from Jen. I had stopped walking and turned to face her. Jen stopped, too. She opened her mouth a couple of times but didn't say anything. I waited her out.

She walked off the trail a bit and leaned against a boulder. She patted the surface of it, the rough edges surely made smooth over centuries of rain, hail snow and wind. I ambled over and leaned with her.

"I never talked about it much, but my dad used to hit my mom." Never talked about it, try she *never* talked about it once. I listened to my inner voice and remained silent so she could share. Jen looked down at her hands and then back up at me, her eyes welling as she tried desperately not to let the tears fall. I put my hand over hers; she clung to it.

"I didn't know what to do, Kate. My mom begged me to leave it be. But I couldn't, ya know? The last time he touched her, I told him I'd call the cops myself, and then I'd leave and go live with you. He was a bully, but my mom, she let it happen, or so I thought. Looking back, I realized she didn't have any other options. She didn't know how to get help, how to support herself and me, how to begin to help herself. There is help out there, now, if you know where to look. That's what I am, well, me and my organization. We're the first step."

I was absolutely horrified on so many levels. I was gutted that Jen's mom had to go through that nightmare that Jen did. I felt awful that I never had any idea that this was going on.

And her organization? What? This was my friend and soulmate, and she was telling me there was a whole world that I didn't know about her. Okay, Kate, take a breath. This isn't about you, I reminded myself.

"Say something, Kate." She squeezed my hand so that she was still clenching.

I leaned over and embraced her. I couldn't speak yet. My own tears were falling. "I'm so very sorry you and your mom had to go through that. I wish I could have helped you. I don't know what I could have done, but I hope it would have been something."

There was silence, but it wasn't awkward. It never was with Jen.

"So, now, I'm involved with, for lack of a better phrase, a domestic abuse underground railroad. The women have to be highly vetted to make their way to us. I won't bore you with our security, but we get them out of the dangerous situation and into a safe environment. If they want to go as far as to disappear, we make that happen too.

"Is it dangerous...for you?" She didn't meet my eyes.

"It has the potential to be."

"And Jeff?" Jen's husband.

"He's never been happy about it, to put it mildly, but he gets it. As long as the girls aren't involved, he can deal with it." Jeff had always been a good guy; I just didn't know *how* good until now.

Oh...my...gosh. This was a lot to take in. First, I heard about Jen's dad and mom, and then the whole 'underground railroad' thing. Even though I had a good idea about it. "Is this legal, Jen." I could feel my forehead wrinkled in concern.

Jen met my worried gaze head-on. "Yes, except if a woman is running with her kids and the father has the right to see them, which happens a lot of the time." Not quite what I expected to hear, but at least I was getting the truth. "And you absolutely can't tell Brian or anyone else because the night of Jack's murder, I was helping a woman who really really needed that help." I wondered if it was Capri's missing bridesmaid, but I knew better than to ask.

"But Jen, it's your alibi! You *have* to speak up!" I decided to take a firmer approach. "Do you want your daughters to visit you in prison?" I gave her the stink eye.

"If my only option to staying out of the big house is to tell my story or part of it, I will. I'll go with Madison, the safe house director, and tell my story if I have to—but I'll do whatever I can to avoid that." She sighed heavily here. Okay. I'd do what I could in the meantime to ensure she didn't have to give the whole organization up to the police. Future good works couldn't be accomplished if she was outed or locked up.

"Madison would alibi me, and hopefully, they wouldn't ask for more corroboration. That's why we have to find out who killed Jack, so I don't have to."

It felt wonderful to hear her say, 'we' again. I had my partner back.

Chapter Thirty-Three

Wednesday, July 15

Consider two sets of chairs if you are being married in the same venue as your reception, vs a religious venue for the ceremony and a different venue for the reception. That way, you don't have to ask either staff or your family and friends for help moving chairs. It will be double your chair rental cost, however.

I awoke to the sound of rain. It had started last night and hadn't stopped. My mind went to Jen. Until the police say Jen is no longer a suspect, I feel obligated to keep trying to find Jack's killer. After all, there's no guarantee the police will believe Jen or Madison, the site leader of Jen's organization, who can alibi her. They could think Madison was lying. Maybe the victim Jen was protecting the night Jack was killed would have to come forward, but I knew both Jen and Madison would hate that. Would they have to go to the police and confirm that Jen and Madison came to the shelter during the night, which could help confirm the alibi, but would the victim in question, be willing to do that? Once Jen outs herself, she potentially would be putting a lot of women in danger—women staying at the safe house, women she's helped before, and women she might be unable to help in the future if it becomes widely known she's involved with this shelter. Overall, there are too many variables. And another worry: would this see Jen in more legal trouble with her clients disappearing? But I have work to do, so while

I wait to hear from Jen about how it went at the police station, I'm going to focus on my business. Life does go on, people still get married, I was still a wedding planner and I have a wedding today. I had to put my concerns aside and do my job. So, this morning, I did just that, but the call I got from the mother of the bride was one no one wants to get, whether you're a wedding planner, guest, or vendor.

"The farm is flooded," wailed the mother of the bride. "The Connecticut River is rising due to all the rain we've been having. The road from one entry into the farm is already closed for guests coming from the east. I just don't know what to do!" I know she was doing her best not to cry. This was as tricky a wedding problem as I've had, because as much as I plan for things, I don't plan a back-up venue for events. Think how ridiculous and expensive that would be. And think of all those brides out there who wouldn't be able to find a venue because someone had booked a 'Plan B' venue that would most likely go unused.

The couple was getting married at a Roman Catholic Church with a reception to follow at a now flooded farm with a tent.

I knew this church. They had a lovely walk-out basement with tables and chairs available for inside use. We are not talking about an old-fashioned church basement here. We are talking a newer church built on a hill, so one entire side was a walk-out. There were nice wrought iron tables and chairs on a covered patio outside, and the landscaping was lush. Many couples who married there had their 'after photos' taken on the grounds.

"How about the church basement, Colby? We did talk about this earlier in the week." I asked the teary mother of the bride.

"I know, and yes, it's still available, but Johnny," (her husband), "said that since he paid all that money for the rentals: tent, tables, chairs, etc., he was going to make sure they use them."

How to be diplomatic here? "I totally get that, Colby, but if your guests can't safely get there, and if they do, they are cold, wet and miserable, that is just not an ideal situation."

Silence.

Now I think I heard soft weeping. "I know," she got out.

"Do you think maybe Johnny could be persuaded to use the church basement?" I gently asked her.

"Well, the thing is, my daughter is set on the farm, too. I can't fight both of them." And then the poor thing really boo-hooded.

I made all the comforting sounds, all the while knowing it was going to be a long day for the guests, the vendors, and me. And it was. The road was blocked off at one end, so anyone coming from the east had to turn around and go all the way around and come in from the west side. People coming from the east were about forty-five minutes late (not everyone attended the church wedding where the directions were announced, and not everyone looked at their text messages where we had sent out a message blast with the emergency update). We really couldn't start the dinner with only half the guests there, so we were forty-five minutes late.

The tent had no floor. It was placed on the grass with a wooden dance floor in the middle. When I arrived in the morning, there were a few puddles, but as the day progressed, the water rose. By the end of the night, we were ankle-deep in water where the guest tables were staged. I had worn my Hunter boots, not all the guests were as lucky; although I have included the suggested footwear in the text message blast to all the guests who had registered their info with the couples wedding website advising of the flooding situation and the wisdom of wearing appropriate footwear. A few had opened the text, many had not even seen it, which I was afraid of. The guests were a group of good sports, and water-logged or not, they were trying to have a good time. Then…the power went out. The farm owners were manning the generators and were not prompt enough in refilling the generator's gas tank. When all went dark, I think that's when it dawned on me.

The night that Jack was killed, the electricity went out. I had gotten up that morning surprised that Ellis was headed into work so early, but as she so sassily told me, it wasn't six in the morning, but nine. The power had been out for three hours at the house the night before (the night Jack was killed). What if the time set on the Bed and Breakfast's security system didn't reset, and it was three hours off? That would explain Lois arriving back at the b and b after midnight, not 9:00 PM. Lois' original alibi was just a matter of

180

chance. WOW. This negates Lois' alibi. Lois and Marjorie never said what time they left for New York for their Spa weekend, but it had to be early, as they didn't know about Jack yet. Maybe Lois's alibi was completely fake. I'm going to have to figure out how to dig deeper into this. Even if there was a different exit at the B&B, it looks odd that Lois was still in town at midnight.

The farm owner arrived with more fuel for the generators, and the wedding finally ended. No one was really interested in an 'after party,' everyone seemed to just want to go home and take a hot shower, me included.

* * *

I was watching a late-night movie after my post-ceremony hot shower. I still couldn't sleep. I was sleep-deprived and had no one to talk to. Well, that wasn't going to happen. I'd just have to rely on myself. Anyway…I was watching this movie, it wasn't that old, and they caught a killer by looking at where he had been on his car's GPS. That started me thinking. Maybe some information could be gleaned by checking the GPS of one of my suspects' cars. I hadn't been poking around Rodney much lately. He would be the most likely of my suspects to drive to the boat house as he lived out of town. So not only did I have to somehow prove that Lois came in late to the B&B, but I was also going to try to access Rodney's car's GPS.

Okay, I saw how hard it would be to get access to Rodney's car GPS, but hey! It had worked for the girl in the movie. She had confirmed that the murderer was indeed the murderer.

So, I'd have to get myself into a situation where I would have access to Rodney's car. I definitely couldn't go to his home and snoop. Too obvious and likely to get caught. I'd just have to get him invited to one of my events. Shouldn't be too hard, he was a local who knew everyone. I just had to think of what events I had this week. Hum…an engagement party, and a wedding. The wedding was a no-go. No one invites someone to their wedding last minute, guest lists are created months in advance. Same was true with an engagement party, although it was a little looser.

Oh well, it was a sound idea. I just couldn't implement it.

Chapter Thirty-Four

Thursday, July 16

Does the weather report predict rain for your big day? If so, have some extra umbrellas on hand—you know the cute ones, the umbrellas like the royals in Britain use, the clear ones. Other items to have one hand? Well, if it's a 'country wedding,' a barn wedding, or any outside component, tell guests to bring their rain boots. They will be glad they did. Nothing like a warm, dry feel to keep one toasty!

The next morning, an incoming text from Ellis: **MOM! I'M AT THE HIGH SCHOOL SCHEDULING MY CLASSES FOR SENIOR YEAR AND I FORGOT MY IPAD.**

I hated when she typed in all caps. So *annoying*. Now I sounded like Ellis. **Use your phone.** I typed back.

I put stuff on my iPad that I didn't back up on 'Word.' Please can you bring it?

Sigh. **Sure, Elle**

I grabbed the iPad that she had left on the kitchen island and my car keys slipped on my All Birds sneakers and headed out the garage door and into my Suburban. Normally, I'd walk, but time seemed of the essence.

I pulled into the school lot and parked. A car pulled into the space next to me. With an empty lot, why would someone do that? I ran the iPad into the high school and then hopped back into my car. I decided to head to Barnes

& Noble and pick up the newest thriller I had been lusting over.

* * *

I pulled into the left turn lane and stopped at the red light. I glanced in my rear-view mirror and who was behind me...but Rodney! 'Is this fate?' I thought about him this morning, and here he is. Oh, who am I kidding? I live in a small town. I went to the Barnes and Noble parking lot, but it looked like he was going to the Stop and Shop lot, so I changed course and parked next to him. He didn't even notice me, but hustled into the store, apparently on a mission. I didn't hear the chirp chirp of a door lock. That means...could he have left it unlocked?

I got out of the Suburban.

I watched him walk into the grocery store. I looked around as inconspicuously as possible and tried to see his driver's door. YES! He had left it unlocked. With a car like this, a gorgeous BMW 7 series, if the car was unlocked, the key fob must be in the car. Otherwise, the car would automatically lock when Rodney walked far enough away from his car. I opened the driver's door all the way,

I took a deep breath. Did I really want to do this? Once I pushed the 'start' button of Rodney's car, there was no going back. If someone saw me... what about my own personal set of ethics? In no realm was this okay. But Jen...

I slipped in the driver's seat, put my foot on the brake (necessary to start the car), and hit the start button. The car powered up with such a delightful purr. What if Rodney came out before I expected him? What would my story be? Oh my gosh, this leather was to die for. I ran my fingers along the upholstery, loving the feel of the buttery leather. What luxury! That would be my story, I thought as my fingers flew over the navigation system. I just had to feel what this luxury vehicle felt like. He really shouldn't leave his car unattended. That's what I'd say. I'd go in all-in, full-on, mom-scolding mode. As they say, the best defense is a great offense. Even though this car was more luxurious than anything I'd ever owned, the nav system wasn't that different from my own Suburban's. I scrolled through the recent trips and found what I was looking for. Rodney *had* been to the Eastbury Boat House the night Jack was killed.

I've got to tell Sarah about this, I thought. WOW…I guess Sarah and I were a team…

Chapter Thirty-Five

Thursday, July 17

Let's talk invitations. What do you think of an e-invite? The beauty of this option is that you can have your guests RSVP online. This makes it easy for them and for you. I initially braced against this option, but now embrace it.

I was walking Chloe that afternoon and came across Claire Gregory, Brian's partner's wife. I was walking along the Connecticut River, and she was sitting on a bench looking out at the view. The last time I had seen her was the barbeque at her immaculate home. She was younger than I was, had two little kids, and, while a seemingly nice person, she appeared exhausted every time I ran into her. But today, she was sporting a nasty bruise on her upper arm. It wasn't a recovering injury. It was fresh, and it was ugly. When she saw me, she pulled her hoodie up to cover it. And then she sobbed.

I rushed to sit next to her and put my arm around her. She fell into the circle of my embrace. I just let her cry. It didn't seem like the thing to ask questions. If she wanted to talk, she would. After what seemed like a long time, she put her head up and sniffed. Let's just say she wasn't a pretty crier; her nose was red and running, and her face was splotchy.

"Are you okay, Claire?" She obviously wasn't. But it had to come from her.

"I, I can't do it anymore, Kate."

"What, Claire?" I had a pretty good idea, but again, it had to come from her.

"He hits me, Kate. It's getting worse. It used to be yelling, then a push, then a punch. Last night, he kicked me."

I was horrified. "have you talked to anyone...the police?"

This got an actual smile. "Come on, Kate. You know how they stick together. They'd never do anything." She pulled out of my embrace and wiped her nose with a crumpled tissue that had seen better days.

"I know someone on the force would have done something. I know *Brian* would have, that he *will* if you confide in him."

"Maybe, but it's too late now."

"It's never too late."

"I have to get away. That's the only way. He'll kill me, Kate. I have the means to do it now. I never would have wished anyone dead, but Jack O'Malley being killed may have saved my life." Claire looked at me with dead eyes. I believed her.

"What in the heck does that mean, Claire?'

"I have to go, and I've already said too much." She got up, I slowly held up my hand to stop her, I didn't want to spook her.

"Before you go, I want to share something about an organization..."

Chapter Thirty-Six

Friday, July 17

An 'After Party' sounds like fun...but is it too much?

A nd that's how I came to be on Gregory's radar. I'm still not sure how Gregory found out that I had given Claire information about Jen's organization. But Claire has disappeared. But here's the thing. Jen knew nothing about her, or her situation. The house manager at the refuge house knew nothing about her. She wasn't with them. Was I worried? Yeah, a lot. She wasn't my responsibility, but we were now tied together.

Sarah was at my house this morning. We were talking about the power outage and how to proceed with the police and the Bed and Breakfast video footage. There was a knock on my front door, not the mudroom door, but the front door, always a bad sign for me in the last few months. When I opened it, there stood Gregory in full uniform.

I answered with trepidation. "Hey, Gregory," He had never been a friendly sort; he most certainly wasn't now. He didn't wait for an invitation to enter, just shouldered his way in.

"Kate," was his only greeting as he walked on my just mopped floor with his muddy boots, grrrrr. He hitched his utility belt up a little, but it couldn't rise above his bulging belly. Why was he in uniform? Brian almost always was in plain clothes, unless a formal event called for a uniform.

Maybe for intimidation purposes?

"I'm not going to beat around the bush. Where is she, and where are my kids?" He looked around, then started to walk into my office.

"Hey, hey," I mistakenly took his arm, which he shook off in anger.

"I said….where…are…they?" His face was now purple with rage.

Never had I been so glad of Sarah's presence. Sometimes, bullies wouldn't act if they had witnesses.

Yes, I had spoken to his wife, Claire.

"Why would you think they're here?" I asked.

"A 'concerned friend' tipped me off. Said you were putting all kinds of crazy thoughts in her head, and that if she wasn't home, she'd be here. Now I've tolerated you, Kate, for Brian's sake, but no one and I mean NO ONE, messes with my marriage. He walked toward me and poked a finger aggressively into my chest. Not okay.

Enter Sarah Deloro. "What's going on in here?"

Gregory turned at the sound of her voice, his mouth agape. He had thought we were alone. His face whitened and then flushed again.

"Hey, Sarah." And then I remembered. Gregory went to school with us, but he was two years ahead, and he had had a massive crush on Sarah. He took a step away from me.

"Kate and I are having a little friendly little chat, that's all." Another step back.

"Come on, Gregory, there's nothing friendly about this call. Look at you all intimidating, or at least you think you are, in your uniform. Does Brian know you're here? I don't think he'd appreciate this call. Unlike you, Brian's a stand-up guy, a good cop."

"Hey, now, Sarah," He took a menacing step toward her.

"Enough, Gregory," now I stepped toward *him*. "you need to leave, *now*."

Gregory looked from Sarah, then to me, and back again. I don't think he knew what to do, what to say. He hesitated and then decided to cut his losses.

"I'm keeping my eye on you, Kate. I won't rest until I find her. I won't let her go. You better tell me where my wife and kids are, or I'll make it look like you had something to do with Jack's murder. I'm not above planting

188

evidence," he claimed. I have it, and I know how to use it." He was enraged.

I was cognizant that he was one bad apple in an otherwise pristine police department, but he sacred me. I didn't want to put Brian in the middle of this whole mess. He was his partner. I think I was bothered all this could be going on right under Brian's nose, and he wouldn't know about it. How could he *not* know? I know that wasn't fair to think that, and not talk to Brian, but I think part of me was afraid of the answers. But then again, that was the nature of the abuse. It was hidden, by the abuser and the victim. It served both. Neither wanted to be outed. The abused by shame, the abuser by fear of censure. I was chilled. That's exactly what Claire had said he would say.

"You have twelve hours." He left, slamming my historic door, which I didn't appreciate.

I turned to Sarah. "Thank you." She just shrugged.

I'll be honest, Gregory scared me.

"Kate, some people blow smoke. Gregory doesn't. Do you have any idea where his wife is? I won't rat you out, but this is not good. You can go to Brian. Gregory is just one bad cop; he's the rarity."

"Gregory will just deny everything." I felt hopeless.

"I'm a witness." Sarah offered.

"You'll be accused of lying to help your friend."

"Who would believe we're friends?" She grinned, trying to lighten the tension.

I almost laughed. "Well, that's true, but it still seems a risk. How do we know Gregory's the only bad cop? What if the chief is a bad guy, too? What if they back each other up? And we have another problem. Claire. How can she be missing? We know she's not with Jen, so where is she? In order to disappear like a ghost, she has to have someone helping her. I want to know who that someone is. And I have this weird feeling that it's somehow linked to Jack's murder."

She cocked a brow at me at the unsubstantiated connection I was making. Okay, I knew it was out of left field.

And that was how Sarah Deloro and I came to be 'in the wind.'

Later that night, Sarah came screeching to a halt in the parking lot of 'The Perk' where we were meeting, her front tires sliding to a scary stop not five feet from me. Yikes! I heard the door locks click to 'unlock,' and I threw my bag in, diving into the car right after it. I was basically on the footwell of the passenger side when Sarah screeched off into the night.

"Where to?"

"I have no idea," I mumbled, hitting my head on the console as she took a corner a little too fast and a little too aggressively. "Ow!" I complained.

"Suck it up, buttercup," Sarah said with no concern at all. She went wildly in the other direction, I think to purposely allow me to bang my head on the door. This time, I didn't react. I wouldn't give her what she wanted. I made my way onto my seat and buckled up. Thank God.

"I didn't think you'd have a plan, so we are putting the Deloro 'Plan B' into operation," she informed me with attitude.

"So, what, pray tell, is the 'Deloro Plan B'? I said with a little snark of my own.

My head banged hard on my passenger window as she went particularly hard around another corner. This was getting ridiculous. I know she was getting a thrill out of this, and it was making me mad.

Before I could say something that I'd regret, for she *was* helping me, or helping Jen, Sarah pulled into the narrow driveway of a storage facility. The 'Stow-a-Way' wasn't as shady as it sounded. It was clean and well-lit. There were even a few young trees planted around the pathways. Ah, New England. Sarah seemed to know where she was going. She pulled around through windy paths until she was in front of the unit. Sarah put the SUV into park and hopped out. "Back in a sec." She went behind the car and opened the tailgate, pulling out an overnight bag and backpack. "Grab your stuff and wait here," she dictated. I complied.

Next, she went to unit 333 and opened the combo lock swiftly, bending down and lifting the heavy garage-type door as if it were nothing. Someone was listening to their personal trainer. It was dark inside the unit, so I couldn't make out what was inside or what she was doing. But boy, was I curious. Good thing I stepped back because before I knew it, I heard an

190

engine start up. A sleek black coupe inched out, it's powerful engine rumbled seductively. The driver's window lowered silently, and Sarah grinned.

"Get in," she said.

I didn't have to be asked twice. I had so many questions. Why did she have a car stored here? Was it hers? Why didn't she drive it on the regular?

She preempted me. "No questions. Now, I have to pull the SUV inside." Okie dokie.

She did just that, quickly. "Beautiful car, Sarah. Where'd you get it? Why's it in storage?"

"You just couldn't wait, could you?' But she laughed. "It was my dad's," all serious now. I remembered that he had died when we were in high school. It was a car accident, his fault, speed, and it was very sad.

"He had just bought it before he died. It only had two hundred miles on it. I could never bear to part with it, but I don't have room to store it at my house. I have my own obsession with cars. So, I rented this space, drive it occasionally, and keep the tags up to date. But it was always my backup plan to 'get out of Dodge' undetected if ever needed. I never thought I would, but there ya go."

"I remember when your dad passed, Sarah. I'm still sorry. He was always nice to me at school events and such."

"Thanks, Kate." And that was all she said.

We drove in silence for a while. But I couldn't stand it any longer. "Where are we headed, Sarah?" I didn't like giving this much control to anyone, much less Sarah Deloro.

"There's a crummy little motel on the Berlin Turnpike that is happy to take cash; in fact, it's preferred. Did you do like I said? Did you go to the Bank of Eastbury ATM and withdraw your daily cash limit?

"Yep," I held my pocketbook aloft where the precious cash was nestled safely. It was nothing short of a miracle that I had been ready in the hour Sarah had given me. Grant had agreed to come pick Ellis up and have her and Chloe stay with him for a couple of days. Wonder of wonders, he didn't grill me as to why I needed him to do this...much. Ellis wasn't thrilled but she complied and didn't throw a million questions at me either. Maybe both could sense my desperation. I didn't tell Sarah that I had also bought a burner phone at the local convenience store, but I was pretty proud of myself.

You didn't tell anyone where you were going? I was silent. I had a daughter. I had responsibilities…

"Kate!"

"The answer is 'no,' but I did tell Ellis and Grant if there was an emergency, to send a DM to my Insta account."

Silence. Then, "Well, I guess that's okay. I doubt the Glastonbury Police force would be skilled enough to track your location via social media if you don't post. I don't even know how that would work…so okay. You're not in hot water with me about it."

"I am *so* relieved," I said with open sarcasm.

Sarah glanced over at me. "Hey, now, who's doing who a favor here?"

"I think we're both doing this for Jen."

"True," she replied, but you're the one who needs to go on the lam now. What were you thinking, being openly hostile to Gregory? Everyone knows he's a crooked cop and apparently now a wife beater to boot. You didn't have to go all Judge Judy on him."

"I also didn't have to go on the lam. I guess we could have told the police chief what Gregory said."

"As you said, why risk that he's dirty too?"

"Right. So, Judge Judy, how does that even make sense?"

"I'm tired." That was enough of an apology for me.

We pulled into the rutted parking area of the Storybook Inn. Believe me, it was no fairy tale. It had seen much better days, from its empty swimming pool (how could that *not be* an insurance liability?) to its water-stained exterior walls. I shivered to think what the inside of the rooms looked like.

I stayed in the car with the 'luggage' while Sarah went to the front desk to pay. She came out only moments later carrying a huge block of wood with what I can only assume, was our room key.

Sarah motioned with her head to come, so I grabbed our stuff while she opened our room door.

"Lucky we got this room," I commented as we entered. She'd pulled in right in front of it.

Sarah laughed harshly. "We could have had our pick of all but two. This place is dead."

I could see why. It was awful. The bedspreads were worn and stained, the carpet threadbare, and the television was something from the 1980s. In fact, I think my family had one, just like it was when I was in high school. If I wasn't depressed before, I was now. Sarah saw my face.

"Let's have a drink." We threw our stuff on a luggage rack; no way was I going to put my things on this floor. Sarah grabbed her Louis Vuitton 'Never Full' pocketbook, (I bet it was a real one, too, not like my knock-off) and pulled out a good-sized bottle of vodka. No wonder Louis Vuitton had named that bag 'Never Full' cause it never was.

"Ice," I said, picking up the grungy ice bucket and looking inside. Yep, there was a plastic bag liner. That would work. "Back in a flash," I said, heading out to the communal ice machine.

When I got back to the room, I gelled my hands from the little bottle of gel hanging from my pocketbook. Sarah hadn't waited for the ice but had opened the sealed plastic tumblers from the bathroom and poured two fingers of vodka into each of them. I poured a little ice in each cup. I was ready to 'clink' glasses with Sarah and say, 'Cheers!' when she shook her head.

"Uh uh." And held a finger up to me. She reached into that bag of hers and pulled out an unopened jar of cocktail olives, I kid you not.

I looked at her. Was this woman for real? "I think I love you," was all I could say.

Sarah laughed. After a refill, neither of us was too worried about the situation, but I knew it was temporary, and tomorrow would find me feeling physically yuck. Dang it!

Chapter Thirty-Seven

Saturday, July 18

If you have a wedding website, use it to alert guests to things like appropriate footwear for women, as they are likely to wear heels if not informed otherwise and the need to bring a sweater or wrap for later in the evening.

The next morning, I found myself feeling yuck, and on top of that, Sarah Deloro snores. I finally threw a pillow at her bed in the middle of the night, and she settled down.

I looked over at her bed when the first light peeped through the skimpy curtains. She had a pink eye mask on…really?

"You snore," I said sourly.

"Well, good morning to you too, Sunshine." She said as she pushed the eye mask on top of her head. Sarah looked as grouchy as I felt. "Dibs on the shower first," and she leapt out of bed. Faker! She wasn't groggy like me at all! But I really didn't care. A few more minutes of sleep for me.

But I did care, thirty minutes later when there was no hot water. Weren't hotels/motels supposed to always have hot water? Well, I guess the answer is, 'No.'

I felt pretty good when I exited the grimy little bathroom, a cold shower wasn't so bad. Sarah sat on her bed with a great haul from the vending machine, consisting of 'Little Debbie' donuts, some peanuts and, bless her, two coffees.

"Where'd you get the coffees?" I was confident the vending machines didn't spit it out.

"Front desk," she winked. "you have to know who and how to ask. I found out they keep a Keurig in the staff back office. And so, it's no surprise, Front Desk agent Tim, may or may not have a crush on me."

If there's cream in my coffee, I'll kiss Tim myself." I grabbed for my cup. And yes, there was cream in it. We were getting entirely too familiar; we were supposed to hate each other. I glared at her; she glared back.

We ate in silence. Then I asked, "Plan for the day?"

"Well, we are here off the grid to get away from Gregory. We want to find out why he doesn't want you checking into his wife and his relationship with her. My guess is that he's knocking her around, and he doesn't want his squad or his commanding officer to find out. That's why he threw down on you and insisted that you drop asking questions about her. But you, of course, won't let it go. So, on top of trying to prove Jen is innocent of Jack's murder, we may have to prove you're innocent, too."

How would Gregory know about me? I'm sure Claire didn't say anything. The only person I talked to about Gregory was Brian. Did he warn him? Did Brian throw me under the bus? My heart broke just a little. Who else could it be?

"Don't be so dramatic, Sarah."

"Dramatic? I was there, or don't you remember? He was so enraged, his face turned purple, and he spit repeatedly in your face as he shouted at you."

What she said was true.

"We need to find Claire. She knows something about Jack and his murder. She said as much to me at the river," I said

"But she really didn't say anything." Sarah hadn't been impressed when I shared what Claire had said about Jack's murder, maybe saving her life. "And why would we be able to find Claire when her own husband, a police detective no less, can't find her?"

"Cause we're women."

Sarah took a big bite of her 'Little Debbie' snack cake and a bigger gulp of

195

coffee and nodded. "I like where this is going."

"So," I started speaking my thoughts out loud. "You've left your abusive husband, and you've been on the run. You apparently didn't do it the right way and get help like I offered. And now you're getting bored, and you're feeling sorry for yourself. And...your kids are getting on your nerves. And let's face it. She didn't have time to plan this out. She left on the spur of the moment, so hasn't gone far."

"Mani-pedi!" Sarah yelled out like she was on a game show.

I took a gulp of my now cold coffee, "Oh, Sarah. You've never been the mother of two small children who have been cooped up. She's either at McDonald's Indoor Playground or Chuck E. Cheese. My guess is Chuck E. Cheese. It's dark, easier to stay hidden."

"What kind of car does she drive?" Sarah asked.

"She won't be driving her own car; Gregory for sure has a BOLO (Be on the Lookout) out for it."

"Do you think there's something more to Gregory threatening you to get them back, or he just wants what he sees as his?"

" I think it's nothing more than that. Let's flip a coin. Heads McDonald's, tails, Chuck E. Cheese."

We couldn't find a quarter, but Sarah had a nickel. I always felt sorry for the nickel. No one liked it. It was heads, but I thought Chuck E. Cheese was a better bet. We googled Chuck E. Cheese and found one in Newington, fifteen minutes away. If they were there, they'd arrive right at opening, 11:00 AM. We would shoot for 11:30.

Chapter Thirty-Eight

Saturday, July 18

Remember, a wedding is just another part of your life, and as with everything in life, you can plan, plan, plan, but that doesn't mean your plans will go off as you wish. What to do? Pivot. Don't be afraid to go to 'Plan B.' Plan B could be making do with the wrong-colored napkins to moving your whole reception to another location due to inclement weather.

D id I really expect Claire and her kids to be at Chuck E. Cheese? Well...It was a pretty good guess, but no, not really. But there they were, right out in the open, having a grand old time eating pizza, playing the games. If she was shocked to see us, she didn't show it. I think she was probably medicated. I bought the kids some tokens for the games and then began quizzing her. I felt a little bad, but not all that much. What surprised me was getting a lot more information than I ever dreamed. I think whatever tranquilizers she was on were my friend. They lowered her inhibitions.

We were seated at a booth way in the back, where we could still see the kids, but were quite alone. There weren't that many people here on a weekday anyway. I think Claire had planned on that.

"I knew it was wrong. But I didn't know what else to do." Yep, that's how Claire opened.

"What was wrong, Claire?" Sarah asked.

"You're here about Lois, right? That's how you found me?"

Sure, we could go with that. LOIS?

"Yes, Claire, I know you were under extreme duress. How did it all play out?" Was that vague enough? I was hoping my show of sympathy and support would encourage her sharing.

"Let me first say I'm not proud of my behavior, Kate. Even though I'm not an attorney, I take our office's position of 'attorney/client privilege' very seriously. It was just part of the deal. I'm sure our office was not an exception." Claire worked as a paralegal at my bride Jane's firm. Unbeknownst to me, Lois had retained Jane to represent the family's interests in Jack's estate, especially Meghan and the baby's, after his death.

"Yesterday, Lois had a meeting with Jane alone, meaning without Meghan, which I thought was strange. Jane asked me to sit in and take notes. I'm still not sure why she didn't just record the conversation the way she often did, but maybe she didn't want a recording out there due to the high profile of the situation. Lois just spilled it all, how Jack started asking questions about the paternity of Meghan's baby, how he was going to change his will if the baby proved not to be his. Lois started to cry, and even to me, it became obvious that she was only worried about herself. Jack had promised her a house, with an allowance, and she wanted to safeguard that. And then it all came tumbling out, how she had called for Jack to meet her out by the river, how she had lured him there about a surprise for Meghan, how he was already there, sitting by the river when she got there, holding his head. He claimed to have had a fight with someone. So she hit him again with the hammer she had brought with her for that purpose. She hit him on the back of the head and then pulled, push and shoved him into the Connecticut River. Jane was stunned, I was stunned, I think even Lois was stunned. We were all in a legal fix, as I couldn't tell anyone, not if I wanted to keep my job, but I wouldn't be disbarred like Jane would be if she talked to the police. Lois knew that, but I think it hit her all of a sudden that she had spoken too much in front of the wrong person, me."

After the big reveal, she looked Jane in the eye and said, "This better be under 'client/attorney privilege,' or I'll see you disbarred." Lois had just confessed to a brutal murder, so Jane knew she was serious, and truth be told, I think she was a little scared of her. 'Of course,' Jane muttered. But she ended the meeting as quickly as she could without arousing suspicion from Lois, but I knew. After Lois left, she kept me in her office, closed the blinds an told me in no uncertain terms that I better keep my mouth shut. I assured her of my loyalty, that I wanted to keep my job, and she seemed placated. The office got busy; one of our clients got into a nasty car accident, there was alcohol involved, and Jane was needed at the police station pronto. I did my best to think about other things but was reminded with brutal awareness as Lois was waiting *in* my house when I got home. I was surprised that she'd do that at a cop's house, almost as much as seeing her sitting in my favorite chair in the living room.

" Come on in, Claire,' she said. She said this in my own home. I was wary, to put it mildly. I entered but didn't stray too far from the front door. I was thankful the kids were having a sleepover with my mom tonight.

"I guess my eyes went once too often to the front door and driveway, cause Lois said with a gloating tone, 'Don't worry about Gregory interrupting our little chat, he's on the graveyard shift tonight. I called the police station. She picked up a glass of red wine from the coffee table in front of her. Yes, believe it or not, she had even helped herself to a glass of wine. 'Want some?' she offered. I just shook my head.

'So, we find ourselves in a little bit of a conundrum. I acknowledge that I never should have confessed to the scuffle with Jack,' *that's* what she was calling her murder of him? I was floored. "But I did," she continued. 'The cat's out of the bag, shall we say. So how to keep little Claire's mouth shut, I keep asking myself."

"Lois, you don't need to worry about me," I promised with a little too much desperation in my voice for my own taste. "I understand the gravity of the situation, and I want to keep my job."

"I'm sure you do, but with a bombshell like this, considering it's Jack O'Malley you might not need any job if you hooked up with the right news outlet, and then I'm sure someone out there is offering a reward for 'any information leading to the arrest and conviction of Jack O'Malley's murderer—'yours truly.' She held the glass of wine to her cheek in a dramatic fashion.

I hadn't thought of all that. I was a cop's wife, after all, and held myself to a high standard. But Lois didn't know that.

Lois set her wine glass down a little too roughly, the first crack in her calm that I had seen tonight. 'So, here's my little plan.

"I saw you at Strawberry Moon. You had on too much foundation near your right eye, but even it couldn't hide the tell-tale bruising. And it wasn't the first time I've seen you with suspicious injuries over the years. I know Gregory is abusing you. I am sincerely sorry for that. No one deserves that." I think she really meant it.

I'll help you disappear, I find myself in the possession of a lot of funds, as long as little Meghan isn't cut off from them, that's what I'm fighting for by the way, the financially security of my daughter and her child.' Yeah, right, I thought.

'You do want to get away, don't you?' Oh, I did, I really did. I nodded my head.

Well, then, little Miss Claire, I'll help you. My only charge is your silence. And here's the thing: if I hear one word of anything regarding Jack in relation to me, I'll tell Gregory where you are. And if he's anything like I imagine, my silence is worth more to you than any amount of money you could score on my story. So, win/win.'

Obviously, I took her up on it until you found me. My plan was to go to Alaska. I hear a lot of people get 'lost' up there. I just needed a day or two to rest a little and get my bearings; then I was headed up there. I obviously didn't go soon enough. Now Gregory will find me, too. And she began to weep.

Sarah and I packed up Claire and the kids and took them to her mom's. We called the local police force in her mom's town and left when they arrived. They assured us they'd take good care of them. We decided our rather impulsive adventure of living off the grid was at an end. Time to get home.

Chapter Thirty-Nine

Sunday, July 19

*What do you think about the rather old-fashioned 'Bridesmaids' Luncheon'?
I think it's a lovely idea, IF you can get all your bridesmaids in before the
wedding. These days, so many of the bridal party are traveling to weddings
from all over the country. How does the 'Bridesmaids' Luncheon' work?
Well, it's just a luncheon hosted by the bride and or her mother where the
ladies are able to celebrate the bride and relax a little. No gifts are expected,
but it IS a nice time for the bride to present her attendants with the
traditional gift from the bride. It's a quaint custom, but one I'd like to see
brought back.*

I got up at 5:00 the next morning and put the percolator on the stovetop. I had used espresso ground coffee this morning. I needed the extra jolt of caffeine I hoped it would provide. I groggily started at the gas flame under the pot and watched it, almost being hypnotized by its blueness in my fatigue. Finally, the coffee had boiled for seven minutes, and I poured myself a cup, adding an overly generous half and half. I took the mug and my phone to the wicker loveseat in front of the fireplace. No fire for me this morning. The weather was finally warm enough that it would not be welcome. I did put my favorite cashmere shall over my legs, though...cozy! I went to Instagram and opened my wedding planner page. I was going to send a DM to Lois and lure her to the boat house where Jack was killed. Did

I really think she would confess? No…but I had to try.

Lois, I want to talk—I have a lot to say, and I think you want to hear it. Meet me tonight at the Boathouse, 10:00."

She responded right away. *I'm not sure what you want but I'll be there.*

* * *

I'd like to say my plan was solely due to my desire to prove Jen innocent, but if I were being completely honest with myself, it boiled down to wanting to wrap this whole mess up in a nice bow. I drove to the boat house at 9:30 PM. It was only five minutes away, but I wanted to be there early. My hands were sweating, and I wish I had worn extra deodorant, I was that nervous. Dang! I parked as far away from the entrance as I could, hoping she wouldn't see my vehicle when she arrived, if she came. The park around the boathouse complex was well-thought-out in its landscaping design, with a lot of lawns and different blooming plants showing their colors all spring, summer, and fall. I loved it under happier circumstances.

What was I trying to gain? She already had an attorney on retainer. She'd never admit to the murder. But I wanted to get her to admit it, record it, and if possible, have a witness. Yes, I'm talking about Brian here.

Brian was to be not only my backup but my witness, too. Even though Brian and I were on/off, hot/cold, I knew that if I called him, he'd come to my rescue, the gallant hero that he was. He had told me to stay out of it, sure, but neither one of us thought I'd do as he asked. Maybe that was part of our problem. Look at me, facing reality.

I was trying to time my call to Brian perfectly, time enough for him to get here, but not time enough to stop me. But then, I still wanted him to hear what I hoped was Lois' confession. I knew full-well that once I was in the middle of trouble, Brian wouldn't take time to scold me but would just come to my aid if needed. Then, when it was all over, I'd catch it. But he would serve his purpose. Only problem? I couldn't reach him. I was really sweating it out now. I knew I had blown it by waiting until the last minute, but I was certain he'd answer. Was he okay? Or was he so mad at me that he wouldn't answer? Neither were particularly wonderful thoughts. I was hiding behind a large hydrangea bush—waiting to go into the boat house and meet Lois. But I knew I couldn't wait much longer, or she'd leave.

I ventured into the boathouse, certain that Brian would eventually pick up, be my wingman, and bail me out if necessary. Or I could just call 911, I thought as I entered the Boathouse proper. I was twenty minutes early, so I had time.

"Stop right there, Kate." Crrrraaaaappp. Apparently, I wasn't the only one who thought it would be prudent to be early. I stopped; of course I did. And oh, how I wanted to turn around. Maybe it was better that I didn't turn around. I reached into my pocket. To heck with Brian, I was going to call 911.

"Uh, uh," Lois said behind me. "No calling anyone. Do you think I'm stupid?" No, I thought, just hoped...

"Hands up."

I slowly raised my hands. No sudden moves for this one. I didn't want to spook her and get shot in the process.

"Okay, now slowly turn around, no sudden moves, or I'll shoot." Boy, it sounded like she was reading a script from a TV cop show.

"So you killed Jack?"

Lois smirked, in fact looked rather proud. "Yep, I did it, he deserved it. I was afraid Jack would find out Rodney was Meghan's baby's father and write her out of his will. He was suspicious. With Jack dead, she'd inherit all his beautiful money. She had made her choice, and she wanted Jack. I probably should have killed Rodney, too," I think she was talking to herself at this point. The gun had dropped, and she was rubbing it against her leg. If there ever was a time for me to make a break for it... But Lois seemed to notice her slip and raised the gun back up.

"Don't even think about it, Kate." Well, there went that slim chance.

Keep her talking, keep her talking, my little inner voice advised. "Well, I guess you answered the 'why,' but how did you do it, Lois? I thought it was claimed that getting Jack into the water would be a major feat. Did you have help? Not that she'd answer me, but it was something to talk about. Quite the little conversationalist, aren't I? It was so dark in this part of the building that I couldn't see her clearly.

"Ironic, you should ask, Kate. It was Jack who paid for my personal trainer, and it was my newfound strength that helped me drag him into the river. He told me I was too young to look so out of shape and frumpy. Can you imagine? The nerve. When it came time to kill him, I just remembered that insensitive, nasty little comment, and then it really didn't bother me much when I dragged him into the river. I did it for Meghan and her baby. I want you to know that. I couldn't risk Meghan being written out of Jack's will. This way, she and the baby inherit everything." And I'm guessing they probably would. Jack was killed before he could change his will.

"But Jack was already down when I found him. I gave him a little bop on the head and drug him into the river to drown. I really think someone else beat me to the punch, but just didn't finish the job. It was up to me to do that." She puffed up her chest. While Lois couldn't inherit from him—if she were caught and convicted of his murder, assuming she was in the will at all—that shouldn't prevent Meghan and the baby from inheriting. Heck, even if Jack wrote in his will that he was leaving money to "his child," and one of Jack's relatives contested that the baby was related to Jack, that wouldn't affect Meghan. She'd still inherit whatever Jack left her—a lot, probably.

"You know all now, Kate. Are you happy? I am. It's nice to be able to show how strong and smart and clever I am." She actually sighed as if contented.

She was a narcissist, pure and simple. She needed someone to admire her and her 'work.' And that was me. Well, I couldn't feel too sorry for myself. I asked for this.

"But now that I've told you, you recognize that you can't live, right? My plan worked so well, I can't leave any loose ends." She looked almost remorseful. "I do feel bad about your kid, though. Your ex-lives close by, right?" What to say?

"Do you want a blindfold or anything?" Really? How do I answer that one?

But I just said, "Sure." Maybe it would take her a minute or two to find a 'blindfold,' and I could try to find a way out of this fix. I looked at my hands. They were shaking, huh? That wasn't good.

But I guess none of this was good. And I started to laugh, from nerves, from fear, from God knows what.

Lois turned from her frenetic, discombobulated search for a 'blindfold. I rushed her then, and we both fell over. We were in the lower level of the Boat House where some of the high school crew team's boats: sculls, surfboats, coxed eight, were stored on racks. We bumped them in our ridiculous scuffle, and I sincerely hoped one…or two wouldn't fall on us.

"What's so funny?" Lois screamed in my face as we rolled around, each trying to get the upper hand. Finally, Lois prevailed, shoving me away from her and once again pointing the gun in my face. I giggled some more. This wasn't a good move on my part. She became enraged, her face flushing scarlet, her mussed-up hair falling in her eyes.

"You think this is funny, Kate?" I'll show you funny. She shot out a window behind me. Oh my God! But maybe the gunshot would be good for me. Someone would hear that gunshot and call it into the police, wouldn't they? I instinctively ducked down, and a few pieces of glass dropped down, crashing around me. I hoped none would fall on me—really? That was my hope.

When I rose from my ducked position, I think a little glass did get in my hair. Lois was standing in a position of shock. She had tucked the gun in the waistband of her jeans and was covering her eyes. "I can't believe I just did that."

She had just been on a rant about killing Jack, but she couldn't believe she had just shot out a window. This lady was one crazy woman!

I couldn't wait for Brian to ride in on a white horse and save me anymore. He wasn't going to call me back. He wasn't coming. I'd have to save myself. I rushed Lois again, and we both went flying with me on top of her. I had a good ten pounds on her and rage. She had new-found strength from her personal trainer workouts. But really, this second scuffle was a lot of slapping and hair-pulling. The gun was bothering me. I wanted it, but the last thing I wanted to do was fight over it. When you did that, it always seemed to go off (at least on TV!), and I wasn't interested in either of us getting shot, especially me. Then, in our struggles, a particularly nasty bop in the nose from me Lois, the gun skittered out of her jeans. I left her and grabbed for the gun. The power had shifted. Lois went completely still when she saw it pointed at her.

"Hey, Siri, call 911," I commanded. Got to love my iPhone.

"Sure thing, Katie," I had programmed her to say.

"911, what's your emergency?"

Chapter Forty

Monday, July 20

Is your wedding budget tight? Then, consider finding a venue that supplies many of the amenities that you would otherwise have to rent. Examples: tables, chairs, restrooms (yes, if you have a barn wedding or a wedding in a remote location, you may have to rent restroom trailers). If you choose a full-service venue, they will supply the above items as well as china, linens, silver, and glassware.

This morning, I had been summoned for a meeting with Rodney. He had been cryptic in his voicemail to me and made it crystal clear that this was one appointment that would be in my best interest to attend.

Rodney leaned back in his desk chair. We were in his home office, the same office where I had 'borrowed' his work cell phone. He wasn't happy with me and made it obvious by not offering me a seat. I was going to have to turn on the 'Katie charm' if I was going to turn this situation around.

I was so mad at Sarah Deloro, I could spit. She had really thrown me under the bus. I'm not sure if she had done it on purpose out of some sort of old 'bad blood' from our former rivalry in high school (I thought we were past all that!) or if she was trying to save her own hide or make a real estate connection. She let it *slip* that I had come into possession of his work cell phone. She wasn't sure 'how,' but she *really* thought Rodney should know in case he needed to change any of his passwords or personal information.

He was a softie. He noticed my discomfort and said with a wave of his hand, "Oh, sit down, Kate." I could tell from here on out I had him. He would be okay with whatever I had to say.

"I know Sarah Deloro told you an ear full."

He gave me a hard stare, leaned way back in his chair, and said, "And then some. Sarah is very good at what she does, but I've long known that she goes about getting her clients and acquisitions in, shall we say, 'unusual ways.' When I started thinking about what she told me about you, I knew it was nothing more than her spinning a small amount of truth to get what she wanted." But what did she want by throwing me to the wolves with Rodney and telling him what I had done with his phone?

"She so wanted to impress me that she had my back, but she would do anything to work with me. I've come into some money recently, and she made it very clear that she wanted my business. I know many people think it's ingratiating to share confidences, but that's not how I roll." He sighed. But I'll probably still end up working with her. She's just that good." He reached over for the coffee service on the right side of his desk, an impressive stainless-steel set. It looked heavy and substantial. The creamer had condensation around it, indicating the cream was cold. He followed my eyes and smiled.

"Would you like a cup, Kate?"

My mouth watered, especially when I spied the coffee cake on the credenza next to his desk. Rodney had some sweet perks. "Yes, please," I finally got out.

Rodney made short work of setting me up with a cup of coffee (I said 'yes' to the cream and 'yes' again to the coffee cake, which proved to be made with about a pound of butter).

"So anyway, Kate, I took what Sarah told me about you and my office phone with a grain of salt."

"Thank you, Rodney. I really appreciate your trust and faith in me. I'm sure Sarah's assumption was innocent enough," why was I covering for her? She was as guilty as I of digging around in his home. Because if I implicated her, I implicated myself. That Sarah Deloro! I was so going to get even with her. Not sure how, or when, but I would. This was war.

"Kate, Kate?" Rodney drew me back to the conversation. "Are you okay? You're kind of flushed."

Not surprised. I was so ticked. "I'm fine, Rodney," I tried to smile. "And you're right. I was looking for the key to the china cabinet in your desk drawer, your friend said it was in there, and Sarah walked in just as I pulled out the phone, checking if the key was under it or behind it. I'm sure it looked funny." I tried to laugh it off.

"I thought it was something like that. What do you think about this coffee cake?"

And we were done with that. But I had some questions of my own. As he wasn't the one who killed Jack, what was his story? He was extremely vicious and intense about his hatred of Jack; would he have acted on that hatred if Lois hadn't beat him to it? After all, he did message Meghan that he wouldn't let Jack win this time, that he'd do whatever it took. AND he had been to the Boathouse, per his car's GPS, about the same time as the murder. How did that figure in?

"Rodney," I began. How did I ask this? I took another sip, okay, gulp of my coffee and a bite of my coffee cake. After this interrogation, I may not be welcome much longer.

"Kate, I have more coffee and cake," he said, laughing.

I'd do it the 'Kate way.' "Rodney, you really hated Jack, right?"

Rodney's face darkened. "Yeah, Kate, I really hated him. He cheated me in the Restaurant real estate deal and took your friend Jen's husband, Jeff Cooper, to the cleaners, too, although Jeff always kept his nose clean. And then Jack stole my girl. The secret's out. Meghan's baby is mine." And here was the first real smile I think I've ever seen Rodney make. I thought I had seen his smile before, but after this luminous grin, I realized I never had. He looked, well, joyful.

"Yeah, I heard. You seem happy, (understatement) congratulations."

"We're getting married as soon as possible, and no offense, Kate, you won't be the planner. It would just be weird."

"None taken. But Rodney, I have to ask, and you can tell me to go jump off a cliff, if you want to, but I know you hated Jack, and it really looked like you were the murderer. What were you doing at the Boathouse the night Jack was killed?

Rodney stood up. I had forgotten how tall he was. I stood, too. I don't think he wanted to talk about this.

"I really should be going…" I began.

"Let's make this simple, Kate."

Then I remembered what Lois had said, that Jack was already on the ground when she had gone to the Boathouse. Why hadn't I put the pieces together? Rodney had hit Jack, maybe even thought he had killed him.

I didn't think, didn't give weight to the fact that maybe I was alone with a man who had tried to kill someone. I just blurted out, "It was you! You hit Jack on the head and left Jack for dead!"

Rodney just laughed and said, "Kate, you're pretty smart. Yeah, I did," he took a bite of coffee cake and smacked his lips. "I did try to kill him. I…wanted…him…dead. I asked him to meet me under the pretense of working out a deal to fix the bank/restaurant debacle. I met him down by the river and soon hit him with all my strength with a wrench that was now at the bottom of the Connecticut River. I did a poor job. I thought he was dead, and he wasn't. Thank God Lois finished the job for me." Yes, the news of Lois' arrest had been all over the news. "It was my first time trying to kill someone, so I'm cutting myself a little slack." He grinned at this. Now, I trust you will keep that juicy little morsel to yourself, or you will find that all your clients and potential clients will hear all about how you rummaged through the private desk drawers of the home of one of your clients. And took a cell phone to use for God knows what purposes." He wasn't smiling. How quickly his mood turned. He scared me, not a little.

I gulped. "Yes," I did my best to assure him; as I crept my way to the office door, I wanted out of there as soon as possible. "We most certainly understand each other." Then I stopped and turned around. "So when we first met at The Perk the day after Jack was killed, and you seemed to know little about the situation, that was all fake?" Why couldn't I keep my mouth shut?

To my relief, Rodney laughed. "You're good, Kate. Let's agree not to work with each other again." And I was dismissed.

Chapter Forty-One

Monday, July 20

Are you planning on live music, (in the manner of a string trio or quartet), for your ceremony or Cocktail Hour? If so, make sure you have shade for the players and their instruments. Sun is not a friend to these fine pieces. It's also important that you provide some sort of cover in case of inclement weather (rain). Chairs without arms are usually needed as well. And don't forget to provide a cool beverage to these talented artists.

After my meeting with Rodney, I went to wish Meghan well, but I had made a mess of it. I could not get her to stop sobbing. We were at her sister's Marjorie's house.

I just can't believe it, Kate! I just can't! Why would she do that? Why? I know she thought Jack was the right one for me. She kept after me and after me that he was a better fit as a husband than Rodney, but Rodney always had my heart."

I took Meghan's hands in mine. My 'why' question was: Did you really not know, Meghan? I guess we will never know. And why was I the person offering her comfort? Not that I was opposed to it. I like to think I am a kind human being, but was I really the best she could do? What about her sister? But Meghan's sister Marjorie had her own story and maybe her own concerns. Her name was the one on the bank business card that Suz, the teller at Middleview Bank, had handed me. I was leaving *that* alone. Was

Marjorie involved with her mother in Jack's murder? Were the three women, Lois, Marjorie, and Meghan, all involved in the plan to get rid of Jack? If so, Lois was covering for them and hadn't implicated anyone except herself. It was time for me to let the professionals hash this whole mess out.

Might as well give Meghan what comfort I could, so I said, "I don't know, Meghan. Maybe in some sort of twisted way, your mom thought she was protecting you. I know she loves you and your little guy," I looked down at her belly.

Meghan's hand went to her baby bump and cradled it gently. This brought fresh tears. I was a little out of my depth here. I was used to comforting distraught brides, not pregnant fiancées of murder victims.

I reached over to the box of tissues on the antique coffee table and handed a couple to Meghan. "Blow," I commanded. And she did.

If word on the street was to be believed, Jack had put Meghan as the sole beneficiary to his estate with no stipulation or mention that the baby was or was not his. Apparently, the paternity of the child was only a recent question in Jack's mind before his death. I think they could have made it work if he had lived. But Lois wasn't going to let that fall to chance.

Time to be off. But before I could make my get-away, in walked Meghan's sister, Marjorie, wearing again another of her lovely knitted creations. This time a cute sweater shell.

"Kate Ludlow. What possible reason can you give that you think it's okay to be here, in my home, after what you've done to my family?" She put her pocketbook down with a thud on the living room coffee table, and an expensive designer pocketbook it was, too. Did she buy it with the money she probably made with the shady deals she was doing with her bank and some of her customers? Probably.

I started to tell Marjorie that I had done nothing to her family, they had done it all to themselves, when Meghan surprised me.

I felt her tense beside me. "Marjorie, you can't blame Kate for what Mom did. Stop. Stop it right now." I squeezed Meg's hand in thanks. I hoped this boded well for the future, that she had grown from this awful situation. Maybe Meghan would be able to stand up to her family, and maybe she

213

would be a better person than one who would try to pass another man's child as his simply for the money.

Chapter Forty-Two

Will you opt to have a second dress for your reception? If so, don't forget to bring it to the reception. Believe it or not, it is the number one thing forgotten on the big day.

Brian...we were headed to New York today, a celebration of sorts. As I waited for Brian to pick me up to head to the train station, I thought about the moments following my 911 call. He had been beside himself when he came to the boathouse.

"Kate, I just don't know what to say. I did see your first call, but I was annoyed and being petty, so I didn't answer. Then my shift started, and I didn't have my phone on me. I'm so, so sorry. I don't know how I would ever forgive myself if something had happened to you." He was actually wringing his hands. Good.

Just then, Grant walked up. He grabbed me and pulled me into an embrace. "Kate," he said into my hair. I gently, but firmly pulled away and gave him a weak smile, pulling the blanket back over my shoulder that a volunteer had given me.

"I'm glad Ellis called me." Ellis, that rat! Why had she called her dad? I smiled a little less warmly. He knew where we stood. He couldn't worm his way back into my heart. I wasn't too happy with Brian, though. He was being a real stink.

Grant took the hint and backed off. Fading into the muddle that was a mash-up of flashing emergency lights, paramedics, law enforcement, and organized mayhem. It was almost as light as day.

Lois was being held in the back of a squad car. She was *not* exercising her right to remain silent. She told everyone who would listen that she was the victim, that she had to kill Jack to protect her beloved daughter and unborn grandchild. Could be that it was all part of an insanity plea. She certainly seemed crazy enough. I gave my statement three times to three different people, and Brian was finally allowed to drive me home. Grant said he'd bring my car to my house and Uber back to the Boathouse to get his own car. He can be a nice guy.

Brian and I were both silent, I for one, didn't even know where to begin. We were not in a good place.

"Katie, let's talk tomorrow. We are both too emotionally spent to get anywhere tonight."

"Agreed," I said. When we got to my house, I opened the car door quickly, almost before he had time to fully stop. The day had been warm, and the night cool. I shivered.

"I'll come around and walk you up to the door," he said. I knew he was hoping to come in so we could have a proper goodbye.

"I've got it," I said softly, with little to no emotion in my voice. If he was disappointed, I wouldn't know as I didn't turn around but limped up my walk and into the house. After I closed my door, I heard him drive off. I'm not sure if I was more mad or more hurt.

* * *

Saturday found us on the train to New York. The ride had been uneventful.

The trains were clean and not overly crowded today. I went back and forth between reading from my Kindle app on my iPhone to thinking of all that had happened in the last several weeks. How so many lives had been changed. This brought my thoughts to Will and Rose. I still didn't know why Will was at the Dodgers Spring Training. But I was fairly certain that it had something to do with Remey being there and that Will had been pestering his employee, Sergio, to cover for him for his cheating, not Jack's murder. I wondered how Will and Rose's marriage would fare from all the sure-to-be fallout. Poor Rose. Brian was on his phone, too, respecting my quiet vibe.

Once we exited our train, we walked the short way to the Oyster Bar,' a NYC institution housed right in Grand Central Terminal. Yes, that was my favorite restaurant in New York and, in my humble opinion, served the best Manhattan Clam Chowder I'd ever had. I loved its tomato base. Manhattan clam chowder is red instead of the more usual white. Still, I was hesitant. I'd seen sides of Brian recently that bothered me. A lot.

* * *

We got to the Oyster Bar a little after it opened for the day. Walking into the restaurant was like walking back in time. It was a beautiful old art deco building. The tiling on the walls was white and crisp, like in a fish market. It was lunchtime, but we both ordered vodka martinis, straight up, and oysters to start—two of my favorites and of course I ordered the Manhattan Clam Chowder as my meal, along with the delicious and darling oyster crackers.

My vodka martini relaxed me, and the comfort food of the chowder warmed my soul. It was a good pick on Brian's part. He knew I was ready to talk, so he dug in.

He picked at the red and white checkered tablecloth. He started with work news. "Gregory is in an anger management program. He and Claire have decided to remain separated for now. I don't think she wants to see him lose his job, so she's keeping quiet so far. Gregory keeping his job is in her and the kid's interest, too. I don't know what's going to happen with them, but I'm getting a new partner." Silence ruled again.

Then, "Katie, would you say we are products of our past our mistakes, and our successes?"

This was an easy one, I thought, but didn't say, as I ate the last of my three olives from my martini.

"I haven't felt secure about us since Grant moved here. I know you've given me no reason to doubt you, but that's the situation. You've had this whole other life, a grown-up life with a mortgage and a child. I think that's what makes me most insecure. Grant is Ellis' dad, and always will be, I get that. It's as it should be." He paused here. He opened his mouth, and nothing came out.

I wanted to urge him on, to encourage him, so I said his name. At least, I intended to. What came out was "Grant." He looked as if I had struck him.

"Oh, my God, Brian. You know I didn't mean that. You were just talking about him...I'm tired. You know this."

Brian shook his head as in disbelief, I felt much the same way. What the heck? What was wrong with me?

Katie, I love you, and I'm not going to let misunderstandings or little slips ruin us again. I'm not seventeen anymore."

"What do you want to say, Brian?" This sounded dire. I was wishing I had another martini but felt fairly confident it would do the opposite of help.

Brian reached across the table and took my hand. "So, we're thirty-eight now, right? You were, what, twenty-two, right out of college when Ellis was born? She's sixteen?"

"You know the answers to these questions, Brian. What are you getting at?" I really wanted that second martini now. Seriously. I was looking for our waiter to flag him down when Brian said, "I want to have a baby of our own, Katie. I want to get married and try for a family of our own." My eyes flew to him. I felt them widen. How did I not see this coming? Of course, he would want a child of his own.

I was struck mute.

"Katie, are you going to say anything?"

I looked Brian right in the eye. There was no avoiding this. "It's not too late, Brian. Lots of women have children at my age and later. The thing is." I stopped and looked down at my empty, licked-clean soup bowl. "The thing is," I repeated, "I'm not sure I want to start over. But, but," I hesitated only slightly. "I would for you. But I saw sides of you recently that really concern me: your jealousy and easy-to-anger vibe. I'm willing to give you another chance. I'm willing to start over with you, but only once I feel certain you're not the same insecure guy. A ring and a baby don't make someone a better person. They just make him a husband and father. And I—and any future children—deserve the better person.

Can you do that?"

Acknowledgements

Thanking everyone for all their help and support is a daunting task. I am blessed to have so many to mention. First of all, thank you to my family: my husband Ken, children: Tyler, Katheen, Maggie, Rob, Tess, Tom and Julia, my grandchildren: Lily, Teddy, Bill and Charlotte, and my almost sisters Kim Davis and Debbie Stauble. Everyone at different times has had to sacrifice a little "Mary, Mom or Belle" time so I could meet a deadline or two!

Thank you for the outstanding support and friendship from Level Best Books, my beyond talented editor, Shawn Simmons, and the wonderful Deb Well.

Love and gratitude to my writer friends, Celeste Connolly, Susan Furlong, Jane Willan, Shari Randall, Ang Pompano and Korina Moss.

Thank you, Barb Goffman for making me a better writer.

And finally, a big shout out to Sisters in Crime Connecticut, especially Tessa Wegert and Elise Hart Kipness.

About the Author

Mary Karnes, a college English major and former teacher, is the mother of four who raised her family though six corporate moves. She always dreamed of being an author and dabbled with writing throughout the years. Once the children were grown and out of the house, she started a wedding planning business, while simultaneously chasing her dream of being a traditionally published author. Her 'Wedding Planner Mystery Series' was born, with her business providing delicious subject matter for her books.

Mary resides in New England with her husband, Ken, and her mini-dachshund, Lucky. Her door is a revolving one with her children and grandchildren visiting frequently. She's busy at work writing book number three in The Wedding Planner Mystery Series, as well as a stand-alone thriller!

SOCIAL MEDIA HANDLES:
  Instagram: @marykarnesauthor
  Instagram: @marypkarnesweddings
  Facebook: MaryKarnesauthor
  TIKTOK: @marypkarnes
  X: @marypkarnes

AUTHOR WEBSITE:
marykarnesauthor.com

Also by Mary Karnes

Wedding Bride and Doom – The first in The Wedding Planner Mystery Series